She flashed a sexy moue. "I'd love to go out on a date with you."

After slipping into his suit jacket, Joseph reached into the breast pocket and handed Crystal his cell phone. "I'm going to need your cell number so I won't have to go through the hotel operator."

Crystal took the iPhone and put in her number. She offered him a tentative smile, handing him back the phone. "Thank you for being a wonderful dinner guest."

Raising her hands, Joseph kissed each of her fingers. "Good night, Crystal."

Her smile widened. "Good night, Joseph."

Crystal felt his loss within seconds of his releasing her hands. Proper etiquette stipulated she walk him to the door, yet her legs refused to follow the dictates of her brain. She didn't know how long she stood there, waiting for the sound of the door opening and closing. When it didn't come, she followed him. He stood at the door, his hand resting on the doorknob.

"Joseph?" His name came out in a shivery whisper.

Without warning he turned and approached her. Crystal didn't have time to catch her breath when she found herself in his arms, his mouth on hers in an explosive kiss that stole the very breath from her lungs. Her arms came up in seemingly slow motion, circling around his neck, holding him fast.

Books by Rochelle Alers

Harlequin Desire

A Younger Man
*The Long Hot Summer
*Very Private Duty
*Beyond Business

*The Blackstones of Virginia

Harlequin Kimani Romance

Bittersweet Love
Sweet Deception
Sweet Dreams
Twice the Temptation
Sweet Persuasions
Sweet Destiny
Sweet Southern Nights
Sweet Silver Bells

ROCHELLE ALERS

has been hailed by readers and booksellers alike as one of today's most prolific and popular African-American authors of romance and women's fiction.

With more than seventy titles and nearly two million copies of her novels in print, Ms. Alers is a regular on bestseller lists, is frequently chosen by Black Expressions Book Club and has been the recipient of numerous awards, including the Emma Award, Vivian Stephens Award for Excellence in Romance Writing, the *RT Book Reviews* Career Achievement Award and the Zora Neale Hurston Literary Award.

She is a member of Zeta Phi Beta Sorority, Inc., Iota Theta Zeta Chapter, and her interests include gourmet cooking, music, art and traveling.

A full-time writer, she lives in a charming hamlet on Long Island.

Sweet Silver Bells

ROCHELLE ALERS

HARLEQUIN® KIMANI™ ROMANCE

Sweet Silver Bells is dedicated to the readers who asked
for more Coles and Eatons.

Recycling programs
for this product may
not exist in your area.

ISBN-13: 978-0-373-86373-0

SWEET SILVER BELLS

Copyright © 2014 by Rochelle Alers

H HARLEQUIN®
™ www.Harlequin.com

Printed in U.S.A.

Dear Reader,

Even before I sat down to plot *Sweet Silver Bells* I knew I wanted to link two members of my favorite fictional families—the Coles and the Eatons. But the question was who I would choose.

You were given brief glimpses of Crystal Eaton in *Sweet Southern Nights* and Joseph Cole-Wilson in *Secret Agenda,* and because both are Floridians I thought, "Why not join these two strangers from prominent Florida families who have more in common than either could have ever imagined?"

Career-driven Crystal finds herself completely enthralled with Joseph, who presents himself as the total package, but for her, the timing is all wrong. A family tragedy forces her to return to Florida, and again fate intervenes when she comes face-to-face with the man whom she will be inexorably linked at Christmas by a love that promises forever.

Read, love and live romance.

Rochelle Alers

www.RochelleAlers.org
Roclers@aol.com

Honor the Lord with your wealth, with the first fruits
of all your crops.
—*Proverbs* 3:9

Prologue

Reunion

"Attention, passengers," the pilot's voice echoed throughout the jet cabin, "this flight to Miami will terminate at Palm Beach International due to a security breach at our scheduled airport. All passengers will be rescheduled to other flights once flights are allowed to land and depart from Miami."

The jet landed smoothly and Crystal Eaton and her baby daughter, Merry, made it into the terminal to find people standing around staring at the electronic boards. All flights to Miami were delayed indefinitely.

"Oh no," she whispered under her breath. That meant she didn't know when she would get home. Sitting and balancing Merry on her lap, she retrieved her cell phone. "Mother, I'm at the Palm Beach Airport. All flights going into Miami are delayed."

"I know, darling. I just heard the news report."

"I'm going to rent a car and drive down. I'll call you again when I get into the city."

"How's Merry?"

Crystal smiled for the first time in hours. "She's a real trouper. She hasn't cried or fussed the whole time."

"Drive carefully, Crystal. Please don't make me worry about you and my grandbaby, too."

"I will." It wasn't until she walked in the direction for car rentals that her mother's plea resonated with her. She professed to worry about her daughter and granddaughter but also about her ex-husband, who'd been admitted to the hospital with chest pains. Several arteries had been found clogged, necessitating immediate heart surgery.

There were long lines at the rental car counters and Crystal set the car seat on the floor. She wanted to put Merry down but decided against it. Her daughter had just taken her first steps several days ago and she didn't trust her not to fall and hurt herself on the marble floor.

The line moved slowly and Crystal wondered if taking a taxi would be a better choice.

She'd just moved out of the line when she went completely still. Walking into the terminal was the man she'd never expected to see again. She turned around, but it was too late.

He'd recognized her.

Closing her eyes, she whispered a silent prayer that he wouldn't make a scene. A shiver snaked its way up her back as his moist breath swept over the nape of her neck.

"You're a liar!" His accusation lashed at her like the stinging bite of a whip.

Crystal turned slowly to face the man who still had the power to make her heart beat a little too fast for her to breathe normally.

She watched Joseph as he stared at her little girl. Even if Crysal hadn't changed, he had. His face was leaner, his cropped hair grayer, and she detected new tiny lines around his large, deep-set, intense eyes. It was as if there was no more boyishness left in Joseph Cole-Wilson.

"I didn't lie to you," she countered.

Grasping her upper arm, Joseph steered her away from the crowd to a spot where they couldn't be overheard. "I asked you to let me know if you were pregnant, and you said you weren't."

When she tried extricating her arm, he tightened his grip. "I'm not going to stand here and debate with you. I have to get to Miami. My father had a heart attack and—"

"I'll take you to Miami," he volunteered, cutting her off.

Crystal shook her head. "That won't be necessary. I'm taking a taxi."

Joseph pushed his face within inches of hers. "Please don't

fight with me, Crystal. As soon as I call someone I'll take you."
Reaching for his cell phone, he punched in a number. "Diego, I
need Henri to come to the airport to pick up Zach. His flight is
due in at any moment. I'm going to call and tell him. Thanks."
He tapped another number. "Hey, bro. I'm not going to be able
to pick you up, but I have someone coming from ColeDiz who'll
meet you. I have a family emergency, but I'll be in touch."

Even though Crystal only heard one side of Joseph's conversation, she knew it was futile to argue with him. He'd said
that he had a family emergency. Well, he was wrong. Raleigh
was her and Merry's family, not his. He might have fathered
her daughter, but legally he had no claim to her.

Joseph extended his arms. "I'll carry her." Crystal reluctantly let him take Merry.

The little girl reached out and patted Joseph's clean-shaven
jaw. "Dada," she crooned, laughing and exhibiting a mouth
filled with tiny white teeth as Joseph buried his face in her
black curly hair.

"Yes, princess. I am Daddy."

Crystal closed her eyes. Merry had a vocabulary of about
twenty words, and Dada had been the first one; Crystal hadn't
exposed her daughter to many men, yet Merry hadn't called
any of them Dada.

Crystal followed Joseph out of the terminal to the parking
lot, strangely relieved that she didn't have to go through the
ordeal alone.

Joseph set the car seat on the second row of seats in the
Range Rover, then placed Merry in it and secured the harness
while Crystal got in beside her. She was exhausted. Not physically but emotionally. She stared at the back of Joseph's head
when he got in behind the wheel and maneuvered out of the
parking lot.

Joseph slipped on a pair of sunglasses as he followed the
signs for the airport exit. Glancing in the rearview mirror, he
noticed Crystal had closed her eyes. "What's her name?"

"Meredith, but I call her Merry."

"How old is she?"

"She turned one October tenth."

He smiled. "An October baby like her mother."

Although he wanted and needed answers, Joseph decided to wait. Crystal's father's health crisis was a lot more pressing than uncovering why she had decided to conceal the fact that he'd fathered a child. Fate had intervened, bringing them together, and he had no intention of letting Crystal walk out of his life again.

Chapter 1
Destiny

Crystal Eaton took a quick glance at the navigation screen on the Ford Escape. She was thirty-three miles from Charleston, South Carolina, less than half an hour from her destination, and if she hadn't had to drive down to Miami earlier that morning, she would've arrived much sooner. As she unclenched her teeth, the lines of tension bracketing her mouth vanished.

Her mother had called crying hysterically as soon as Crystal had maneuvered out of the parking garage at her Fort Lauderdale condo. She hadn't been able to understand a word her mother was saying, and in a panic she'd driven south instead of north.

It wasn't the first time in her life Crystal wished she hadn't been an only child. If Jasmine Eaton hadn't been able to reach her, then she would have been forced to contact her son and/ or other daughter whenever she had an emotional meltdown.

If it had been a medical emergency, Crystal would have postponed her plan to meet with the owner of several luxury hotels, but she then discovered the cause of her mother's latest hissy fit. Jasmine's current boyfriend had refused to take her with him on a business trip to Las Vegas, leading Jasmine to accuse him of cheating on her.

Biting her tongue and instead of telling Jasmine she was too old for adolescent histrionics, Crystal smiled, issuing her usual mantra, "Mother, this, too, shall pass."

This was followed by another crying jag until Crystal reminded her mother that her eyes were swollen and her cheeks blotchy.

It was as if someone had flipped a switch when Jasmine raced to her bathroom to examine her face, declaring no man was worth sacrificing her beauty.

Crystal knew her own reluctance to marry was because of her parents' inability to form lasting relationships. Her fifty-four-year-old father had been married four times and her mother, only a year younger than her ex-husband, had had so many dates with a steady parade of men coming and going that Crystal stopped counting.

However, Jasmine was quick to inform anyone who labeled her a serial dater that she was very discriminating when it came to sleeping with a man. Jasmine's gratification came from being seen on the arm of a handsome gentleman, not sleeping with him.

Crystal's cell rang and she glanced at the number on the dashboard. Activating the Bluetooth feature, she said, "Hey, Xavier."

"Where are you, Criss?"

"I'm about forty minutes outside the city."

"Selena and I expected you hours ago."

She'd promised her cousin she would stop and spend some time with him, his wife and their toddler daughter. "I would've been here sooner if I didn't have to drive to Miami and check on my mother. She just broke up with her latest male *friend,* and that always sends her into drama mode. I believe she liked this one more than she's willing to admit."

"Isn't she a bit too old to have tantrums?" Xavier asked, chuckling softly.

Crystal rolled her eyes, although her cousin couldn't see her. "Please, Xavier, don't get me started. My mother should've become an actress instead of an art dealer."

Xavier laughed again. "Your mother is drama personified."

Crystal frowned. "I don't know why I mentioned her, because talking about my mother's antics always gives me a headache. It's too late to stop by tonight," she said, deftly changing the topic of conversation, "so I'm going directly to the hotel. I have meetings tomorrow and Friday, but I'm free this weekend."

"Why don't you come spend at least Saturday or Sunday with us?"

"That sounds wonderful. I'll call to let you know when I'll be there. See you soon."

"We'll be here," Xavier said.

Tapping a button on the steering wheel, Crystal ended the call. Crystal smiled for the first time in hours. She was about to embark on a project she'd dreamt about since decorating her first dollhouse. But this project wasn't about dollhouses but two historic landmark buildings the owner planned to turn into an inn and a bed-and-breakfast.

The original owners of the three-story, early-nineteenth-century structures had used them as their secondary residences whenever they relocated their families from the cotton, rice and indigo plantations built along the creeks and marshes in order to escape the swamp fevers so prevalent at the time during the intense summer heat.

She knew she'd taken a big step when she left her position with a prestigious Fort Lauderdale architectural and design firm to set up her own company—Eaton Interior and Design. She'd come to the realization she'd been overworked, overlooked for promotions, underpaid for her expertise, all the while being subtly sexually harassed by one of the partners. Rather than initiate a lawsuit against him and the firm, she'd decided it was time to leave.

Despite Jasmine's occasional histrionics, Crystal had to thank her mother for giving her the encouragement she needed to strike out on her own. Jasmine might have been impetuous when it came to her relationships, but she was the complete opposite when buying and selling art. Jasmine revealed that she, too, was thirty when she'd sold her first painting, so it would stand to reason that her daughter would start up her own company at thirty.

Two years later Jasmine opened a thriving and exclusive art gallery in an upscale Miami neighborhood with a growing clientele that included celebrities who wanted to decorate the walls of their sprawling mansions with works of art.

Crystal didn't have a shop—not yet—but she did have recommendations from several of her father's clients and one from her mother. Not once had she harbored any guilt about using her parents' name to further her career. It was the least they could do for emotionally abandoning her as a child. She'd found herself competing with her father's wives for his attention, while her mother had never recovered from losing her husband, the man she considered the love of her life.

Crystal spent more time at her cousins' house than she did her own. Levi, Jesse and Carson Eaton were more than cousins. They had become her surrogate brothers.

The lights of downtown Charleston came into view as she listened to the automated voice issuing directions, driving through cobblestone streets lined on both sides with elegant homes still festooned in Christmas lights and decorations. It was the second week in January and it was as if the residents were reluctant to let go of the holiday.

Maneuvering up to the hotel's entrance, she slowed, coming to a complete stop in front of a valet wearing a white shirt, red bow tie, black vest and slacks.

"How long are you staying, ma'am?"

"I'll be here for a couple of months."

"Are you Ms. Eaton?" the young man asked.

She nodded. "Yes, I am."

The valet opened the driver's-side door. "I'll park your truck and have someone bring in your luggage." Reaching into the back pocket of his slacks, he removed a walkie-talkie. "I need a bellhop out front."

Crystal reached for her handbag and the tote with her laptop and then slipped from behind the wheel. She managed to smother a moan. Her legs were stiff and her shoulders ached. She'd driven nearly six hundred miles, stopping in St. Augustine to refuel and order a fruit salad. The entire drive had taken her nearly twelve hours.

What she wanted now was a leisurely bath before climbing into bed to sleep undisturbed throughout the night.

She made her way into the lobby and over to the desk to

check in, admiring its sophisticated opulence. Marble flooring, several glittering chandeliers and a massive glass-topped table in the center of the lobby cradled an enormous hand-painted ceramic vase filled with fresh flowers. Queen Anne chairs were positioned at round pedestal tables for guests to sit and relax.

A woman with flawless brown skin, neatly braided hair and an infectious smile greeted Crystal as she approached the front desk. "Welcome to the Beaumont House. How may I help you?"

"I'm Crystal Eaton," she said, "and—"

"Oh, Ms. Eaton, we've been expecting you," the woman said. "Your accommodations will be handled by concierge." She picked up the telephone, speaking quietly into the mouthpiece.

In less than a minute, a tall man in a black tailored suit approached the desk. There was something about his bearing that reminded Crystal of her father. Raleigh Eaton's good looks, refinement, charm, and legal and financial acumen had made him a very wealthy man *and* a magnet for women regardless of their age.

Two years ago he'd divorced his fourth wife, and his current fiancée was thirty-five, only five years older than Crystal. Wherein Raleigh might have been unable to maintain a successful marriage of any duration, he wasn't so reckless as not to have had his prospective wives sign a prenuptial agreement. The exception had been his first wife. The alimony payments deposited directly into Jasmine's bank account like clockwork afforded the mother of his only child, coupled with her successful art business, a very comfortable lifestyle.

The concierge extended his hand, while offering Crystal a friendly smile. He lowered his gaze rather than let her see the admiration in his gaze. Crystal Eaton was stunning. Her pixie-cut hairstyle, unblemished face, the color of polished mahogany, radiated good health, and her dark brown wide-set slanting eyes, pert nose and full, sensual mouth were enthralling.

The perfection of her body matched her face: tall, slender and curvy in a pair of fitted black jeans, matching pullover sweater and leather flats.

"Welcome, Ms. Eaton. I'm John Porter, your personal concierge. Mr. Beaumont has asked me to take care of all of your needs during your stay."

Crystal took his hand, finding it as soft as her own.

"Thank you so much, Mr. Porter."

John reluctantly withdrew his hand. "Mr. Beaumont has arranged for you to stay in the penthouse. You will have the privilege of twenty-four-hour room service that includes laundry, dry-cleaning, housekeeping and meals." He angled his head, smiling. "All of which are gratis. The penthouse staff is aware they're not to accept tips from *you*. Don't look so alarmed, Ms. Eaton," he said when Crystal's gave him a stunned look, her delicate jaw dropping. "They are compensated far beyond what the other employees earn," he added when her mouth closed.

She forced a smile she didn't feel at that moment. "That's good, because I wouldn't want to take advantage of their services."

John cupped her elbow, directing her to the bank of elevators, and stopped in front of one with a sign indicating floors 8-PH. "Mr. Beaumont treats all of his employees quite well. I'm going to give you two room card keys. The red one will permit you elevator access to your floor and the green to your apartment."

He handed her an envelope with her name, punched the button and waited for the doors to open. Crystal walked into the car. He entered behind her and, reaching into the pocket of his suit jacket, removed a master key and inserted it into the PH slot. The doors closed, and the car rose silently.

When she agreed to the terms in the contract between Beaumont Hotels and Eaton Interior and Design in which the owner of the hotel chain would provide lodging for the duration of the project, Crystal had expected to occupy a suite, not a penthouse apartment. She knew Algernon Beaumont was anxious for her to decorate the two boutique hotels before spring and the influx of tourists to the Lowcountry, and because she wasn't married, didn't have a fiancé, boyfriend or children, Crystal was able to accept the commission that would take her away from home for weeks at a time.

The elevator doors opened and she stepped out into a carpeted hallway.

John remained in the elevator. "You're in penthouse two, which is on the left," he informed Crystal. "The bellhop will bring up your luggage. If you need anything, please dial fifteen and either I or someone from my staff will procure it for you."

Crystal smiled at the very formal man. "Thank you. I doubt if I'll need anything tonight." All she wanted was a bath and a bed. Anything she did need would wait until the next day.

John nodded. "Good night, Ms. Eaton."

"Good night, Mr. Porter."

She walked the short distance to the door labeled PH 2, opening the envelope and taking out one of the card keys.

Crystal's hand halted as she caught movement out the corner of her eye. She stole a glance at a tall, slender man dressed in a pair of cutoffs, a T-shirt and flip-flops closing the door to the other apartment as he walked toward the elevator. The contrast of the white shirt against his olive complexion was attention-grabbing. He was like a bronze statue come to life.

After several seconds Crystal realized she was staring when their eyes met and held. Even from the distance she noticed the perfection of his features.

"Good evening, neighbor," he said.

She went completely still as a shiver of awareness swept over her body. The man's voice was deep and as utterly sensual as he appeared to be. "Good evening," Crystal replied, smiling.

"Are you checking in?" She nodded. Closing the distance between them, he extended his hand. "Joseph Cole-Wilson."

Shifting the card key to her left hand, she took the large, groomed hand with long, slender fingers. "I'm Crystal."

"It's nice meeting you, Crystal."

Nodding, she withdrew her hand from his loose grip. "Are you Joseph or Joe?"

He smiled, drawing Crystal's gaze to his sensual mouth and the slight cleft in his strong chin. "I've always been Joseph. I'm not going to hold you up settling in, but I just want you to know I'll be next door if you need anything."

Crystal wanted to tell Joseph that if she *did* need anything, all she had to do was pick up the telephone and dial two digits. She didn't know if Mr. Drop-Dead Sexy was attempting to come on to her, but at present his mojo definitely wasn't working. She was much too tired to carry on an exchange of witty repartee with him, and the reason she was in Charleston took precedence over any- and everything in her life.

"Thanks, Joseph. I'm sorry, but I have to get some sleep or I'm going to fall on my face."

Joseph's eyebrows lifted a fraction. Light from a wall sconce illuminated the face of the tall, slender woman with the killer body. Only those in his family knew his legal name: José Ibrahim Cole-Wilson. His mother had always called him Joseph, so the name stuck.

Crystal put up her hand to smother a yawn, and it was then he noticed her exhaustion.

"I'm sorry to hold you up. Have a good evening." That said, he turned and walked to the elevator.

Crystal stared at him until he disappeared into the car. Then she inserted the card key into the slot, waited for the green light and pushed open the door.

If the furnishings in the lobby reflected a bygone era, it was the same in the penthouse. The chairs, tables, lamps, wall mirrors in the living and dining rooms were uniquely art deco, one of her favorite decorating styles.

Dropping her handbag and tote on an oversize ottoman, she walked into a modern, state-of-the-art kitchen with double stainless steel sinks, cooktop stove, double oven, eye-level microwave, dishwasher, French-door refrigerator/freezer, trash compactor and cooking island. There was also a fully stocked wine cellar with three dozen bottles.

Crystal opened the refrigerator stocked with dairy products, the vegetable drawers with fresh fruit and salad fixings. The freezer was also filled with packaged and labeled meat. The shelves in the pantry were stocked with everything she would need for breakfast, lunch and dinner. A door off the kitchen revealed a half bath.

She continued her tour, mounting a flight of stairs, discovering two bedroom suites with adjoining baths. Each bedroom was constructed with sitting and dressing areas. Wall-to-wall silk drapes were open to offer an unobstructed view of nighttime Charleston and a lit rooftop deck.

She returned to the first floor at the same time the bell chimed throughout the apartment. She opened the door and the bellhop carried her bags up the staircase, leaving them in the hallway outside the bedrooms. He returned, gave her a slight bow and then left, closing the door behind him.

Crystal turned off all the lights on the first floor with the exception of the table lamp in the entryway. Her footsteps were slow as she climbed the staircase for the second time, wondering if she would remain awake long enough to take a shower.

After a hot shower, she crawled into bed, pulling the sheet and comforter up to her neck.

She hadn't drawn the drapes. Daylight coming in through the windows would become her alarm clock. Eight hours of sleep would give her everything she needed to face the day and the most comprehensive commission of Eaton Interior and Design thus far.

Chapter 2

Joseph lost count of the number of times he swam the length of the Olympic-size swimming pool on the lower level of the Beaumont House. He'd also stopped cursing his cousin for banishing him to South Carolina to start up ColeDiz Tea Company, ColeDiz International Ltd.'s first U.S. mainland venture since their great-grandfather established the company ninety years ago. He was solely responsible for the oversight of the ongoing operation of the tea garden, as well.

This wasn't his first trip to the Lowcountry. Two years ago, Joseph had met with Harry Ellis to survey one hundred acres of land between Kiawah and Edisto Islands the real estate agent had purchased on behalf of the Cole-family-owned conglomerate. Not only had Harry bought the land, but five years earlier he'd also brokered a deal with a Ugandan cotton grower for Diego, making ColeDiz the biggest family-owned agribusiness in the United States.

Subsequently an engineering company had drained the swampy area to prepare it for growing and processing tea leaves, all the while Joseph insisting they not upset the ecological balance of region's indigenous wildlife.

He'd argued with his cousin that he was a lawyer, not a farmer, but Diego was quick to remind him that he also wasn't a farmer, yet had familiarized himself with the entire process of growing and harvesting coffee, bananas and cotton. Joseph had been under the impression that tea wasn't grown in the States, but Diego told him about the tea garden on Wadmalaw Island, South Carolina. Once ColeDiz Tea Company harvested their first yield, there would be not one, but two tea gardens in the United States.

It'd taken him a while, but he had adjusted to spending the last two years of his life in Belize, Mexico, Jamaica, Puerto Rico and Brazil, educating himself with the cycle of planting, cultivation, harvesting and processing coffee and bananas in order to learn everything he could about the different varieties.

It hadn't been only about planting trees, but also soil quality, insect control and irrigation. He had logged thousands of hours in the air, crossed various time zones and grown accustomed to sleeping in strange beds and ordering room service. Several of his college buddies and fraternity brothers claimed they envied his jet-setting lifestyle, but Joseph had been quick to remind them it was work and not fun.

However, he did take time off to have some fun when he stayed with his landscape-architect cousin Regina Spencer in Bahia, Brazil. Regina and her pediatrician husband hadn't been to Carnival in years, yet had offered to accompany him. Joseph witnessed firsthand the once-in-a-lifetime frivolity. Partying nonstop for three days offset the months, weeks, days and hours he spent learning to become a farmer.

Now he was back in Charleston to oversee the first planting of ColeDiz Tea Company's tea garden. He'd grown fond of the incredibly beautiful historic port city and its friendly populace. He returned not as an attorney but as a farmer and an astute businessman. Although assigned to the legal department, he'd been groomed to eventually take over as CEO when Diego retired. His cousin failed to realize that Joseph preferred the legal component to running a company. Whether it was negotiating contracts or spending hours researching and interpreting international tariffs, law had become his jealous mistress.

He didn't want to think about jealous mistresses or past relationships. His four-year liaison with Kiara Solis had run its course the third day into a two-week Hawaiian vacation when he'd tried to make the best of what had become a highly volatile situation.

Kiara had been under the impression they were going on a romantic holiday where he would propose, although he'd told her repeatedly he hadn't been ready for marriage. At twenty-eight his life wasn't stable. He'd just resigned his position clerking for a Florida appellate judge to join ColeDiz. He had also purchased land in Palm Beach with plans to build a home, but even that had been placed on hold until after he curtailed traveling.

Joseph's father had lectured him about dating a woman for more than two years without committing to a future together. His father failed to understand that although he loved Kiara he hadn't been in love with her. If he had, there was no doubt he would've married her.

Joseph swam the length of the pool, then pulled himself up at the shallow end. He was breathing heavily, his chest rising and falling from the exertion. Picking up a towel from the stack on a wooden bench, he dried off before pulling on his shorts and T-shirt. Swimming was the perfect alternative to sitting up watching late-night infomercials.

Joseph walked to the bank of elevators. Living in the penthouse wasn't a perk but a requisite befitting his lifestyle. He'd grown up privileged, and having the best life had to offer was something for which he never apologized. As a Cole and a member of the purportedly wealthiest African-American family in the country, he accepted everything that went along with the distinction.

Kiara had called him a "spoiled rich boy" and a few other epithets that he would never repeat to anyone, and it was her vicious and spiteful outburst that reminded him why he'd been reluctant to ask her to marry him. It hadn't been the first time Kiara had gone off on him when she couldn't get her way, but it was the last time Joseph decided to turn the other cheek. Although laid-back and easygoing, he wasn't a masochist.

He was certain his parents had had their disagreements, yet he couldn't remember a time he was privy to them. Joseph shook his head as he stepped out of the elevator car, and walked to his apartment, unlocking the door. He vowed to remain single until he met the woman with whom he felt he wanted to spend his life. After all, he was only thirty and in no immediate hurry to settle down and start a family.

Climbing the staircase to the second level, he stripped off

his clothes, leaving them in a hamper, and then stepped into the shower. By the time Joseph got into bed, he had mentally prepared himself to oversee the project he'd been entrusted with. Despite his initial objection to setting up a tea garden, he knew failure was not an option.

Crystal woke rested and clearheaded. Her appointment with Algernon was scheduled for nine in the hotel restaurant; he'd informed her they would meet with the contractor in downtown Charleston to inspect the interiors of the recently restored properties.

When she first came to see the abandoned buildings, she'd found herself hard-pressed to contain her excitement. Despite the faded, peeling wallpaper, warped floors, weakened window sashes and the pervasive odor of mold, she was able to imagine the beauty and elegance of the renovated spaces. Algernon, or Al, as he insisted she call him, wanted the interior to replicate the furnishings of 1800s Lowcountry city residences.

After brewing a cup of coffee, she unpacked, putting everything away, then stepped into the Jacuzzi for a leisurely soak. The hands on the clock on the bathroom's vanity had inched closer to eight-fifteen when she stepped out of the tub. At eight forty-five she entered the restaurant off the hotel lobby, the hostess greeting her with a friendly smile.

"Good morning, ma'am. Are you a guest?"

Crystal nodded. "Yes, I am."

"What is your room number?"

"I'm in penthouse two."

The hostess punched several keys on a computer. "Ms. Eaton?"

"Yes," she confirmed. "I have an appointment to meet Mr. Beaumont here at nine."

"Ms. Eaton, I don't know if anyone told you, but as an elite guest you'll take your meals in the private dining room. Mr. Beaumont will meet you there." The young woman motioned to a passing waiter. "Patrick, please escort Ms. Eaton to Mr. Beaumont's table."

Crystal followed the waiter to the rear of the restaurant and to a door with a plaque reading Elite Hotel Guests Only. The space was half the size of the restaurant for other hotel guests and the general public, and furnished in the manner of a formal dining room with cloth-covered tables and place settings of china, silver and crystal. Classical music flowed from hidden speakers as waitstaff moved silently, efficiently picking up and setting down dishes.

She thanked the waiter when he pulled out a chair at a table in an alcove, seating her at the same time her cell phone chimed softly. Reaching into her handbag, Crystal retrieved the phone and glanced at the display. It was Algernon. Tapping in her pass code, she answered the call.

"Good morning, Al."

"Crystal. I'm glad I reached you. I rang your room, but it went directly to voice mail. I'm on my way to the airport to catch a flight to Vancouver. My daughter was injured on a movie set, and even though I'm told it isn't serious, I need to see her. I'm not certain when I'll be back, but I'll keep you updated. I'm sorry you had to come and—"

"Please don't apologize," Crystal said, interrupting him. "Take care of your daughter and don't worry about me. I'll be here when you get back. The last time I was in Charleston I didn't get to do much sightseeing, so I intend to tour the city until you return."

"Thanks, Crystal, for being so understanding."

"Have a safe flight and I'll see you when you get back."

She ended the call, exhaling an audible sigh. Although anxious to see the restored buildings, Crystal also understood an unexpected personal predicament. And taking care of your family always took precedence over everything. There were Eatons living in different parts of the country, but whenever there was a significant occasion, they all came together as one whether it in sickness, tragedy, marriage or a new birth.

She'd attended so many weddings over the years Crystal needed a scorecard to document which first cousin had married whom. It began with Belinda marrying her brother-in-law sports attorney/agent, Griffin Rice. Belinda and Griffin had become guardians of their twin nieces after the death of their parents, who were Belinda's sister and Griffin's brother. Belinda made Griffin a biological father for the first time after giving birth to a baby boy.

The marriage bug then bit Belinda's brother, Myles, when he married his ex-fiancée after a ten-year separation. Myles hadn't known Zabrina was pregnant with his son, because she'd been blackmailed into marrying another man. They added to another generation of Eatons with a daughter.

Myles and Belinda's sister Chandra married celebrated playwright Preston Tucker, and they were now the parents of a daughter, and Xavier and his wife, Selena, also had a daughter. All the Eatons were wagering whether Denise and Mia and their husbands would have boys once they decided to increase their family, because it looked as if girls were outnumbering boys in the latest generation of Eatons.

Crystal still did not picture herself a wife or a mother. The closest she'd come to a committed relationship was when she lived with a man after enrolling in graduate school. Her parents disapproved of her living or *shacking up* with a man, because they claimed they'd raised her better than that.

Jasmine lamented, why would the man want to buy the cow when he could get the milk free? Her comeback was that she didn't want to be bought, because her goals did not include becoming a wife.

Her relationship with Brian worked well; he also didn't want to marry or father children. As a child he'd been physically abused by his parents, spent years in foster care and feared he would turn out like them. He and Crystal had lived together for three years before Brian was offered a teaching position at a Los Angeles college. Crystal encouraged him to accept the position, and after graduating she gave up their miniscule New York City Greenwich Village studio apartment and moved back to Florida.

She lived with her mother until she secured employment with a Miami-based design firm. Once she transferred to their

Fort Lauderdale office, she purchased a two-bedroom condo in a gated community.

Living alone was a wake-up call that she was in complete control of her life and future.

She beckoned a waiter as he finished filling a water goblet at a nearby table. "Is it possible for me to change tables? Mr. Beaumont won't be joining me." Crystal didn't want to sit in the grotto-inspired alcove alone.

The waiter glanced around the room. "There's an empty table near the window."

Crystal nodded. "I'll take it."

It wasn't until she was seated near a wall of glass that she saw her penthouse neighbor. Joseph sat at a table several feet away. Their eyes met and she returned his open, friendly smile with one of her own.

"Good morning, neighbor," Joseph said in greeting.

Her smile grew wider. "Same to you, neighbor."

"Did you sleep well?" he asked.

"Yes, I did. Thank you for asking."

Joseph stared boldly at the woman, who'd exchanged her jeans and sweater for a navy blue pantsuit and white silk blouse. A light covering of makeup enhanced her best features: eyes and mouth. His gaze lingered on Crystal's flawless dark complexion. He took a quick glance at her hands. She wasn't wearing a ring, but that still didn't mean she wasn't married or involved with someone.

His interest in the woman occupying the neighboring penthouse was a reminder of how, for the past two years, his life had not been his own to control. He hadn't found time to embark on another relationship since his breakup with Kiara, but now that he was stateside his days and nights were more predictable.

"Are you expecting someone?" he asked Crystal.

"No, I'm not. Why?"

"I see several people waiting for tables, and if we sit together, it would free up one for them."

Crystal's gaze shifted from Joseph's deeply tanned face to the couples standing at the entrance. She was seated at a table for two while he sat at a table seating four. "You may sit with me."

As he moved over to sit opposite her, Crystal inhaled the subtle scent of his masculine cologne. It was if she were seeing Joseph for the first time. Last night she hadn't realized he was so tall. She was five-nine in her bare feet, and estimated he had to be at least three or even four inches above the six-foot mark. He was casually dressed in relaxed jeans, black Timberland boots and a white button-down shirt, opened at the collar under a navy blue blazer.

The hint of a smile softened her mouth. "I see you're Greek."

Attractive lines fanned out around his large dark eyes when he smiled. "Alpha Phi Alpha," he said proudly, glancing at his belt buckle with the Greek alphabet. "Are you also Greek?"

Crystal nodded slowly. "Alpha Kappa Alpha."

Joseph smile grew wider. "Well, Miss AKA, where did you go to school?"

"Howard. And you?"

"Cornell."

Her eyebrows lifted. "So you're an Ivy Leaguer. I'm impressed." It wasn't often she met many African-American men who'd attended Ivy League colleges. Most she knew had enrolled in historically black colleges. "Are you active?" she asked Joseph.

He flashed a set of straight white teeth. "Active *and* financial." Since his return to the States, Joseph had rejoined his local chapter. He planned to drive to West Palm Beach one weekend each month to attend chapter meetings.

Crystal glanced at a spot over Joseph's broad shoulder. She didn't want him to think her rude for staring. Despite the stubble on his lean jaw, there was something about his features that made Joseph almost too pretty to be a man. "I'm financial but inactive. Unfortunately," she admitted, "I don't have the time to attend my chapter meetings."

"Where is your chapter?"

"Miami."

Leaning back in his chair, he crossed his arms over his chest. "So you're a Gator."

Crystal wasn't able to discern from Joseph's expression whether he was being derisive or complimentary. "Is there something wrong with being a Gator?" she asked defensively.

"Hell no, because you're looking at a fellow Gator. Palm Beach," he said before she could ask.

She laughed softly. "It looks as if we're truly neighbors in every sense of the word." Crystal paused, and then asked, "What are you doing in Charleston?"

Joseph picked up the menu, studying the selections rather than looking at Crystal. He'd never been one to engage in what he deemed inane repartee in order to glean information from a woman, yet that was exactly what he was doing with Crystal.

"I'm here on business."

"So am I," Crystal concurred.

He glanced up, meeting her direct stare. "It appears we have a lot in common. We're both Greek, Floridians and we're in Charleston on business."

"That's three for three."

Joseph angled his head. "What about your marital status?"

"What about it?" she asked, answering his question with one of her own.

"Are you single?"

"I'm single *and* unencumbered."

A beat passed. "Is that the same as not having any children?" Joseph asked

"It is."

He went completely still. "That's four for four."

"What else do you want to know about me, Joseph?"

There was another pause before he asked, "How long do you plan to be here on business?"

"I estimate a couple of months."

The slow smile that spread over his features did not reach his eyes. Joseph thought about the odds of meeting a woman, an incredibly beautiful woman who was staying in the same hotel as his, on the same floor and with whom he shared much in common. If he'd signed up with an online dating service, Crystal would've been the perfect candidate. He wasn't looking for a relationship, but friendship—something he hadn't had in a while.

And for him it had never been about how many women he could sleep with, because there had been more than he could count or remember who were more than willing to become his dessert after he'd taken them to dinner. He didn't know why, but Joseph always thought about his sister and the lengths he would go to if some man sought to take advantage of her. His mantra of protect a woman as if she were your sister was never that far from his mind, and he knew that was why he'd continued to stay in his past relationship longer than necessary.

"Five for five," Joseph drawled. He'd planned to live at the hotel for the next four months; the tea garden's manager who was overseeing wanted to return to Nebraska with his wife, where she would give birth to their first child.

Crystal smiled as she glanced at the menu. It appeared as if she had more in common with Joseph than she'd had with Brian. The man with whom she'd lived eschewed fraternities and sororities, claiming they were socialized cults. The subject always started an argument where they wouldn't speak for days. It wasn't their only disagreement, but it was one subject she refused to allow him to vilify. Her mother had been an AKA and her mother before her.

Her stomach rumbled loudly and she hoped Joseph hadn't heard it. She motioned to a waitress standing several feet away. "I'm ready to order now. I'll have grits with soft scrambled eggs and one slice of buttered wheat toast."

The waitress scribbled on her pad. "Would you like coffee, tea or juice, ma'am?"

Crystal closed the binder. "I'd like green tea and grapefruit juice." Joseph had just given the woman his order when an ear-shattering piercing sound reverberated throughout the room.

The waitress slipped her pad into the pocket of her apron. "I'm sorry, but you're going to have to leave the hotel. That's the fire alarm."

As if on cue, everyone began filing out, Joseph reaching for

Crystal's free hand as she gripped her handbag with the other. Hotel personnel were escorting guests down the staircases, because the elevators were shut down, through the lobby and out to the parking lot. The wail of sirens in the distance came closer and closer. Members of the police and fire departments were now on the scene, urging everyone to leave the parking lot and move across the street.

Joseph tucked Crystal's hand into the bend of his elbow as they followed the crowd away from the building. An elderly woman complained loudly that someone on her floor had been smoking in their room and she thought it shameful they'd ignore the hotel's smoke-free policy.

"It looks as if we're going to have to forgo breakfast," Joseph said softly, leaning closer to Crystal.

Her stomach rumbled again at the mention of breakfast. "Maybe you can, but I have to get something to eat. The last time I had solid food was more than eighteen hours ago."

He went completely still, his eyes meeting hers. "Do you have an eating disorder?"

Chapter 3

It took several seconds for Crystal to process what Joseph had just asked her. She wasn't underweight and she definitely didn't look emaciated, either. "No!" she said. "I didn't get a chance to eat yesterday. I drove up from Miami and I wanted to get here before nightfall," she explained when he continued to stare at her. "And there's nothing anorexic-looking about me."

Joseph blinked slowly before a slow smile spread over his features. His gaze moved over her body. "No, there isn't." He sobered quickly. "I know of a small restaurant not far from here."

Crystal wasn't immune to the hungry look in his eyes, and wondered if Joseph knew how much his eyes mirrored what he was feeling. It was apparent he hadn't learned to hide his emotions behind a facade of indifference. "How far is not far?" she asked.

"It's about ten blocks. If we start out now, maybe we can get there before it gets too crowded."

Crystal eased her hand from his loose grip, reaching into her handbag for her phone. She had no intention of walking ten blocks in four-inch heels. "I have a cousin who lives downtown and I'm going to call him and let him know to expect us."

Joseph narrowed his eyes. "Are you certain he's not going to be put out with bringing a stranger into his home?"

"He's not going to be put out. We *Eatons* have an open-door policy when it comes to family." She'd proudly stressed her family's name.

His smooth brow furrowed when she mentioned the name Eaton. "Are you related to Judge Solomon Eaton?"

"You've heard of him?" Crystal asked.

"Are you kidding?" Joseph couldn't keep the excitement out

of his voice. "I clerked for him for a year before joining my family's business."

Crystal couldn't stop her hand from shaking as a shiver of unease eddied up her back, making her more than apprehensive. She did not want to believe she was indirectly connected to a man she'd met less than twenty-four hours ago. "You're a lawyer." The query was a statement of fact.

He nodded. "Yes."

"And you're certain it was my uncle you clerked for?"

"Yes," Joseph said emphatically. "We happen to be fraternity brothers."

She ran a hand over her short hair. Her uncle had pledged Alpha Phi as a Howard University undergraduate. "This is much too weird. If I didn't know better, I'd say you were stalking me."

Crossing his arms over his chest, Joseph gave her a direct stare. "I can assure you that I'm not stalking you. In fact, I didn't know you existed before last night. And the name Eaton isn't that common. And with you being from Florida, I just assumed you were related."

His former boss had distinguished himself as a federal prosecutor before he was appointed to the bench, and still held the distinction of presiding over more drug cases than any other U.S. attorney in south Florida's history. He indicted a drug kingpin, several traffickers responsible for high-end deals and midlevel dealers caught with large amounts of cocaine and marijuana.

"Solomon Eaton is my uncle," she confirmed. And he was also Levi, Jesse and Carson's father.

Reaching into the breast pocket of his blazer, Joseph retrieved his cell phone. "I'll call a car service while you call your cousin."

Walking away to put some distance between them, Crystal turned her back, tapping the screen for Xavier's number. "Good morning, Crystal," Selena answered in greeting.

"Good morning to you, too," she replied. "Selena, I'm afraid I'm going to have to take you up on your offer to hang out with you guys earlier than I'd anticipated." She told her cousin's wife about her aborted meeting with the hotel owner and having to evacuate the hotel because of a fire situation. "I hope you don't mind if I stop by for breakfast."

"Crystal, please. You know you don't have to ask."

"I'm asking because I'm bringing someone with me."

"That's not a problem. I was just preparing brunch for Xavier. He doesn't have classes until this afternoon. I'll hold off cooking until you guys get here."

"Thanks, Selena."

Crystal ended her call at the same time Joseph ended his. "My cousin says you're welcome to come with me."

He smiled. "Thank you. The car should be here in about fifteen minutes."

Staring at him in the bright sunlight, she noticed flecks of gray in his coarse, cropped black hair. Crystal doubted whether he was that much older than she, which meant he was graying prematurely. She also wondered how many times Joseph came to Charleston on business for him to have had a local car service programmed into his phone.

There was so much more she wanted to know about him, yet was reluctant to ask. She just wasn't prepared to accept any more revelations. And because he knew her uncle, there was also the possibility he had been familiar with her aunt and cousins.

She wrapped her arms around her body as much to ward off the morning chill as to protect herself from someone she wasn't prepared to possibly become involved.

What-ifs nagged at her like exposed, inflamed nerves. If her mother hadn't had a meltdown delaying her arrival, she would've spent the night with her cousins instead of the Beaumont House. If Algernon hadn't had a family emergency, she would have shared a table with him instead of Joseph. Now she was exacerbating the situation by inviting him to meet her cousins.

Crystal didn't get the overt vibe that Joseph was coming onto her, but even if he was, she knew his efforts would be fruitless, and not because she had qualms about establishing a friendship with a man.

Her sole focus was the exclusive commission to decorate the

historical structures with exquisite antiques and reproductions. She'd spent months in furniture warehouses and at estate sales looking for pieces with which to decorate a nineteenth-century Lowcountry residence. It wasn't just furniture she'd sought but also accessories, including candlesticks, vases, rugs, apothecary jars, clocks, linens, teapots and other collectibles.

She'd recommended Algernon rent a storage unit. Several pieces she had purchased at an estate sale were carefully wrapped, crated and shipped to him at the Beaumont House, where he arranged for them to be stored in the unit that was quickly filling up with sets of china and silver. Once she inspected the restored buildings, Crystal would be faced with what to put into each room. And in keeping with the time period, she'd planned for the walls to be covered with wallpaper, tapestries or even fabric.

She was anxious to begin her first significant commission.

"A dollar for your thoughts."

Joseph's soft, drawling voice shattered her reverie. Smiling, she turned to face him. "I thought it was a penny."

"That was before inflation," he countered. Slipping out of his jacket, he placed it over Crystal's shoulders. "You look cold."

Tugging on the lapels, she inhaled the cologne clinging to the cashmere fibers. "Thank you, but aren't you going to be cold?" She had on a suit, while he was in his shirtsleeves.

"No. After spending so many winters in upstate New York with lake-effect snow, I rarely feel cold."

"When I was here last January it was much warmer than it is now."

"Last year was unusually warm." Joseph stared at Crystal's distinctive delicate profile. "Did you bring winter clothes with you?"

Crystal nodded. "Yes. However, I didn't expect to stand outside when I got dressed this morning." Her wool gabardine pantsuit wasn't adequate for the low-forties temperature. As someone who lived in Florida year-round, anything below fifty degrees was cool to her.

A Lincoln Town Car maneuvered up to the curb, and Joseph, resting his hand at Crystal's waist, led her to the rear of the limo as the driver alighted. "I'll get the door, Mr. Wilson," the chauffeur called out.

Joseph stepped back, permitting the driver to open the rear door. Crystal got in first, and he followed, sitting beside her on the leather seat. Waiting until the man was seated behind the wheel once again, she gave him the address to her cousin's house.

Sitting close to Crystal, feeling her feminine heat and inhaling the hypnotic scent of her perfume was a bonus Joseph hadn't anticipated when he suggested they share a table.

The ride was much too short when the driver stopped in front of a classic example of a Charleston single house. The wrought-iron and stone pinecones atop ornate brick gates guarded the three-story structure with tall, narrow black-shuttered windows and first- and second-story white porches. The street address and 1800, the year the house was erected, were engraved into a brass plate affixed to one of the brick gate columns.

"Nice," Joseph crooned sotto voce. The house was surrounded by palmetto trees and several ancient oaks draped in Spanish moss.

Crystal smiled. His reaction was similar to her own when she first saw Xavier's house. "Wait until you see inside." Selena had decorated the interiors in an iconic Lowcountry style.

The driver came around to open the door and Joseph stepped out, extended his hand and assisted Crystal until she stood beside him. Reaching into the pocket of his jeans, he removed a money clip, peeling off a bill and handing it to the man. "I'll need you to take us back to the Beaumont House later this afternoon."

The chauffeur pocketed the money, smiling, then handed Joseph a business card. "Thank you. Call me when you're ready to go back."

Joseph put the card and money clip in his pocket. He rested a hand at the small of Crystal's back as they walked together to the front door. He stood off to the side. She'd just raised her hand to ring the doorbell when the door opened.

Ex-marine Major Xavier Eaton smiled at Crystal. He shifted the little girl he cradled on one hip. Extending his free arm, he pulled Crystal close and kissed her forehead. "Welcome back to Charleston."

Crystal pulled back, staring at Xavier's deeply tanned face. He wore a white tee, jeans and running shoes, and his ramrod-straight posture signified he'd had military training. "Thank you. You wear your vacation well."

Xavier, Selena and their daughter, Lily, opted out of spending Christmas with the extended family when they'd flown down to Puerto Rico to stay with one of Xavier's Marine Corps buddies who'd retired there once he was medically discharged. Xavier was also forced to resign his commission after a bullet had shattered his leg when he was deployed in Afghanistan. He'd been the quintessential bachelor whose dimples winked whenever he smiled until he stared through the plate glass of Sweet Persuasions to catch a glimpse of Selena Yates, the owner of the patisserie on King Street.

He laughed softly. "I'm still in vacation mode."

Crystal rubbed noses with Lily Eaton, eliciting high-pitched giggles from the toddler. "Hi, sweet Lily." Shifting slightly, she smiled at Joseph. "Xavier, I want you to meet a…a friend." She didn't know why she was stammering, but for an instant she didn't know how to introduce him. "This is Joseph Wilson." Reaching for Joseph's hand, she eased him closer. "Joseph, this is my cousin Xavier Eaton. And the beautiful little girl is his daughter, Lily."

The two men shook hands. "Nice meeting you, Xavier."

"Same here, Joseph. Welcome and please come in."

Xavier noticed Crystal was wearing Joseph's jacket over her suit, wondering if the man was the reason his cousin had changed her mind, deciding instead to spend several nights at the hotel. He successfully hid a smile. It'd been a while since Crystal appeared remotely interested in a man, and if she'd decided to bring Joseph to meet her relatives, he suspected he was more than a *friend*.

He was deployed when his sister told him Crystal had relocated to New York to pursue her graduate studies, and Xavier found it hard to accept that she was living with a man, because it had been drilled into the heads of every Eaton, every generation whether male or female, if a man or woman was good enough to live with, then he or she was good enough to marry.

Crystal slipped out of Joseph's jacket, handing it to him as they followed Xavier along the length of the porch and through another door leading into an entryway with a solid oak table cradling a collection of woven sweetgrass baskets. Selena's decorating trademarks were everywhere in the carefully chosen furnishings in the expansive living and formal dining rooms. She'd teased her cousin's wife that if Selena retired as a patissier, she would hire her as an assistant.

"Did Selena tell you we had to leave the hotel?"

Xavier glanced over his shoulder as he led them down a narrow hallway to the kitchen. "She mentioned something about a fire but didn't go into detail. What happened?"

"Joseph and I overheard one of the guests complaining about someone smoking in their room."

"If you guys can't get back into your room, then you're more than welcome to stay here."

Crystal exchanged a glance with Joseph. She noticed Xavier said *room* instead of *rooms*. He assumed she and Joseph were sharing a hotel room. "I don't think that's going to be necessary—"

"What's not necessary?" asked a familiar feminine voice. Selena stood at the cooking island in a bibbed apron, her hair concealed under a blue-and-white-checkered scarf as she sprinkled flour on a ball of dough. Her lips parted in a wide grin. "Wow!" she drawled. "Look at you. You cut your hair."

Crystal smoothed down the short strands on the nape of her neck. "I decided I needed a new look." She'd affected a hairstyle that was virtually maintenance free. She didn't have to use a blow-dryer, curling iron or flatiron. It was what she thought of as wash and go. A trim every six weeks kept the style fresh.

Wiping her hands on a towel, Selena approached Crystal, arms outstretched. "Good seeing you again. He's gorgeous," she whispered under her breath, hugging her husband's cousin tightly.

Crystal knew Selena was referring to Joseph, and she had to agree with her. He *was* gorgeous. "Selena, I would like you to meet Joseph Wilson. Joseph, this is Selena, who just happens to be the best pastry chef in the entire city."

Smiling, he took Selena's hand. "My pleasure. Your home is beautiful."

Selena's dark, almond-shaped eyes in a face the color of toasted hazelnuts crinkled attractively when she smiled. "Thank you. It's going to be at least fifteen minutes before everything is ready, so if you'd like, Xavier can give you a tour of the house." She cut her eyes at her husband. "Honey, please put that child down. Once you leave she's going to wild out because I refuse to carry her around."

Xavier tightened his hold on Lily as he gestured for Joseph to follow him, deliberately ignoring Selena. "If you don't have any plans for Super Bowl Sunday and if you're going to be in Charleston, then I'd like you to come over for a little get-together."

Crystal waited until she was certain the men were out of earshot before turning to look at Selena, who'd opened the refrigerator/freezer, taken out a small dish filled with freshly cut fruit, set it and a fork in front of her and then gone back to rolling out dough for biscuits.

Sitting on a stool at the island in the ultramodern chef's kitchen, she said, "It's not what you're thinking."

Selena met her eyes. "What exactly is it I'm thinking, Crystal?"

Between bites of cantaloupe and honeydew, she carefully formed her thoughts. "There's nothing going on between me and Joseph." She told Selena how they met and what they'd discovered about each other while sitting in the hotel's restaurant. "Belonging to a sorority or fraternity isn't extraordinary, but knowing he'd clerked for my uncle is eerie."

"It's not as eerie as it is serendipitous. It's as if you were destined to meet," Selena drawled, trying not to laugh.

Slipping out of her suit jacket, Crystal draped it over the back of the stool. "I don't believe in serendipity."

"What do you believe in?"

It was a full minute before she said, "I believe everyone is born with certain gifts and it's up to us or for others to recognize those gifts in order to make the world a better place."

Selena picked up a pastry brush, dipping it into a bowl of melted butter, and then brushed the tops of the biscuits in a baking pan. "What about love, Criss?"

"What about it?"

"Don't you believe in love?"

Crystal smiled. "Of course I believe in love. Look at you and Xavier. You guys are living proof of the adage 'love at first sight.'"

Selena placed the baking sheet on the shelf of a heated eye-level oven. She wiped her hands on the towel tucked under the ties of the bibbed apron. Resting a hip against the countertop, she angled her head. "You're talking about me and Xavier, but what about you, Criss? I heard about the man you lived with when you went to school in New York. Were you in love with him?"

"I don't think so. My relationship with Brian was more of convenience and companionship."

"For whom?"

Crystal stared at the granite countertop. "Brian and I were like a two-headed coin. We were interchangeable." A wry smile flitted over her lips. "He wasn't looking for a serious relationship, and it was the same with me. I didn't want to get married and neither did he. He also didn't want children, because he'd grown up in an abusive home and he feared he would also abuse a child, while I definitely wasn't and still am not looking to become a mother."

"You don't want to get married or have children?" Selena asked.

She wasn't marriage-phobic, but she didn't see it in her immediate future. "Right now I'm concentrating on growing my business. We didn't have to go looking for a date, and whenever men tried coming onto me, I told them the truth. I was living with a man," Crystal continued as if Selena hadn't broached the subject of marriage and children. "We were museum junkies. When Brian wasn't teaching and when I didn't have classes, we spent all of our free time seeing how many museums we could visit. One summer we drove to Vermont and hit every museum as far south as D.C."

Selena's eyes grew wider. "It sounds as if you had the perfect relationship. Didn't you ever argue?"

"Oh, we had our disagreements but nothing that monumental. He didn't believe in sororities or fraternities and he invariably left the toilet seat up and dirty dishes in the sink."

Scrunching up her nose, Selena drawled, "Thankfully Xavier is a neat freak. Now back to Joseph. It looks as if you two have a lot in common, so if he does ask you out, would you accept?"

"I think my busybody cousin already took care of that. Unless Joseph gives him the four-one-one about us, Xavier assumes we're sharing a hotel suite. And I'm certain you heard *your husband* invite him here for the Super Bowl party."

Selena sucked her teeth. "You didn't see it the last time you were here, but we turned the top floor into a theater and media room. I told Xavier if any of his friends have too much to drink and can't make it downstairs, then they're going to stay up there until they're mummified."

Crystal laughed until her sides hurt and tears ran down her face. She and Selena were still laughing when Joseph and Xavier entered the kitchen, both holding Lily's hands as she urged them to swing her higher.

She stared at him, marveling that he appeared so comfortable with her family. When Xavier released his daughter's hand, Joseph swung Lily up as she emitted a high-pitch squeal of delight. Black curls had escaped the two elastic bands holding her hair in place, and in that instant Crystal wondered if Joseph would be a stern or indulgent father. Judging from his interaction with the toddler, she knew it would probably be the latter.

Lily, breathing heavily, her face flushed, screamed, "I have to do potty!" Joseph set her on her feet and she raced to the half bath off the kitchen.

"She goes by herself now?" Crystal asked. Selena had begun toilet training her daughter at fourteen months, but Lily refused to sit on her potty unless her mother sat in the bathroom alongside her, reading fairy tales and nursery rhymes.

Selena chuckled softly. "Miss Grown wants to do everything by herself now that she's two. Every morning we bump heads because she wants to pick out her own clothes."

"What's wrong with that?"

"She forgets we're in Charleston and not Puerto Rico. She wants to wear sandals, shorts and bathing suits. I try to tell her we're not in the Caribbean, but she doesn't seem to understand." Lily emerged from the bathroom, her hands dripping water, and Xavier handed her a paper towel. The toddler dried her hands and then ran over to Crystal, raising her arms for her to pick her up.

Selena shook her head in exasperation. "When it gets to the point where I'm not going to be able to do anything with her, I'm going to send her to Florida to spend time with you."

Cradling the little girl to her chest, she dropped a kiss on her hair. "You know I'd take her in a heartbeat. Titi Criss will make certain she'll have the most tricked-out dollhouse imaginable."

Lily clapped her chubby hands. "I want a dollhouse."

Joseph sat on the stool next Crystal. "You build dollhouses?"

Xavier cracked eggs into a mixing bowl, then whisked them until they were light and fluffy before turning them onto a heated stove-top griddle. "You didn't know your girlfriend is an interior decorator?"

"I'm not his girlfriend," Crystal countered quickly.

"My bad," Xavier said with a sheepish grin.

Joseph stared at Crystal's profile. He didn't know why, but he wanted her to be his girlfriend only because he felt they were destined to connect. "I never would've thought you were a decorator."

She shifted slightly to look at him. "Why not?"

He lifted a shoulder. "Somehow I got the impression you were in Charleston to audit some company's books." There was something about her demeanor that called to mind the no-nonsense accountants at ColeDiz.

"You're not even close. I'm here to decorate the interior of an inn and B and B for the owner of Beaumont House," Crystal said.

Now he knew why she was living in the penthouse. He stayed at the Beaumont House because it was rated as one of the best hotels in Charleston. And if the owner of the hotel had elected to have Crystal decorate his other establishments, then there was no doubt she was at the top in her field.

"Congratulations."

She flashed a wide grin. "Thank you."

Thoroughly exhausted, Lily pushed two fingers in her mouth and closed her eyes. Within seconds she was asleep as Crystal savored the warmth of the small body molded to her chest. She closed her eyes for several seconds and when she opened them she was shocked by the tender expression on Joseph's face as he watched her rock the child. Seconds ticked as they continued to stare at each other.

Xavier shattered the spell as he gently extricated his sleeping daughter from Crystal's arms. "Let me take her."

"Does she usually take a nap this early?" Crystal asked him.

"Her sleep patterns have been haywire since we came back from vacation."

Xavier placed Lily in a playpen in the corner of the kitchen while Selena removed the pan of golden-brown biscuits from the oven, setting them on a warm plate. Temporarily fortified by the dish of fruit, Crystal stood up, washed her hands and assisted Selena in setting a bowl of grits and a platter with crisp bacon, julienned ham and country links on the table in the breakfast nook in the large eat-in kitchen, while Xavier ladled fluffy scrambled eggs into a serving bowl. Crystal had to do something so as not to sit and stare at Joseph.

* * *

Joseph, seated next to Crystal, took surreptitious glances at her. Each time she asked him to pass her a dish, their shoulders brushed, making him more than aware of her feminine scent.

He was surprised at how comfortable he felt interacting with her and her cousins.

It had to be an Eaton thing because he had experienced the same thing when meeting Solomon for the first time. He'd been referred to the judge by one of his law professors who'd attended law school with Solomon.

Although passing the bar on his first attempt, Joseph found himself mildly intimidated working for the former celebrated U.S. prosecutor, who struck fear in defendants and the opposing counsel whenever he entered the courtroom. Solomon never went to trial unless he was certain of a victory. Joseph's mentor jurist treated him as an equal, and he learned more about the law working with Solomon than he had in three years of law school.

Joseph swallowed a forkful of grits and eggs, savoring the piquant flavors. "Do you guys eat like this every morning?" he asked.

"I wish," Xavier intoned. "Most mornings I have breakfast at school. It's not as appetizing as it is health-conscious."

Selena smiled at Joseph. "I save the grits, eggs and pork for the weekend or whenever we have houseguests. If I ate like this every morning, I'd end up going back to bed instead of working."

Joseph slathered apple butter jam on a fluffy biscuit. "Xavier told me you have a home-based mail-order business."

She nodded. "Yes, I do. I closed my shop on King Street and went completely mail order after Lily was born. We expanded the house and installed a commercial kitchen. Working from home allows me to spend time with Lily and to do what I love."

He picked up the small jar of jam, staring at the label printed with the Sweet Persuasions website. "Do you sell these, too?"

Selena nodded again. "Those I give away as complimentary gifts for first-time customers. Most times they order the larger size whenever they place subsequent offers."

"Do you also make them?"

"No," Selena said, smiling. "I can't take credit for the jams, jellies and preserves. My grandmother makes them for me and I sell them in two-, four- and six-ounce sizes."

"How large an order can you accommodate?"

"How large are you talking about?" Selena asked.

"I'd like to begin with an assortment of at least five hundred jars. My family own and operate a number of vacation resorts throughout the Caribbean, and a variety of gourmet jellies and preserves would be perfect for breakfast breads and high tea. The larger sizes could be sold in the gift shops."

"Which resorts?" Crystal had asked the question before a seemingly stunned Selena could respond to Joseph's offer.

"ColeDiz International Limited." Joseph's expression was deadpan.

A soft gasp escaped Crystal's parted lips. "You're one of *those* Coles?" Even though it'd never been substantiated, the Coles were purported to be the wealthiest African-American family in the United States. It was then she remembered he'd introduced himself as Joseph Cole-Wilson.

The hint of a smile flitted over his mouth. "And you're one of *those* Eatons."

Xavier's gaze shifted from his cousin to Joseph. "Am I missing something here?"

Joseph told Xavier he'd been a law clerk for Solomon Eaton and that they also belonged to the same fraternity. "Now I'm a true believer that it's a small world, but I never would've expected to meet the judge's niece when I checked into the Beaumont House."

Xavier nodded. "Fate is a fickle woman. You never know what to expect from her."

"Why does it have to be a woman?" Crystal and Selena chorused in unison. Sharing a wide grin, they exchanged a fist bump.

"I think we'd better quit while we're ahead, brother," Joseph suggested, as he and Xavier executed their own handshake. He redirected his attention to Selena. "Do you think you'd be able to meet my request?"

She closed her eyes for several seconds. "I…I don't know. I have to think about it."

He nodded. "Take all the time you need. However, I'd also like to invest in your company. Just name your price. While you're thinking about it, can I place an order and have you overnight it to Diego Cole-Thomas. He's the CEO at ColeDiz."

A heavy silence descended on those sitting in the kitchen as Crystal stared at the contents of her plate instead of the man sitting next to her. He definitely was one of *those* Coles, she mused.

She didn't know if Selena was willing to give up a portion of a business she'd worked to grow over the past three years, and if she did agree to Joseph's offer, then the Eatons and Coles would be linked even further.

Crystal knew Joseph's family guarded their net worth like a top-secret government document, and had elected to remain a private company instead of going public like many billion-dollar conglomerates. People such as Joseph sealed deals with a single phone call or with a stroke of a pen.

And he had it all: looks, brains, wealth and power. Something told Crystal to run in the opposite direction, that when they returned to the Beaumont House she should end her association with him. But realistically she knew that wasn't possible. Xavier had invited him to their Super Bowl party.

Although Crystal did not want to become involved with Joseph, fate, destiny, providence or external circumstances had intervened. He would become a part of her existence while in Charleston and possibly beyond because of her uncle.

Chapter 4

It was after one when Joseph and Crystal returned to the Beaumont House.

When he called the front desk and was told the smoky condition had been extinguished, Joseph made arrangements for the driver to take them back. They hadn't exchanged a word during the return ride.

He reached for Crystal's hand, guiding her through the throng of guests to the elevators. Aside from reconnecting with his parents and siblings, he couldn't remember when he'd spent a more enjoyable morning since returning to the States.

The cooking skills of the owner of Sweet Persuasions were superior and the interchange between Crystal and her cousins light, lively and easygoing. He listened closely when Xavier talked of his intent to become a career officer, but after being seriously wounded he'd smoothly transitioned to civilian life and moved to Charleston to teach military history at a prestigious military prep school.

His interest in history was evidenced by the memorabilia in Xavier's home/office that included military maps, books on military history and black-and-white photographs of players from the Negro Leagues, and different countries and cities he'd taken while on leave.

Selena recounted her career from actress to pastry chef, and now mother of a precocious two-year-old. She admitted to being a frustrated interior decorator, teasing Crystal that whenever she decided to give up her mail-order enterprise she wanted to assist her at Eaton Interior and Design.

Joseph had waited patiently for Crystal to open up about her life and career, but she appeared more interested in her cousins talking about themselves. He still didn't know her age, if she'd been married or why she'd decided to become an interior decorator. He was also puzzled about her reaction when he'd revealed he was a Cole. He felt her withdraw when it was quite the opposite for him once she revealed she was an Eaton.

Both of them belonged to prominent black Florida families but hadn't crossed paths. He'd come to Charleston to oversee a business venture and had unknowingly come face-to-face with his mentor's niece. Joseph wasn't certain what she'd heard or read about the Coles that made her refer to his name with so much aversion.

It was another five minutes before they were able to squeeze into one of the three elevators. His arm went around her waist, easing her back against his body as a large man settled his bulk against Crystal's slender frame. His sigh echoed hers when they finally exited the car at their floor.

When he'd gotten up earlier, Joseph had planned to eat breakfast and then drive over to the tea garden to meet with the manager of the tea garden, not spend the morning and early afternoon with a woman who was as intriguing as she was stunningly beautiful.

Reaching into her handbag, Crystal removed her card key, while the hint of a smile played at the corners of her mouth. "Let's hope the rest of the day goes a lot more smoothly than this morning."

Joseph wanted to tell her there was nothing remotely wrong with his morning. Circumstances beyond his control had connected him with his penthouse neighbor and a plan he never would've been able to devise even if he'd mulled it over for days.

"It wasn't a total loss. At least not for me," he added, smiling. "And thank you for allowing me to tag along with you for brunch. I'd like to return the favor and prepare dinner for you tomorrow night." He'd heard Crystal tell Selena she would see her Saturday afternoon.

Crystal's fingers tightened on the card key. "You can cook?"

His expression changed, vertical lines appearing between his eyes. "Why would you ask me that?"

Cocking her head to the side, she drawled, "Your being a Cole, I thought you would've grown up with live-in cooks and housekeepers."

Joseph's frown vanished quickly. "So you think because I'm a Cole I'm completely helpless and that I need someone to cook and pick up after me?"

"I don't know what to think," Crystal countered. "What I do know is that you've overdosed on entitlement pie. You hadn't known my cousin an hour before you expected her to accept your offer to invest in her company."

Joseph stared at the carpeted floor for several seconds; then his gaze came up and his eyes met Crystal's. "I asked her because I'm a businessman."

"I thought you were a lawyer."

"I am a lawyer, a farmer and also a businessman looking for new opportunities in which to expand my family's company." He realized that two years ago he never would've admitted to being a businessman or a farmer. Joseph had challenged the CEO of ColeDiz when Diego gave him the responsibility of adding the tea company to the list of other ventures under the corporate umbrella with the argument that he wasn't a farmer.

The disclosure that he was a farmer shocked Crystal. "What are you growing?"

Joseph's expression closed. "We can discuss that when you have dinner with me. Tomorrow night, seven o'clock, my place, casual attire."

Much to her chagrin, Crystal laughed. She'd just accused Joseph of having OD'd on entitlement and he'd just assumed she would share dinner with him because he wanted it. "What you need to consider is eating a slice of humble pie," she said laughingly.

Splaying the fingers of his right hand over his heart, he managed to look contrite. "I'm so very sorry, Miss Eaton, but will you do me the honor of sharing dinner with me?" He lowered his hand. "Is that humble enough?"

"It'll do—for now," she said, biting back more laughter. Even though she thought Joseph slightly arrogant, she had to add charming to his other obvious assets.

"Do you like Italian food?"

"I love it."

"Then Italian it is," he said with a wide grin.

"Do you want me to bring anything?" she asked.

"No. I have everything I need."

"Tomorrow night at seven," she repeated.

Turning, she walked the length of the hallway to her apartment. Crystal felt the heat from Joseph's gaze on her back, and seconds before she slipped the card key into the slot, she turned to find him watching her. He hadn't moved. Their eyes met, gazes fusing for a nanosecond; she glanced away, opened the door and then closed it behind her.

Kicking off her shoes, she placed the card key on the table in the entryway and set her handbag on the leather-covered bench seat next to the table.

Walking on bare feet, she made her way into the living room. Flopping down on an inviting club chair, she rested her feet on the matching ottoman and closed her eyes at the same time her cell phone chimed. Pushing off the chair, Crystal went to retrieve the phone from her handbag.

Swallowing back a groan, she tapped the screen. "Hello, Mother."

"Why did I have to wait almost twenty-four hours just to hear your voice?"

Walking back to the chair, Crystal sat down again. She'd promised her mother she would call her once she arrived in Charleston, but she didn't because she didn't want to hear Jasmine go on about her latest breakup. "Mama, please don't start."

"Please, Crystal. You know better than to call me by that tacky title."

She rolled her eyes upward even though Jasmine couldn't see her. "How are you today?"

"Wonderful. I'm leaving for the airport to fly out to Vegas

to meet Philip. He called early this morning to say he wants me to join him."

Crystal clenched her teeth to keep from spewing curses. She didn't want to believe she'd driven down to Miami to console her mother just to have her reconcile with her latest beau the very next day. "What happened to you breaking up with him, Mother?"

"I changed my mind. Of all of the men I've dated, Philip is someone I'd actually consider marrying."

"He must really be exceptional if you're willing to give up your alimony payments."

"I did say *consider*."

Crystal stared at the chipped polish on the big toe of her right foot as her mother talked incessantly about the plans Philip had made for them. "I told him I wanted to take a flight over the Hoover Dam and Grand Canyon," Jasmine continued without pausing to take a breath, "but he said he's not certain whether we'll have enough time."

"When are you coming back?"

"Wednesday night. Enough talk about me. Have you seen Xavier and his adorable baby daughter?"

Smiling for the first time since answering the phone, Crystal said, "Yes. But Lily's not a baby anymore. She's a toddler who's walking, talking *and* potty-trained."

"I really miss seeing Raleigh's family."

She registered the longing in Jasmine's voice. "Remember, Mother, you divorced Daddy, not the Eatons. Whenever they invite you to family reunions, you always decline. And I've lost count of those who've asked about you year after year."

"I don't come because I can't abide those tramps hanging on to Raleigh as if they can't breathe without him. He needs to be told to stay away from strip joints when looking for a new wife."

"You're preaching to the choir, Mother." Crystal didn't understand how her father could take up with women who were the complete opposite of his first wife. Jasmine had more class in her little finger than all of her ex-husband's ex-wives collectively.

"I know you don't like talking about it, but why don't you ask Xavier to introduce you to some of his single guy friends? If you're going to spend a couple of months working in Charleston, you should have some fun, too."

Crystal rolled her eyes upward again. "I came here to work, not look for a boyfriend."

"There's nothing wrong with a little casual dating."

"I'll think about it, Mother," Crystal lied smoothly.

Two months was hardly enough time for her to meet and become romantically involved with someone, and what Jasmine termed as casual dating usually meant seeing someone for a month. It would take her more than a month to truly feel comfortable enough to take their casual dating to the next level.

"Hold on, darling. The gatehouse is ringing me." Seconds later, Jasmine said, "I have to go. My driver is here."

"Have fun, Mother."

"I will. Love you, darling."

"I love you, too." She ended the call, staring at the live fern in a painted glazed pot on a corner table. The words her mother found so difficult to say when Crystal was a young girl now came so easily from Jasmine. She'd wanted Jasmine to be like the mothers of her friends and cousins who got up and prepared breakfast before seeing their children off to school. Or when she came home after classes, she wanted to find freshly baked cookies waiting for her as she sat down to do her homework.

What she did remember was Jasmine sleeping late, chain-smoking and visiting her therapist, while handing over the responsibility of taking care of her daughter to a series of nannies. Once Crystal turned eight, there was no longer a need for a nanny or babysitter; she had unofficially moved in with her uncle Solomon and Aunt Holly.

Shaking her head to banish painful childhood memories, Crystal pushed off the chair and climbed the staircase to the upper level. Restlessness assailed her, akin to an itch she couldn't scratch. She needed a full-body massage. She didn't know why, but she always experienced unease whenever Jasmine called her because she never knew what to expect. Why, she mused, couldn't they just have a normal mother–daughter discussion without Jasmine bringing up the topic of dating?

What the older woman did not know was that she did date, although it had been a while. Over the years she'd dated a few handsome and not-so-handsome men, those who were well-to-do and others whom she suspected lived from paycheck to paycheck. Their looks and the size of their bank accounts were never prerequisites for Crystal to agree to go out with them. It was always their confidence and manners—the latter taking precedence over the former. Even before she was old enough to date, her mother had lectured her constantly about home training.

Even behind closed lids Crystal could still see the image of Joseph's deeply tanned face, his dark eyes and tall, toned slim body. He was the epitome of tall, dark and handsome. And the fact that he was wealthy didn't begin to play into the equation.

She didn't want to think about Jasmine or Joseph. Rolling her head, she attempted to ease the tight muscles in her shoulders and upper back. It was time for a massage. Having access to an on-site health club was one of the reasons, along with the unisex salon, spa and boutique, was why she'd decided to buy property in the Fort Lauderdale gated community.

Picking up the phone, she dialed the number to the hotel's Serenity Silk Day Spa. Her call was answered after the second ring. "Good afternoon, Ms. Eaton. How may I help you?"

"I'd like an appointment for a facial and a mood-makeover massage. Is it possible for me to combine the massage with hot stones?"

"Of course, Ms. Eaton. What time would you like to come in?"

Crystal glanced at her watch. "I can be down in less than half an hour."

"We'll be waiting for you."

Ending the call, she went upstairs to her bedroom to change out of her suit and into a pair of sweatpants, a shirt and a pair of flip-flops. The sound of something hitting the windows caught her attention. It was raining. Even if she'd wanted to do some sightseeing, Crystal realized she would've had to change her plans.

She slipped the two card keys, a credit card and cash onto a wristlet before leaving.

Crystal walked across the marble floor of the lobby to the spa discreetly located at the end of a narrow hallway. She felt the calming atmosphere the instant she opened the door to the candlelit space, finding herself enveloped in the sounds of a waterfall, soothing New Age music flowing from hidden speakers and the tantalizing scent of essential oils.

The white-coated receptionist escorted her to a dressing room, where she stripped down to her panties and put on a thick terry cloth bathrobe. She was given a cup of herbal tea and a questionnaire asking about her health status, including whether she was pregnant and/or had any implanted devices.

Twenty minutes later Crystal knew she'd made the right decision visit the spa. Her face anchored in the cushioned doughnut on the massage table, she closed her eyes and moaned softly when hot stones lined the length of her spine. She had her mother to thank for her turning her onto the practice of using heated stones dating back five thousand years to the Ayurveda, an ancient Indian healing tradition.

She found herself succumbing to the strong fingers of the masseuse easing the tightness in her shoulders and upper back, falling asleep and waking only when told to turn over.

The hot stone massage was followed by the application of oils made up of lavender and patchouli, and then a shower and a facial that left her moisturized face glowing. She lingered long enough for a mani/pedi.

After paying for the services, Crystal gave the masseuse and esthetician generous tips, feeling better than she had in weeks.

As she left the spa and walked through the lobby, Crystal had to decide whether she wanted to cook dinner for herself, order room service or eat in the hotel's restaurant. Her step faltered as she headed in the direction of the elevators to find Joseph in a passionate embrace with a petite woman with a café-au-lait complexion and hair the color of ripened wheat.

Joseph lifted the woman off her feet at the same time his eyes met Crystal's. She saw an expression of surprise freeze his features as he stared at her. She didn't know why, but she felt like a voyeur even after she'd pulled her gaze away from the couple. Joseph had promised to cook for her the following day, and she wondered if the attractive blonde would join them.

Entering the elevator, she inserted the card key into the PH slot. *Two's company and three is a crowd.* The familiar adage came to mind as the car rose quickly to the top floor.

Perhaps, she mused, Joseph should've waited to invite her to dinner before checking whether his girlfriend would show up. It was obvious her neighbor was faced with a dilemma, and because Crystal detested confrontation she was more than willing to accept his suggestion to cancel dinner. The ball, as the saying goes, was definitely in his court.

Joseph went completely still as he held his sister. When Bianca called from the concierge's desk asking him to come down, he'd been surprised to hear from her. Then he saw Crystal stroll across the hotel lobby in sweats and flip-flops.

Once he and Crystal returned to the hotel, he hadn't been able to stop thinking about her, or comparing her to Kiara. He found himself transfixed by her soft drawling voice, her low, sensual laughter, the genuine affection she appeared to have for Xavier and Selena and the sparkle in her eyes whenever she interacted with Lily. He was completely mesmerized by the confidence and poise that seemed to come so naturally to her. And after comparing her to Kiara, he realized he'd wasted four years of his life with a woman with whom he had so little in common.

As a Cole, he would always put family first, but not with Kiara. Once she left Baltimore she refused to return or interact with her parents or anyone in her extended family. And whenever he mentioned meeting her family, she would fly into a rage, then not speak to him for days.

"Joseph, please put me down." Bianca's command broke into his musings.

"Sorry about that." He gave her a long, penetrating stare. "How did you find me?" he asked.

A slight frown appeared between Bianca Cole-Wilson's brilliant gold-green catlike eyes. "Diego told me you were going to be here for a few months. I need to talk to you."

Joseph hadn't seen his sister since Thanksgiving. Bianca, a premed senior at Duke University, hadn't celebrated Christmas and New Year's with the family because she'd spent the holiday in California with her sorority sisters with whom she shared off-campus housing.

Holding on to her hand, he steered to the bank of elevators. "We'll talk upstairs."

Bianca pulled back. "Can't we talk down here?"

He gave her a questioning look. "What's the matter?"

"Henri is waiting in the parking lot to drive me back to college."

"Why are you going back so early? Don't you have another week before classes begin again?"

"Yes, but I need to clean up my bedroom. I left clothes everywhere. It's also my week to clean the kitchen and bathroom."

"Why aren't you flying up?"

"The jet is being serviced."

Joseph nodded. Henri had been hired as Diego's driver and bodyguard. The mandate that anyone with Cole blood was prohibited from flying on a commercial carrier was still in effect more than forty years after Regina Cole's kidnapping. Instead of arriving at the airport hours before departure time, or going through long lines at the security gate, Bianca and her sorority sisters were seated in the Gulfstream G650 business jet within minutes of arriving at the Raleigh-Durham International Airport for their nonstop flight to LAX.

"Okay," he said conceding. "We'll talk in the lounge area. Would you like me to order something for you to eat or drink?" he asked when they were seated next to each other on a tan leather love seat.

"No, thank you. We stopped to eat in Savannah, so I'm good."

Joseph wanted to tell his sister that aside from her deep suntan, she didn't look that good. Standing five-four and usually tipping the scales at one ten, she appeared much too thin. The natural blond hair she inherited from her Puerto Rican maternal grandmother made her a standout among the many dark-haired, dark-eyed Coles.

"Talk to me, Bianca."

Lacing and unlacing her fingers together on her lap, Bianca revealed she had second thoughts about going to medical school. "It's not that I don't want to become a doctor, but I'm thinking of taking a year off after I graduate in May."

Joseph's expression did not reveal his shock at this disclosure. For as long as he could remember, Bianca had always talked about going into medicine. "Are you pregnant?" he asked. It was the first thing that popped into his head.

She gave him an incredulous look. "No!"

He angled his head. "Then why the change of mind?"

Bianca closed her eyes. "I think I'm burning out." She'd accelerated in high school taking advance placement classes, graduating at fifteen, and would be a month shy of her twentieth birthday when enrolling in medical school. "My brain is fried, Joey," she whispered under her breath. Bianca was the only one in the family who shortened his name.

Draping an arm around her shoulders, Joseph eased her closer to him and pressed a kiss on her hair. "Should I assume you haven't mentioned this to Mom and Dad?" She nodded. "Have you decided what you want to do while you're taking the year off?"

Bianca's cheeks puffed up as she emitted an audible sigh. "I want to spend six months in Brazil with Regina and Aaron, and the next six in New Mexico with Emily and Chris."

"Why are you telling me this instead going directly to Dad?" Joseph asked. "After all, he's still legally and financially responsible for you."

Bianca raised her chin, staring directly into the eyes of her favorite brother. It wasn't that she didn't love her other three brothers, but it was Joseph with whom she felt closest. Nathan, Harper and Anthony, who were twenty-six, thirty-two and thirty-five respectively, never seemed to find the time to play or listen to her.

"I have saved some money, and I would've had more if I hadn't gone to L.A., but what I need is your reassurance that you'll loan me enough to hold me over for the next year because Daddy's going to cut me off once I drop out of school."

Orthopedic surgeon José Cole-Wilson Sr. laid the ground rules for his children with regard to their education. He would underwrite the cost of their college, law or medical school tuition, provide them with a car and gas cards and deposit enough money into a checking account to take care of personal incidentals. And if she did take a year off, then she would be forced to move back home and rely on her parents for her day-to-day support.

"You're not dropping out, Bianca," Joseph argued softly. "You'll graduate in May."

"But I don't plan to go to medical school for a year, and for Daddy that's the same as dropping out."

"I think you're being a little overdramatic, Bibi."

She closed her eyes. "You know I'm not."

"If you decide to take a year off, I doubt Dad will cut you off financially. But if that's what you believe, then I want you to open a separate account when you get back to Durham. Call me with the account number and I'll arrange to transfer money from my account into yours. How much do you think you'll need?"

She opened her eyes, smiling. "I'm not certain, because I'll be staying with Regina and Emily."

"Have you told them of your plans?"

Bianca nodded. "They're both in agreement. What I have to do is tell Dad."

"When are you going to do that?"

"I'm going home for spring break. I'll tell him then."

"Do you want me to be there when you tell him?"

Bianca kissed his stubble. "No. I don't think I'm going to need backup, but thanks for offering."

Joseph rested his chin on her head. "Regardless of what happens I want you to remember that I'll always be here for you."

She smiled, willing the tears pricking the backs of her eyelids not to fall. She came to Joseph rather than her other brothers because she knew he would not only hear her out but also take her side. Nathan, Anthony and Harper were too involved in their careers and whatever woman they were dating at the time.

"I know that." Bianca glanced at her watch. "I think I've kept Henri waiting long enough."

"I'll walk you to the car."

Joseph put his arm around Bianca's shoulders. He'd always felt very protective of his sister from the moment his parents brought her home from the hospital.

They reached the parking lot and as if on cue Henri exited the limousine, opening a large black umbrella. A rare smile parted his lips with his approach as he extended his free hand. "Good afternoon, Mr. Wilson," he greeted in slightly accented French.

Joseph grasped the proffered hand in a firm handshake. "Good afternoon, Henri. How have you been?"

He hadn't seen the driver/bodyguard since before the Christmas holiday. The man with the shaven dark brown pate and strong features reminiscent of carved African masks appeared as taciturn as his boss. He and Diego were well suited for each other; both were men of few words—Henri even less than Diego. Only Diego knew his last name, and whenever he picked up the phone to call Henri he made himself available twenty-four/seven.

"Bien, señor."

Joseph smiled as Henri lapsed fluidly into Spanish. There were occasions when he overheard the man speaking fluent French, Creole or Spanish. He shifted his attention to Bianca. "Call or text me when you arrive. And don't forget about the account number."

Going on tiptoe, she kissed his chin. "I will."

Taking a step back, Joseph watched Henri hold the umbrella over Bianca's head as they walked to the black Mercedes. He stood in the same spot watching the red taillights disappear before going back into the hotel. He had to come up with a menu for a dinner he would prepare for the most beguiling woman he'd ever met. The South Carolina Eatons had offered him their Southern hospitality, and in a little more than twenty-four hours a Palm Beach Cole would return the favor when he prepared dinner for Crystal.

Chapter 5

Crystal massaged scented cream cologne over her body, followed with dots of a matching perfume at all of her pulse points. She'd taken a bubble bath, luxuriating in the Jacuzzi until the candles lining the bathtub's ledge flickered wildly, then sputtered out.

The clock on the table in a corner of the expansive bathroom chimed the half hour. It was six-thirty—thirty minutes before she was scheduled to meet Joseph for dinner.

He planned for a casual encounter, and after going through her closet she selected a pair of black stretch cropped slacks, matching long-sleeved cashmere sweater and black leather ballet flats.

As promised, Algernon had called, giving her an update. He planned to return to Charleston late Monday evening; the contractor overseeing the renovations to the adjoining historic buildings would meet with her and the owner Tuesday at noon.

Anxious to begin decorating the rooms for the inn and B and B, Crystal estimated completing the project hopefully within eight weeks.

Her next commission would take her to New York City, where the owner of a one-hundred-fifty-seven-year-old Tribeca residence planned to turn the town house's basement into a late-night jazz club; she looked forward to returning to the city she'd called home while attending Parsons New School for Design, where she'd earned an MFA in interior design.

Pushing her arms into the sleeves of a thick terry cloth robe, Crystal belted it and sat at the vanity; picking up a sable brush, she opened a makeup palette with foundation, concealer and bronzer in shades matching her skin tone and another with eye shadows in muted shades ranging from sienna to smoky grays and black.

Adjusting the lighting around the perimeter of the mirror, she lightly swept the tip of the brush over the foundation, gently blew off the excess and then dusted the velvety bristles over her forehead, cheeks and chin.

Peering closely at her reflection, she surveyed her final handiwork, pleased with the results. The smoky gray shadow on her lids and the soft black mascara on her lashes made her eyes appear larger, dramatic. The coat of raspberry lip gloss matched the barely perceptible matching blush on her high cheekbones.

Staring at her reflection, she recalled Joseph hugging the blonde. She'd expected him to contact her to cancel their date, but as the time drew closer she went through with the motions of readying herself as originally planned.

Crystal experienced a range of emotions whenever she thought about Joseph. Despite his being born into wealth and privilege, there was nothing ostentatious about him, and if he did give off vibes of entitlement she credited it to his being a Cole. And she was also curious to find out more about his family. Even with their supposedly great wealth, they'd managed to remain discreet, inconspicuous, unlike some privileged scions stalked by the paparazzi.

What truly puzzled her was his disclosure of being farmer. Why, she mused, would he give up practicing law to farm? And what was he growing? Crystal hoped she would have the answers she sought before the night ended.

The chiming of the doorbell echoed throughout Joseph's apartment. Taking long strides, he crossed the living room to the entryway and opened the door, certain Crystal could hear his audible intake of breath when he stared at her upturned face. Her dramatic yet subtle makeup, her black attire, the modified spiky hair style and the scent of her perfume silently screamed *sensuality.* It took herculean strength for him to pull his gaze away from her mouth.

"Am I too early?" she asked.

Crystal forced herself not to gawk at Joseph. The absence of stubble made him appear boyish. He'd exchanged his jeans and boots for a pair of dark blue tailored slacks and black leather slip-ons. His light blue shirt with white contrasting cuffs and collar was open at the throat.

Joseph blinked as if coming out of a trance. "No...not at all." Stepping aside, he opened the door wider. "Please come in."

Crystal handed him the decorative bag with several bottles of wine. Not wearing heels made her aware of the differences in their heights. The top of her head came to his chin. "I didn't know if you were serving meat, chicken or fish, so I brought zinfandel, pinot noir and a sauvignon blanc."

He peered into the bag. "Thank you, but I have wine."

"Please keep it," she said when he attempted to give her back the bag. "I have more than I'd ever attempt to drink in a year."

Placing the bag on a side table, Joseph escorted Crystal into the living room, seating her on the love seat facing an unlit fireplace. The layout and furnishings in his apartment were identical to hers. He hadn't drawn the wall-to-wall drapes, and lights from office buildings and streetlights shimmered eerily through the nighttime mist. A steady downpour had left the city with more than two inches over a twenty-four-hour period.

Her gaze shifted to the table in the dining room set for formal dining with china, silver and crystal. It was apparent dinner was going to be anything but casual.

She turned to face Joseph staring at her, wondering what was going on behind his dark eyes. Crystal asked herself why she'd accepted his invitation when it would have been so easy to decline. As soon as the thought entered her head she knew the answer. Not only was she curious about Joseph, but she also had to acknowledge the physical attraction. Everything about him: face, body, the hypnotic scent of his cologne and the sensual timbre of his voice radiated blatant sensuality.

"Did you ever work in a restaurant?" she asked him.

Folding his hands together behind his back, Joseph angled his head. "Yes. Why?"

"Just asking."

A smile tilted the corners of his mouth. "Why are you 'just asking'?"

Pushing to her feet, Crystal walked into the dining room. "Only someone with restaurant or catering experience would know how to arrange silver and glassware for a formal dinner." The place settings included salad, dessert and fish forks and dinner and butter knives, water goblets and red wineglasses.

Joseph followed Crystal, resting his hands on her shoulders. "My mother owns a restaurant. The year I turned fifteen I worked there as a dishwasher. At sixteen it was busing tables, and at seventeen I'd graduated to waiting tables."

She froze for several seconds before relaxing under the light, impersonal touch. Crystal peered at him over her shoulder, smiling. She'd misjudged him. He wasn't a rich kid whose parents had indulged his every whim. Washing dishes and busing tables were the least glamorous jobs in the restaurant business.

"Where's her restaurant?"

"Palm Beach. It's called Marimba in honor of my grandfather who was a percussionist with a Latin band back in the day."

"You're Cuban?"

Tightening his hold on her shoulders, Joseph turned her around to face him. "I'm African-American, Cuban and Puerto Rican." Reaching for her hand, he laced their fingers together. "Come with me into the kitchen and I'll give you a brief overview of the Cole-Wilsons."

The sight that greeted her in the gourmet kitchen rendered her temporarily mute. He'd prepared an antipasto with prosciutto, Genoa salami, roasted peppers, mixed olives, fresh mozzarella, sliced tomatoes and a Caesar salad topped with parmesan shavings. There were also small cubes of marinated beef kabobs on a plate next to the stove-top grill.

Moving closer to the cooking island, she stared at a baking sheet with risen dough sprinkled with garlic, rosemary, olive oil and coarse salt. Joseph had poked shallow indentations and sprinkled grated Parmesan over the top of the focaccia bread.

"There's a lot of food here," she remarked.

He pulled out a high stool at the island, seating her. "It looks like a lot because I enjoy different courses. I grew up eating soup, salad, bread, rice, beans, meat, chicken or fish for dinner, plus dessert. There's enough here for two servings from each course."

Joseph continued to surprise Crystal. His culinary prowess was definitely impressive. "You must have spent all day putting this together."

"I got up early to put up the dough, but it took me less than half an hour to make the antipasto and salad. I cooked the main dish of baked rigatoni with a tomato-basil sauce and meatballs last night, so it just has to be reheated."

Resting her elbows on the granite countertop, Crystal watched Joseph unbutton and roll back the cuffs on his shirt. Her gaze lingered on his hands. They were as exquisite as his face. "Who taught you to cook?"

"*Mi madre y abuela*. My mother and grandmother," he translated quickly. "I hope you brought your appetite."

"I did," Crystal answered truthfully. Her caloric intake for the day included yogurt topped with granola, an apple and bottled water.

Joseph opened the refrigerator and removed a pitcher of clear liquid filled with sliced white peaches and green grapes. "We'll start with peach sangria and the beef kabobs."

She stood up. "Do you need help with anything?"

Leaning closer, he ran his forefinger down the length of her nose. "Yes. I want you to help me eat this food."

Crystal rolled her eyes at him. "That's not what I meant and you know it."

"Do you know that you're real cute when you pout?" he whispered, filling two glasses with sangria and handing her one. He touched his glass to hers and took a swallow.

For several seconds she had no comeback. "I never pout."

"Yeah, you do," Joseph insisted. "You push out your lips and roll your eyes upward."

"Pouting is sucking teeth, closing your eyes, while rolling your head on your neck. Like this," Crystal added, demonstrating the motions.

Throwing back his head, Joseph laughed loudly. "You remind of Wanda. The Jamie Foxx character from *In Living Color*."

Crystal's laughter joined his. "I love watching reruns from *In Living Color* and *Martin*. And to see those actors transform themselves into characters that became icons is genius."

"Now, that takes real talent," Joseph agreed. Turning on the stove-top grill, he sprayed the surface with cooking oil. "How do you like your meat cooked?"

"Well. How do you like yours?" she asked.

He placed the skewers on the heated surface. "Why? Do you plan to cook for me?" he teased with a wide grin.

Crystal flashed a sexy moue. "Could be yes, could be no."

"Which one is it, Crystal?"

The uneasiness she'd felt when first walking into Joseph's apartment disappeared, replaced by an easygoing emotion that made her feel as if she'd met him weeks ago instead of two days. "I'll cook for you if you want."

His wide grin showed straight white teeth. "I want."

"Are you certain your girlfriend won't mind?"

The teasing glint in Joseph's eyes vanished. "Why would you mention a girlfriend?"

Crystal also sobered. "You said you're single, but you could still have a girlfriend."

He lifted a skewer, testing the meat for doneness before turning it over. "I don't have a girlfriend."

"Do you like women?"

Joseph's expression was a mask of stone as he glared at Crystal, unable to believe she would ask him something so ridiculous when he was practically salivating over her. It had taken every ounce of his self-control not to kiss her and satisfy the yearning to see if her mouth tasted as sweet as it looked.

"Yes, I like women. In fact, I like them a lot. It's just that I'm not seeing anyone right now."

"And why not?" she asked, pressing the issue.

Joseph turned four of the eight skewered cubes of beef over. He preferred his meat medium-well. "I was in a relationship for four years."

"What happened?"

"She wanted marriage and I wasn't ready for it at that time." Leaving his position at the courthouse to work for ColeDiz entailed longer work hours and a great deal more responsibility.

Crystal recoiled as if she'd been struck across the face. "You date a woman for four years and then decide she's not worth marrying?"

A frown furrowed Joseph's forehead. "Don't put words in my mouth, Crystal. I never said she wasn't worth marrying."

"What exactly are you saying, Joseph?"

"Kiara and I met in law school. We saw each other off and on, then hardly at all after graduation because I was studying for the bar. We reconnected when she relocated from Baltimore to Orlando. She was offered a position with the public defender's office at the same time I began clerking for your uncle."

"Had you moved to Miami?"

He shook his head. "No. I kept my West Palm Beach condo."

"You commuted the seventy miles between West Palm and Miami?"

He nodded. "Driving a minimum of three hours roundtrip every day isn't what I'd call a walk in the park, but I did it because I loved what I was doing." Joseph exhaled an audible breath. "I regretted having to resign clerking for Judge Eaton because criminal law had taken over my life. I ate, breathed and slept it."

Crystal took a sip of sangria, waiting for Joseph to continue. She wondered what would make a woman date a man for four years hoping, wishing and praying he would marry her. "Why did you resign?"

"Unfortunately, ColeDiz's general counsel was murdered when he walked in on a home invasion, and my cousin Diego needed someone in the legal department he could trust because he'd restructured to take the company global. I was able to set up an African international division, which allowed Diego to pay cash on delivery to a Ugandan cotton grower with an extralong staple crop. It resulted in ColeDiz becoming the biggest family-owned agribusiness in the States. I traded commuting for jetting around the world.

"One month I'd be in Mexico or Belize. Then a couple of months later it was Jamaica, Brazil, Puerto Rico or Africa. Kiara complained we didn't see enough of each other, but there was nothing I could do about it because of my commitment to ColeDiz. I took her to Hawaii for a vacation to try and make up for the time when we couldn't be together, but she misconstrued my intent, believing I was going to propose marriage. When I didn't, all hell broke loose. The only thing to do was cut the trip short and return to the mainland."

"You never reconciled?"

"No." The single word was adamant. Joseph would never reconcile with Kiara because she had cursed not only him but also his entire family.

A beat passed before Crystal spoke again. "What else are you involved in besides cotton?"

"We have banana plantations in Belize and coffee in Mexico, Jamaica, Puerto Rico and Brazil. Two years ago we established Cole Tea Company, our first North American–based enterprise. It's only the second tea garden in the United States."

Crystal stared, surprised. "You're growing tea here in South Carolina?"

An expression of triumph brightened Joseph's eyes. "Yes."

"That means you're going to compete with the Charleston Tea Plantation."

Joseph sobered. "I don't know about competition, but ColeDiz has done very well with coffee, so tea was the next logical choice. Our tea garden covers one hundred acres between Kiawah and Edisto islands, and we plan to harvest our first crop in a couple of months."

Crystal sparingly sipped the sangria. "Is that what you meant when you said you were a farmer?"

"I now think of myself as a farmer because before the tea garden I knew absolutely nothing about bananas, coffee or tea except to eat or drink them. I spent a couple of years studying everything I could find about irrigation, soil composition, disease control and various methods of planting and harvesting these crops."

"Why did you decide on South Carolina? Why not Georgia or Florida?" she asked.

"The Lowcountry has the perfect environment for tea because of its sandy soil, subtropical climate and an average rainfall of over fifty inches a year. And there's a common myth that different types of teas are produced from different tea plants."

"Aren't they?" she asked.

"No. All types of tea are produced from the same plant, although there are two different varieties. The differences between them are the result of the different processing procedures. Sinensis sinensis thrives in the cool, high mountains of central China and Japan and sinensis assamica in moist, tropical regions of northeast India, the Yunnan provinces of China and here in the Lowcountry."

Crystal's eyebrows rose in amazement. "Are you saying green, black and oolong tea all come from the same plant even though they don't taste the same?"

"Yes. If you have some free time I'd like to take you to see our tea garden."

Although Crystal wanted to see the tea garden, she knew it couldn't be this weekend because she'd promised to spend that time with Xavier and Selena, and she was also scheduled to meet Al and the contractor Tuesday afternoon. "Monday is the only day I'm free this coming week."

"It's all right. We can put it off until a later date. By the way, do you have boots?"

Crystal nodded. "I have a pair of rain boots."

"They'll do because most times the island is a little muddy."

"What about your resorts?"

"What about them?" Joseph countered.

"How many do you have?"

"Eight. That's why I offered to invest in Selena's company. Her gourmet jams and jellies when marketed as duty-free souvenirs will make her a very wealthy woman. ColeDiz of course will be responsible for exportation, tariffs and other fees."

Crystal closed her eyes for several seconds. Now she understood how the Coles had amassed their wealth, and she wondered how many people outside their family were privy to this information. When she opened her eyes Joseph had placed four kabobs on a plate with a tiny cup of dipping sauce for her along with a knife and fork.

Setting down the glass of wine, she picked up the knife, cutting a slice of the grilled meat and popping it into her mouth.

"Oh my word!" she gasped. "This is so good."

Joseph dipped his cube into the leftover marinade, slowly chewing the tender buttery sirloin. It was only the second time he'd attempted the recipe, and he had to admit to himself it was delicious. "Not bad."

"Don't be so modest, Joseph," Crystal chided. "You're an incredible chef."

"Cook," he corrected. "My mother is the professional chef. Enough about me," he said, deftly steering the topic away from him. "Is there someone special in your past?"

Crystal stared at the precisely cut raven-black hair lying close to Joseph's scalp, wondering, if he let it grow, if it would curl or stand up like brush bristles. The seconds ticked while she composed her thoughts.

"I lived with a man for three years when I was in graduate school." The disclosure seemed to shock Joseph. "Brian taught art at New York University. We met at a sports bar in the Village where students and faculty from NYU and Parsons hung out on weekends."

"If you lived together for three years, why didn't you get married?"

The censure in Joseph's voice sounded so much like Raleigh Eaton she thought she'd conjured him up. "There were a number of factors. I was twenty-three and felt I was too young to settle down. Brian was thirty-nine and he didn't want children."

"Damn, the dude was too old for you."

"He wasn't *that* old." Crystal knew she sounded defensive, but it wasn't what it seemed. Brian might have been sixteen years her senior, but he looked years younger.

"I still say he was too old for you," Joseph whispered under his breath. "Should I assume you wanted children?"

"Not then. However, I'd like to have one or two sometime in the future."

"Why did you break up?"

Crystal caressed the granite surface under her fingertips. "We really didn't break up. He was offered a teaching position in California and I encouraged him to take it. After I graduated I gave up our Greenwich Village apartment and moved back to Florida."

Joseph placed his hand over Crystal's. "How did your family react to you shacking up with a man?"

She rolled her eyes at him again. "You could've said cohabitating instead of shacking."

"It is what it is, Crystal."

"To answer your question—my parents didn't like it for a number of reasons. First, they felt I was too young to *shack up* with a man and second, Brian was too old for me. It was sort of a test for me because I grew up as an only child and if it hadn't been for my aunt, uncle and cousins I probably would've had abandonment issues. My parents divorced not only each other but also me. They were so caught up in their own lives at that time they'd forgotten they had a child."

He tightened his grip when she attempted to extricate her fingers. "How old were you when they divorced?"

"Eight."

Joseph stared at his hand covering her much smaller one. "That's very young."

Crystal smiled wryly. "I managed to survive without having to spend thousands of hours on a therapist's couch. Now that I'm an adult, I'm cool with my parents. It's better they're not married because they get along better as friends than husband and wife."

"Did you ever think you lived with a man who was that much older than you because you were looking for him to replace Daddy?"

Crystal clenched her teeth as she gave Joseph a long, withering stare. "I definitely wasn't looking for another father. Brian and I were together because we offered each other what we needed at that time in our lives.

Joseph released her hand. "Sex?"

In spite of herself, Crystal burst out laughing. "Is that all you men think about?"

His gaze traveled over her face, then moved slowly to her chest before reversing direction. "It's not all *I* think about, but it is necessary if you want a satisfying physical relationship."

Resting an elbow on the countertop, she cradled her chin on the heel of her hand. "I prefer a *healthy* physical relationship to a satisfying one. Don't forget there are methods men and women can use to bring themselves to climax or ejaculate."

Choking sounds came from Joseph as he reached for his glass of sangria and took a deep swallow.

"Did I embarrass you?" Crystal laughed. "Come, now, Joseph. We're both adults, so the subject of masturbation shouldn't be off the table." Growing up around three male cousins and overhearing them talk about sex helped her to have a healthy attitude about what went on between men and woman in the bedroom.

Joseph narrowed his eyes. "I'm not embarrassed," he said defensively. "I just didn't expect us to talk about masturbation."

"You were the one who mentioned sex."

"You're…" His words trailed off when the phone rang. "Excuse me, Crystal, but I have to answer that." It wasn't often someone called him on the hotel's line. Striding across the kitchen, he picked up the receiver to the wall phone. "Hello."

"Hi, Joey. I tried calling your cell, but it went to voice mail."

Joseph was too annoyed with his sister to tell her he left his cell phone in the bedroom. She had promised him she would call when she got to Durham. "Don't tell me you're just getting in, because I left you a voice mail this morning."

"I got in last night but couldn't call you because one of my sorority sisters found out that her boyfriend got another girl pregnant and we were up all night talking her off the ledge. She's threatening to buy a gun to shoot him and the girl."

"Tell her to save her money and the bullets because neither of them is worth her spending the rest of her life in prison."

"That's what we've been saying. Hopefully it will sink in. By the way, you don't have to send me any money. I spoke to Daddy a few minutes ago and told him everything."

He smiled. Apparently Bianca had decided to take a stand with their father. "How did it go?"

"He wasn't too happy, but said he understood where I was coming from. He must be mellowing out in his old age."

"Dad's only sixty-two, so he's not that old." Joseph half listened to his sister talk nonstop about the plans she'd made when she took the year off as he stared at Crystal, watching him. There was no doubt he'd misjudged her. Under her reserved exterior was a woman who wasn't afraid to speak her mind. And she was right when she accused him of bringing up the topic of sex.

"Joey, are you still there?"

"Yeah, Bibi. I'm here."

"You sound distracted. Do you have company?"

"Yes."

"Why didn't you say something?" Bianca admonished. "I'll text you with an update on the drama that's going on here."

"Tell your soror that I'm not licensed to practice law in North Carolina, so she shouldn't do anything crazy. Remind her if she's charged with murder one, that carries a life sentence or the death penalty."

"I'll let her know. Bye, Joey. I love you."

"Love you, too, Bibi."

Joseph ended the call, returning to the cooking island. "That was my sister. I told her when she came to see me yesterday to call when she got back to school, but she had other pressing issues than phoning her brother."

Grimacing, Crystal bit down on her lower lip until she felt a pulse. "That was your sister I saw you with in the lobby yesterday?"

"Yes. When I introduce Bianca as my sister, folks always ask if she's adopted. My brothers and I tease her saying we found her on the back porch and decided to take her in."

"I guess you and your brothers look alike."

"We look like most Cole dudes, while Bianca resembles the Reyes side of the family. At almost twenty, she's the mirror image of our Puerto Rican grandmother at the same age." Joseph noted the time on the microwave. It was almost eight o'clock. He and Crystal had spent the past hour talking. Rounding the island, he eased her off the stool. "It's time I feed you or you'll think I'm a terrible host."

Chapter 6

Dinner concluded, Crystal sat across the table from Joseph wondering if she'd been involved with him at twenty-three how different her life would be now. She knew he never would've agreed to live together without marriage. And if they'd married they would have at least one child.

Unlike his ex, she wouldn't complain about not seeing her husband enough. Growing up an only child, she learned early on to entertain herself. Whenever she wasn't with her cousins, she escaped between the pages of a book. In middle school she began making up stories, filling volumes of cloth-covered journals.

Once she entered adolescence, subscribing to magazines had become her drug of choice. She filled out countless order cards and when the first issue arrived along with the bill, Crystal gave it to her father, who promptly wrote a check.

Stacks of magazines devoted to fashion, travel, cooking and design and architecture eventually took over all the available closet space in her bedroom. Then her mother issued an ultimatum: get rid of all but her favorites. She bundled all except the issues devoted to décor and design. Thus began her love affair with interior decorating.

"What made you decide to go into interior decorating?"

Joseph's voice broke into her musings. It was as if he'd read her mind. "I love beautiful things," she said, smiling. "I suppose it comes naturally because my mother is an art dealer."

Leaning back in his chair, Joseph angled his head. "A lot of people like beautiful things, yet they don't become decorators."

"For me it is taking an empty space and filling it up with

pieces that not only complement one another but also reflect the owner's personality."

"I'm planning to build a house."

Crystal sat up straight. She didn't have to be clairvoyant to know Joseph was going to ask her about decorating ideas. "What do you want to know?"

"Will you consider decorating it once it's completed?"

She schooled her expression so as not to reveal her excitement. Joseph asking her to decorate his home, if she accepted the commission, would be her first nonreferral. "If you hadn't met me, who would you have chosen?"

"My aunt, who just happens to be a retired decorator, gave me a list of recommendations. She stopped working for the family a couple of years ago because she's spending more time with her great-grandchildren."

"Who did she recommend?" A cold shiver snaked its way up Crystal's spine when Joseph mentioned the architectural and design firm in Fort Lauderdale where she'd been sexually harassed.

Joseph's expression mirrored confusion. "What's the matter, Crystal?"

"What are you talking about?"

"You look as if you just saw a ghost when I mentioned Bramwell and Duncan Architectural and Design."

She lowered her eyes, staring at the tablecloth. "I used to work for them before I went into business for myself."

Joseph leaned over the table. "Why did you leave?"

"I was passed over for promotion one too many times."

"What else, Crystal?"

She looked up at him, meeting his eyes. "What makes you think there's something else?"

"I may be a few things, but a fool is not one of them. I saw something in your eyes that says there's bad blood between you and your old employer."

Crystal had underestimated Joseph. It was apparent he was quite perceptive. "One of the partners sexually harassed me, and rather than sue, I resigned."

"You never told anyone?"

She shook her head. "No."

"You leave so he can sexually harass another woman?"

Joseph's accusatory tone grated on her nerves. "You have no right to be judgmental when you don't know all of the facts. I wasn't the first woman to be targeted, and there's no doubt I won't be the last. An assistant architect told me in confidence that another woman had threatened to sue, but she was paid well for her silence. Bramwell and Duncan have deep pockets and enough clout to keep any case tied up in the court for years. And because I wasn't willing to take a bribe, I left. Think about it, Joseph. How many companies would hire someone with a history of suing her employer?"

Joseph ran a hand over his face. "I suppose you did the right thing when you resigned."

"Even if I didn't do the right thing, I know I made the right decision to go into business for myself."

"Lucky me," he drawled. If Crystal was good enough to decorate hotels for the preeminent Charleston hotelier, then she had to be very good at what she did. "Now, Miss Business-woman, will you accept the commission to decorate my house once it's completed?"

"What's the projection date for completion?"

"It probably won't be until sometime next year."

Crystal traced the design on the handle of the dinner fork with her forefinger. She did not want to commit to decorating a home that was still in the planning stages. "We'll talk once you get closer to completion. No more, please," she said, plac-ing her hand over her wineglass when Joseph attempted to refill it. Smiling, she said teasingly, "If I drink any more I'll have a problem making it down the hall."

Light from the overhead chandelier bathed Joseph in gold as he ran a forefinger around the rim of his wineglass. "You don't have to go home. I do have an extra bedroom."

Her gaze grazed his mouth. "I was only teasing about not making it back to my apartment. What I'm not is much of a drinker."

His eyes opened wider. "And I'm serious about you staying over. If or when you can't make it back to your place, I'll either carry you or put you up here."

A shiver of awareness snaked its way up Crystal's back when she realized she was about to embark on something for which she wasn't quite ready. Joseph embodied the essence of the perfect bachelor—if there was such a thing. He was tall, dark, handsome, intelligent, elegant and wealthy. "Is that something you do with women who've had too much to drink? Put them up at your place?"

Joseph dabbed the corners of his mouth with the linen napkin. "No. I can't afford to have an intoxicated woman in my home and later on have her accuse me of taking advantage of her. When I suspect she's had too much to drink I usually call a car service to take her home. The driver knows not to leave them until they're safely behind a closed and locked door."

She gave him a bright smile. "I don't think you'll ever have to deal with that problem with me, because two drinks is usually my limit."

He gestured to her glass. "You only drank half your wine."

Crystal touched her napkin to her lips. "That's because I had the sangria."

His expression didn't change. "Are you ready for dessert?"

She looked at Joseph as if he'd suddenly taken leave of his senses. "I'm so full I'm going to have to pass on the dessert."

Rising, Joseph came around the table and pulled back Crystal's chair. He hovered over her head longer than necessary, her warmth and scent wafting to his nostrils. "I'll wrap it up so you can take it with you."

Crystal stood, resting her hand on his shoulder. "I'm not leaving yet. I'm going to stay and help you clean up."

He shook his head. "No, you're not. Someone from housekeeping will take care of everything." A knowing smile played at the corners of Crystal's mouth, bringing his gaze to focus there. "What's so funny?"

She averted her head to conceal her smirk. Joseph had denied having someone pick up after him. "Nothing. No!" she screamed. He'd picked her up, holding her above his head as if she weighed no more than a child. "Put me down, Joseph!"

"Apologize."

Crystal closed her eyes, praying he wouldn't drop her. "For what?"

"For what you were thinking."

"What was I thinking!"

"You know right well what you were thinking."

"Okay. I'm sorry." She shook uncontrollably when he finally lowered her until her feet touched the floor.

Joseph felt her trembling. Pulling her against his chest, he pressed his mouth to her forehead. "It's okay, sweetheart. I wouldn't have dropped you."

Crystal curved her arms under his shoulders, holding tightly as if he were her lifeline. Temporarily traumatized, she couldn't react to the softly whispered endearment. "I'm afraid of heights," she admitted tearfully.

Cradling the back of her head, Joseph closed his eyes. "I'm sorry. I didn't know." Lowering his head, he pressed a kiss to her ear, and then trailed kisses along the column of her neck. "Will you forgive me?"

Crystal sniffled. "I'll think about it."

Joseph cradled her face in his hands. His heart turned over when he saw the unshed tears in her eyes. He touched his mouth to hers, making certain not to increase the pressure to where she'd pull away. "I'm very, very sorry," he whispered over and over, placing light kisses on her parted lips.

The soft caress of his mouth reminded Crystal of the gossamer wings of a butterfly brushing her face when she'd lain on the grass long ago, staring up at the clouds in the sky. At first it'd startled her, but it flew back and landed on her forehead; she lay completely still so it wouldn't fly away again. Those were the happiest days in her young life—before her parents' divorce.

It had been a long time, much too long since a man had held and kissed her. Before she'd slept with Brian, there had been one man—a student at Howard University—and no one after Brian. She dated a few men but refused to sleep with them because she'd convinced herself she didn't have time for romance in her life when she had to concentrate on her career.

Spending the past few hours with Joseph had proven her wrong. She wanted romance, passion and to experience again why she'd been born female. Lowering her arms, she pushed against his chest. "I think I'd better go now."

Reluctantly, Joseph released her. "Don't you want to wait for your dessert?"

A rush of heat suffused her face as she grew conscious of his scrutiny. "Will it keep?"

"Yes."

Crystal forced a smile. "Bring it to my place Monday. If you don't have anything planned for Monday evening, then I'd like to have you over for happy hour."

His eyes caressed her face. "What time does happy hour begin?"

"Five."

"I'll be there."

Rising on tiptoe, she kissed his cheek. "Thank you for a wonderful evening and an incredible dinner."

Joseph stared at her, committing everything about her face to memory. Resting a hand at the small of her back, he led her out of the dining room. "I'll walk you back to your place."

"Don't be silly. I'm less than two hundred feet from you."

He took her hand. "Didn't I tell you I always make certain my date gets back home safely? And because I don't have to call a driver, I'm going to see you to your door."

Crystal realized it was futile to argue with Joseph. "I didn't know I was your date."

"You don't get out much, do you?"

She gave him a sidelong glance. "Why would you say that?"

"When a man invites you to share dinner with him, it's a date."

"What if I invite you to dinner? Is it still a date?"

"Yes, ma'am."

Crystal stared at the toes of her shoes for several seconds. "I'm glad we cleared that up."

Joseph left his door unlocked as he walked with Crystal to her apartment. He waited while she took the card key from the pocket of her slacks and slipped it into the slot. The light glowed green. Reaching over her head, he held the door open for her. "I'll wait until you close and lock the door."

Crystal didn't understand Joseph's rationale for escorting her to her apartment. The penthouse floor was the most secure one in the hotel; they were the only guests occupying the apartments, and only employees assigned to the floor were allowed access. "I think you're being ridiculous."

"Please indulge me."

"Good night. And thank you again for a wonderful night."

Joseph winked at her. "You're welcome, beautiful."

She closed and locked the door; pressing her back against the solid surface, she slid down to the floor, her heart hammering against her ribs. *I like him. I really like him!* She'd come to Charleston to decorate hotels, not become involved with a man who'd claimed confidence as his birthright.

"If you're going to spend two months working in Charleston, you should have some fun, too." Her mother's words came rushing back in vivid clarity. "Well, Mother," she whispered, "I'm about to have some fun."

Joseph picked up the iPhone, answering before it rang a third time. He knew it was Diego. *"Hola, primo. Cómo estás?"*

"That's what I should be asking you, *primo*. I left a couple of voice mails for you to call me back."

Joseph had been watching a comedy on television

"I was indisposed, Diego." It was a half-truth.

Diego's resonant chuckle came through the earpiece. "I hope she was good."

A shadow of annoyance crossed his face. "It's not what you think." He and Crystal had shared dinner, not a bed, and if she'd been any woman other than the niece of Judge Solomon Eaton, Joseph definitely would've made it known to Crystal he was romantically interested in her.

While in college he'd had one-night stands, but they usually left him unfulfilled. Waking up next to a woman he'd just met hours before, unable to remember much about her, sometime not even her name, was relegated to his undergraduate party days.

"Lo siento, José. Quise decir sin faltarle el respeto," Diego replied in Spanish.

"No disrespect taken," Joseph countered.

"Who is she, Joseph?"

"What makes you think it was a she?"

There came another chuckle. "If it wasn't a she, then you would've said you were tied up with something."

Joseph smiled. "You think you know me that well?"

"Well enough since you decided to leave the dark side and work for ColeDiz."

"I didn't have much of a choice when it came to leaving the dark side as you call the justice system. If you hadn't lost Barry I still would be helping to lock away the dregs of society for lengthy sentences."

There came a pause, and then Diego said, "I really like your suggestion about selling the gourmet jams, jellies and preserves in our resort gift shops."

It was apparent Diego had received the order he'd placed with Sweet Persuasions. "Have you sampled them?"

"Hell yeah. That's why I'm in agreement. Do you have a firm offer from the manufacturer?"

"Not yet," Joseph said confidently. He knew he had to create a business plan, outlining their partnership before meeting with Selena.

"You're a brilliant lawyer, but you've also become a helluva businessman."

There was another pause, this time from Joseph. "Are you all right, Diego?"

"Of course. Why?"

"You usually don't give out compliments." Diego had a reputation as a hard-nosed, take-no-prisoners businessman. He wouldn't let anything or anyone stand in his way if he wanted something. A few of the employees referred to him as the SOB instead of the CEO, but never to his face. Diego expected those who were fortunate enough to work for ColeDiz to give the company 110 percent effort. However, their hard work was always rewarded with generous year-end bonuses.

"I shouldn't have to blow up your ego because we're *sangre*."

Joseph nodded, although Diego couldn't see him. They were blood, and for a Cole that meant everything. Anyone with even a drop of Cole blood was *familia.* "Word."

"I had a long talk with Vivienne a few days ago and I want you to be the first know that I'm thinking about going into semi-retirement at fifty and retire permanently at sixty. That means you should prepare to become CEO-in-training."

Joseph held his breath, not exhaling until his lungs were close to exploding. Diego held the distinction of being the fifth CEO of ColeDiz since Samuel Claridge Cole had established the company in the mid 1920s.

"Are you sure there's nothing wrong with you? Vivienne? The kids?"

"Slow down, Joseph. There's nothing wrong with either of us. I suppose you can say I had an epiphany."

"What about?" he asked, listening intently as his cousin talked about making changes in his life.

"I'd like to spend more time with my family before my kids grow up and have lives of their own. In ten years they'll be teenagers and will probably want nothing to do with their old man except use me as their personal ATM. I don't want to miss their soccer and Little League games or dance and music recitals because Daddy always has to work."

Joseph tightened his grip on the phone. He wasn't ready to assume control of a billion-dollar international conglomerate. He didn't need that responsibility, even if shared. When would he find the time to complete the construction on his home? And when finished, would he have time to enjoy it?

"What if we compromise, Diego?"

"How?"

"I limit my traveling to South Carolina, Puerto Rico and Jamaica. No more crossing time zones and datelines. Even though I'm not married or have children, I'd like to think about having them by the time I'm thirty-five. And that's not going to happen if I continue to jet around the world at a moment's notice."

"Have you met someone special, Joseph?"

Joseph's jaw clenched. *If* he had met someone special he doubted whether their relationship would be deemed even close to normal. What woman would be willing to put up with him not celebrating her birthday with her because he was thousands of miles away? And if married, miss the birth or birthdays of their children?

"No," he said emphatically.

"Are you looking?" Diego asked.

"Not consciously, but I don't want my life so bogged down with work that I won't be able to give her the emotional support she's entitled to as my wife. I bought that parcel of land almost a year ago with the intent of building a house, yet it hasn't happened. I've put off meeting with the architect so many times he probably thinks I'm crazy. I'm scheduled to meet with him once again, but it'll have to be after the tea harvest."

"I didn't realize you were ready to settle down."

"It's not so much about settling down as it is experiencing a semblance of normalcy. Hanging out here in Charleston for the next three months is the first time since I joined ColeDiz that I can actually plan what I want to do two or three days in advance. I may not have a family, but I do have a life. When you asked me to come and work with you I didn't hesitate because you're *familia*. And now you want me to take on more responsibility."

"It won't be that much more."

"That's bull, Diego, and you know it. I'm not agreeing to anything unless you're willing to compromise."

"Let me think about it."

"You do that," Joseph countered. Diego wasn't the only Cole with a stubborn streak a mile wide. "I'm going to draft a proposal for Selena Eaton, so hopefully we'll be able to invest in her company. I'll send you a copy before I present it to her."

"Eaton? Is she by chance related to your Judge Eaton?"

Joseph's annoyance with his cousin eased with the mention of his former mentor. Diego knew how he had felt when he had to resign his position at the courthouse. But instead of pouting and sulking he sucked it up and did what so many in his family did when summoned to come work for the family-owned business. They did it without question.

"Yes. She's married to his nephew."

"Damn, *primo.* It looks as if you can't get away from the Eatons."

A wide grin spread across Joseph's face. He doubted if he would ever have met Selena if it hadn't been for Crystal. "You're right about that. I guess you can say it's a small world."

"When it comes to you and the Eatons, it's a small, small world," Diego countered. "And there's no need to send me a draft of the proposal, because you'll just have to explain the legalese, which by the way bores the hell out of me. And, Joseph?"

"What, Diego?"

"I'm going to check with H.R. to see who in legal would like to do a *little* traveling every now and then."

"Gracias, primo. Adios."

Ending the call, Joseph wanted to remind Diego that it wasn't just a little traveling, and whoever he selected would probably have to renew their passport every two to three years instead of the requisite ten. He also realized he'd turned a page on a chapter in his life when he'd challenged Diego. It was something he wouldn't have thought of doing two years ago. However, Diego wasn't the only one who'd had an epiphany. It was time he took control of his life *and* his future.

Palming the phone, he made his way to the area where a home/office had been set up. Instead of using the hotel desktop, he opened his laptop and entered his password.

Hours later Joseph printed out the draft agreement. He would wait a day or two and then review it for additions and/or deletions.

Chapter 7

Crystal dropped her overnight bag on the floor in the entryway, her gaze lingering on the exquisite bouquet of flowers on the table.

"Gorgeous flowers," she remarked as she followed Selena through the living room.

"They're a gift from Joseph," Selena said. "He sent the flowers along with a dozen honeybell oranges as thank-you gifts for brunch. It's nice to find a man our age with some home training. Most times they want to take from a woman instead of giving or sharing. In my opinion he's a keeper."

Crystal placed a hand over her mouth to conceal a yawn. She'd spent a restless night, tossing and turning, then finally getting out of bed after recurring dreams about Joseph. In one of them they were in bed together, limbs entwined, while his mouth explored every inch of her body. In another she saw herself walking away from him while he yelled at her to come back. The visions were both erotic and frightening, foreshadowing a short-term relationship.

"I can't keep what I don't have."

Reaching for her hand, Selena led her into the kitchen. "But you could have him. I saw the way he was looking at you."

"Which way was that?"

"Like he couldn't believe what he was looking at. Would you go out with him if he asked you?"

Crystal didn't tell Selena that although she would go out with Joseph she definitely wasn't looking for something long-term. "Why not? After all, it's not as if I have a trail of men knocking on my door. And as you said, he does have home training."

"You should have a trail of men knocking down your door,"

Selena said, giving her a sidelong glance. "Everyone says you and Mia are the family's high-fashion models."

"Yeah, right," Crystal drawled. "It's because we're so tall." The former Mia Eaton had relocated from Dallas to Jonesburg as a medical resident. She fell in love and married Selena's cousin Kenyon Chandler, sheriff of the historic Mingo County, West Virginia, mining town.

"Tall and beautiful," Selena continued as if Crystal hadn't spoken. "In fact, you and Mia look enough alike to be sisters now that you've cut your hair. I know you said you had breakfast, but will you join me for a cup of latte?"

Settling herself on the chair at the table in the eat-in kitchen, Crystal nodded. "Of course." She looked around, not seeing any of the toys usually scattered about the floor. "Where's Lily?"

"Out with Xavier. He took her to Murrells Inlet."

Crystal stared at her cousin's wife in a pair of gray sweatpants and an oversize white tee. She'd pulled her hair back into a ponytail. "What's there?"

"Brookgreen Gardens. It has nature trails, sculpture gardens and the Lowcountry Zoo. Lily's a little young for the trails and gardens, but I'm certain she'll enjoy the zoo."

Crystal smiled. "So the outing is more for Xavier than Lily?"

Selena turned on the espresso machine. "You really know your cousin. Every Saturday he takes Lily out to give me a break. Even though he selects places that are child-friendly, they still appeal to him if they're connected to history. And that means you and I have the rest of the day to ourselves."

"Don't you have orders to fill?"

Selena opened an overhead cabinet, taking down two mugs. "I stayed up late last night making six dozen chocolate amaretto and coffee-flavored truffles for a customer who'll pick them up in an hour for her twin daughters' twenty-first birthday."

"Have you given any thought to Joseph's offer to invest in Sweet Persuasions?"

Selena nodded. "Xavier and I talked about it, and he's warming to the idea. I called Myles and spoke to him about it. He said not to commit or sign anything until he looks the agreement. It pays to have a lawyer in the family."

Crystal agreed with Selena. There were a number of Eatons who were doctors, several lawyers and teachers and her CPA/financial analyst father. "If Myles gives you the go-ahead, will you be able to meet the demand?"

Resting a hip against the countertop, Selena gave Crystal a direct stare. Her expression changed, her gaze softening. "That depends. I'd have to hire someone, even if it's part-time, and buy several automatic jam and jelly makers. The machine can produce about four half pints of each at a time. The problem is I don't want to give up being an at-home patissier, because it would mean putting Lily in day care."

"What would you do?"

"I may have to expand the commercial kitchen."

"How long does it take for a batch of jam to cook?"

"About thirty minutes. One machine can produce one hundred twenty-eight ounces an hour. Multiply that by four hours and you have five hundred twelve ounces. Packaging them in two-ounce jars will yield more than two hundred fifty of them. I have Grandma's recipe, so there's not a problem of duplicating the final product. I thought about copackaging it, but the recipe is a closely held secret, and it would take years to get a patent, so I have to keep it in the family."

Crystal smiled. "Good for you." Her smile faded. "What about your employee? Will he or she be privy to the ingredients in the recipe?"

"No. They'll know everything but the ingredients for the pectin. That's Grandma's secret." Selena waved her hand. "Enough about me. What do you want to do today?"

"Shopping."

"I was hoping you'd say that," Selena said, smiling. "There's a new boutique that opened a month ago off Calhoun Street that I'd like to check out."

Crystal's smile grew wider as she cupped a hand to her ear. "I can hear it calling my name."

* * *

Joseph eased off the accelerator, slowing the Range Rover as he maneuvered along the narrow, rutted, unpaved road leading to the tea plantation.

Each time he came to the sparsely populated island during the summer months, Joseph felt as if he had stepped back not only in time but also into another world. It was primordial with ancient live oaks draped in Spanish moss, towering cypress trees, swamps and marshes teeming with poisonous snakes, alligators, snowy-white egrets and eagles. Eagle Island—one of more than a thousand in the Lowcountry running from Charleston, South Carolina, to Savannah, Georgia—was environmentally sensitive, and the engineers ColeDiz hired for the tea garden were instructed to clear land only necessary for planting.

The summer air—heavy and dense—always seemed to smother him like a leaded blanket, making it difficult to draw a normal breath. But in autumn it changed, becoming clearer, softer and lighter, although the mornings were heavy with dew. The winter months were Joseph's least favorite time of the year. What had been lush and alive now appeared gray, bleak.

He drove past a small house erected on stilts, returning the wave of the elderly man sitting on the porch. Several hundred feet away stood another house, this one larger with a screened-in wraparound porch. There were more houses, all built off the ground in typical Lowcountry architecture. Most front doors were painted light blue, which at first he found odd until the proprietor of the island's only store explained it was a Gullah custom. The color blue kept away the bad spirits.

If Joseph thought many of the Gullah customs and traditions peculiar, it was their language he found intriguing. The term Gullah, believed to be derived from Angola, was an English dialect interspersed with several African languages. Books devoted to the Gullah culture and language now lined the shelves of the bookcase in his ColeDiz office, along with those devoted to every country and culture he'd visited. Joseph knew success only came from immersing himself in the culture of the country or region in which he conducted business.

A road sign pointing the way to the Cole Tea Company came into view. Reflective letters warned it was private property and trespassers were subject to arrest. Unseen to the naked eye were close-circuit cameras protecting the property and monitored by a local resident who also worked for the tea company.

Executing a smooth left turn, he maneuvered over a wide, paved roadway and then came to a complete stop. A carpet of green stretched across the landscape for as far as he could see.

Seeing acre upon acre of tiny shoots pushing up through the damp earth made two years of sacrifice all the more profound. Joseph had given up the career he coveted since he was a child to take his place in the family-owned company. He'd sacrificed years of not having a normal relationship with a woman because of his commitment to a project initially he wasn't certain would come to fruition. Twenty-six months, to be exact.

Staring at the tea plants filled him with an indescribable feeling of pride. A law degree notwithstanding, Joseph had become the latest farmer in a family spanning five generations.

Pulling into the driveway alongside a modern two-story Lowcountry house, he turned off the engine. The sound of a door opening and heavy footfalls caught his attention as he stepped out of the Range Rover. Joseph's smile matched the wide grin belonging to the man who'd taught him everything he needed to know about growing tea.

Standing six foot six and tipping the scales at two sixty, raven-haired former NFL defensive tackle Shane Knox was an imposing figure.

Extending his hand, Joseph mounted the porch steps. "Happy New Year."

Ignoring the proffered hand, Shane pulled him close in a rib-crushing bear hug. "Back at you, Wilson. How the hell have you been?"

Joseph pounded his back. "Yo, man, ease up before you break my ribs."

A rush of color suffused Shane's face. "Sorry about that."

"How's Marci?" The move to the Lowcountry hadn't been easy for Shane's wife. She missed her family, and the isolation was exacerbated by a pregnancy plagued with nausea and vomiting.

Shane ran a hand over his face. "She's resting. Her sleep patterns are off because the baby sleeps during the day and does gymnastics at night. Do you want me to let her know you're here?"

Joseph shook his head. "No. Let her rest." Reaching into the breast pocket of his jacket, he handed Shane an envelope. "These are your arrangements. Someone from the car service will call you tonight to confirm the time you and Marci will be picked up Sunday morning. The jet will be at the airport when you arrive. The only thing you'll need to board is your ID. I've also arranged for a doctor and nurse to be onboard if Marci needs medical assistance."

Shane tapped the envelope against his palm. "I hate to leave now with harvest only months away. What if I send Marci now, and fly out closer to her due—"

"Come on, man, let's not go through this again," Joseph said, cutting him off. "Your wife has been begging *you* to take her to see her parents—her mother in particular—because Marci needs to see and talk to someone other than you. This tea garden will not wither and die because you're not here. Mervin, Willie and I will make certain of that."

"But—"

"No buts, Shane" he interrupted. "If your ass isn't on that plane tomorrow morning, then you're fired!"

When Shane asked him if he could take Marci home to Nebraska to await the birth of their son, Joseph quickly approved the request.

The blood drained from the former athlete's face, leaving it an ashen shade. "You're kidding," he whispered.

A scowl distorted Joseph's features. "Do you see me laughing?"

A beat passed. "No, I don't," Shane countered.

"So we're in agreement?"

Shane offered his hand. "Yes."

Smiling, Joseph took his hand, then landed a soft punch on Shane's hard-rock shoulder. "Thank you." His smile vanished, replaced with a hardened expression belying his youth. "My grandfather told me a long time ago that nothing, and that includes personal desires, is more important than family. Marci and that baby she's carrying are your family. *They* are your priority, not this tea garden. Take care of them."

That said, Joseph turned and walked back to his truck. Pressing a button on the remote device, he started the engine. He'd questioned his cousin's management style over and over, and within the span of thirty seconds he'd threatened a prospective father with dismissal because Shane challenged his mandate.

He hadn't wanted to step into the role as a badass, but if the tea garden failed he would be culpable, not Shane. Diego had entrusted him with the venture, and no one wanted the tea garden to succeed more than Joseph, but not at the expense of a man neglecting his family.

Crystal took a step back, surveying her handiwork. The smile parting her lips reached her eyes. She hadn't lost her touch. All of the dishes on the buffet server had met, and several exceeded, her expectations.

Rather than offer Joseph the usual happy hour fare, she decided on a cheese platter with red and white seedless grapes, sliced strawberries and stone-ground crackers. There were hot and cold hors d'oeuvres with a Mediterranean medley of grape leaves, red sweet peppers, pepperoncini and mixed pitted olives. Cocktail meatballs, sesame shrimp toast, pork dim sum and barbecue spare ribs cut into bite-size pieces were kept warm atop an electric buffet server.

Housekeeping had come earlier that morning to dust, vacuum and clean the apartment while Crystal made a supermarket run to purchase the items she didn't have on hand. Her decision to cook for Joseph was twofold: she wanted to return the favor of his preparing a scrumptious dinner for her, and she wanted to see if she hadn't lost her touch hosting a dinner party.

The doorbell chimed and she walked out of the dining room to answer the door. She opened the door to find Joseph leaning against the door frame, grinning from ear to ear.

"Welcome to Club Chez Crystal." She'd affected a French accent.

He inclined his head. *"Merci, Mademoiselle Eaton,"* he replied, extending his right hand with the bag with the wine she'd given him. "I thought you could use a little more libation." He tightened his grip on the handles of the smaller bag in his left. "This one has a cannoli, your dessert from the other night, and a few samples of gelato from your favorite shop."

Crystal's jaw dropped slightly as she stepped aside to open the door wider. "Paolo's?" Joseph nodded. "Who told you it was my favorite?"

Joseph smiled, glancing around the candlelit living room. She hadn't drawn the drapes, and the light coming in through the wall-to-wall windows lent itself to an evening for romance.

His gaze shifted to linger on her, moving slowly from her face to her shapely bare legs in a pair of black pumps that put her height close to the six-foot mark. He smiled again. It was obvious she was very secure about her height. "Xavier."

Crystal took the bag with the dessert from his outstretched hand. "You and Xavier were talking about me?"

"Not really. I asked him if I wanted to take you out what restaurant was your favorite. And he said you really liked 39 Rue de Jean on John Street, and you never ate dessert there because you preferred ordering gelato from Paolo's."

Her eyes narrowed in suspicion. "Is that all you talked about?"

Taking several steps brought Joseph mere inches from her. His hands went to her bare shoulders. The ubiquitous little black dress hugged every inch of her tight body, making him more than aware of her feminine curves. "That's all," he said softly. "I like surprises."

Crystal froze. There was something so potently masculine about Joseph she found it difficult to draw a normal breath whenever he touched her. She'd lived with a man many years older than her, yet she never felt this uncomfortable around Brian.

She closed her eyes for several seconds. "You think of me as a surprise?"

He dipped his head and pressed a kiss alongside her neck. "Everything about you is surprising," he whispered against her silken skin. "When you opened the door I didn't know what to expect, but it certainly wasn't to be wined and dined at Chez Crystal by the owner herself."

Crystal let out an inaudible sigh, grateful he'd said wined and dined and not seduced. Seducing Joseph wasn't something she consciously thought about, because that had never been her style. She liked dating and courtship.

"I had to do something to try and match your incredible cooking prowess." Her smile and the timbre of her voice belied her quaking innards. Everything about Joseph seeped into her: the warmth of his body, the feathery touch of his mouth against her neck and the scent of his sensual cologne.

Joseph's hands moved up, cradling her face. "There shouldn't be a competition between us, Crystal."

Her gaze searched his face, lingering on the cleft in his strong chin. "What do we have?"

A sweep of long black lashes concealed his innermost feelings for a woman whom he felt he'd known forever instead of less than a week. "Something very special," Joseph said after a pregnant silence.

Another beat of silence ensued. "And what's that?" Crystal asked.

"A family connection."

She didn't know what she'd expected him to say, but he was right. Neither knew of the other days ago, yet circumstances beyond their comprehension deemed one day their paths would cross. "How true. You're going to have to let me go so I can put the gelato in the freezer before it's a soupy mess."

It was with reluctance Joseph lowered his hands. If possible, he would hold her indefinitely. "Do you want me to help you with anything?"

"Yes. I want you to help me eat this food," she said, repeating what he'd told her Friday night.

Joseph had no comeback as he watched the sexy sway of Crystal's hips and her long legs that seemed to go on forever. He watched her walk, and suddenly it hit him. He wanted to make love to Crystal. The image of her lying naked in bed, arms outstretched to welcome him into her embrace, flooded his mind like fast-moving frames of film.

Making love with Crystal was something he didn't want to think about only because it would ruin their easygoing friendship. Besides, she was the first woman he'd known since becoming sexually active with whom he could be himself. He'd long tired of women who either were vapid or came on too strong, and Crystal was neither. Shaking his head as if to banish the erotic musings, he followed her into the kitchen.

However, he felt like a voyeur, staring at the outline of her firm backside in the fitted dress as she leaned over to place the gelato in the freezer drawer. Turning around, he walked out of the kitchen and into the dining room, not trusting himself to occupy the same space with Crystal. He had to leave or she would've seen his growing erection. Buttoning the suit jacket, he stood at the window staring at the many steeples of the churches in the Holy City.

"Would you like something to drink?"

Not willing to risk turning around to face Crystal, Joseph smiled at her over his shoulder. "I'll have what you're having."

She moved closer, standing next to him. "I'm going to make a virgin planter's punch because I have to work tomorrow and I need to be clearheaded."

It seemed like an interminable length of time before he was able to look directly at her. "I'll have the same."

Looping her arm over the sleeve of his jacket, Crystal steered Joseph over to the bar. "Whenever I want to drink something nonalcoholic I usually ask for a virgin planter's punch or piña colada."

Joseph watched, awed as she measured orange juice, lemonade and grenadine syrup into a shaker filled with ice. Once the shaker was frosty she added ginger ale, then poured the concoction into two ice-filled Collins glasses, finishing them off with a pineapple spear, a maraschino cherry and an orange slice.

"Where did you learn to tend bar?"

Crystal handed him a glass. "I used to fill in at my mother's gallery whenever her regular bartender couldn't make it to the openings."

He shook his head in amazement. "What did I say about surprises? It probably would take me years to figure you out."

"I'm not that complicated, Joseph. What you see is what you get." She touched her glass to his. "To happy hour."

Joseph smiled. "Here's to more surprises."

Crystal took a sip of her drink. It was perfect. "I don't know about you, but I'm ready to eat."

Moving over to the buffet server, he picked up a napkin and a plate. "What can I serve you?" he asked her.

"I'll have one of everything, thank you."

Joseph and Crystal cuddled spoonlike on the sofa, his chest rising and falling against her back. She'd kicked off her shoes and lay on the sofa after what had become a leisurely eating affair, and he knew he'd surprised her when he joined her on the sofa, molding her body to his like a trusting child.

Many of the candles lining every flat surface in the living and dining rooms were sputtering and going out, leaving the space in near darkness. Twin lamps on either end of the table in the entryway provided the only illumination on the first floor. Joseph was loath to move because he didn't want his time with Crystal to end. Lowering his head, he pressed a kiss to her soft, fragrant hair.

"Are you going to sleep?" he whispered.

Crystal opened her eyes, smiling. She felt the strong beating of Joseph's heart against her back. Happy hour had stretched into more than two, and unlike Joseph, who'd prepared enough of each course for two servings, she had plenty of leftovers.

"No, but I don't know how long I'll be able to stay awake, because I'm as full as a tick."

Throwing back his head, he laughed loudly. "It's been years since I've heard that expression."

She giggled like a little girl. "Well, I am. You know I'm going to have to stop hanging out with you, because every time we get together we eat."

"What's wrong with that?"

"What's wrong is I won't be able to fit into my clothes, and I don't have the money to replace some of the garments in my closet with a bigger size."

"Not to worry, sweetheart. If I'm responsible for you gaining weight, then I'll buy you a new wardrobe."

Crystal pulled her lower lip between her teeth. This was the second time Joseph had called her sweetheart. She wondered if it was just a slip, or if he called all of his female friends sweetheart, or did he actually think of her as his sweetheart? She didn't know if she wanted to be his sweetheart, because it'd been too long since she'd been physically close to a man to whom she found herself attracted.

And she didn't want or need Joseph to pay for her clothes or anything else. All of her life men had indirectly taken care of her. Although her parents were divorced, her father had made certain to provide for her financial support. Then it was Levi and his brothers who put the word out that no one better mess with Crystal or they would have to answer to them. It continued with Brian, offering her his protection months after she'd moved to New York City.

However, the one time she needed a man to take care of her, he wasn't there. She knew that if she had made it known that she was being sexually harassed, things would've turned out differently for her. The partners would not have retaliated by firing her, but no doubt would've made certain she would never advance at the firm.

"I'm not a pauper, and the clothes I have I like very much."

Joseph kissed the nape of her neck. "And you look incredible in your clothes."

A wave of heat swept up her chest to her hairline. "Thank you. Maybe that's because they fit."

"But you have to admit we make a pretty good pair when it comes to throwing down in the kitchen. I'd prepare the entrées and you the hors d'oeuvres and cocktails."

Shifting, Crystal turned to face Joseph. "Yeah, we could hire ourselves out as caterers for small, intimate dinner parties," she said, laughing.

He traced the curve of her eyebrow with his forefinger. "That sounds like a plan."

"That sounds crazy. I like cooking, but not enough to give up decorating interiors."

Joseph stared at Crystal's upturned face in the diffused light, committing it to memory. He wanted to remember everything about her: face, voice, body and mannerisms. Once she completed her commission he didn't know when or whether their paths would ever cross again. Although he'd talked about her decorating his home, he knew that was just conjecture. The architect still had to draw up plans for the proposed property. And once it was completed, there was no guarantee she would accept his offer or be available for the project.

"It could be your Plan B once you decide to give up decorating."

A shimmer of amusement filled her eyes. "I'm still working on Plan A while you're talking about a Plan B. The difference between you and me is that you're involved in a successful family business at the same time I'm growing mine."

"If you're looking for clients I'm certain I can send a few your way."

Crystal wanted to tell Joseph that if she needed referrals, all she had to do was call her parents. She forced a smile she didn't feel. "Please don't think I'm ungrateful, but I'd rather build a reputation based on referrals from prior clients. Eventually I want Eaton Interior and Design to be a brand."

Joseph stared at her, complete surprise freezing his features. "Are you in business to make money or become a brand?"

"Both," she confirmed.

"If that's what you want, then why wouldn't you accept help from someone who could help you—"

"Stop it! Please stop," she pleaded in a softer tone. "I have to do this my way." Pushing against his shoulder, Crystal slipped off the sofa, coming to her feet. "Excuse me, but I'm going to clean up the kitchen."

He also stood. "I'll help you."

"No, you won't. I know you don't like washing dishes."

Taking a step, Joseph curved his arms around Crystal's waist. "Are you that perceptive, or am I that transparent?"

Resting her hands on his chest, she rose on tiptoe and brushed a light kiss to his cheek. "You are very, very transparent, Joseph Cole-Wilson."

Transparent enough to see that I want to make love to you, he thought. He found himself so physically attracted to Crystal it was palpable. "You're right," he confirmed. "I don't like washing dishes."

"And you don't have to, because I don't mind doing them." She paused, suddenly at a loss for words. Crystal knew when Joseph walked out the door it would be a while before they would get together again. It probably wouldn't be until Super Bowl Sunday. Decorating the historic residences meant conferring with workmen and visiting antique shops and furniture warehouses as far as away as North Carolina. "Would you like me to pack up some of the leftovers?" she asked after an uncomfortable silence.

Joseph moved even closer, their chests a hairbreadth apart. "No, thank you." Placing his hands over hers resting on his chest, he gave her fingers a gentle squeeze. "Thank you for an incredible happy hour. And if you can find time in your very busy schedule, would you be opposed to taking in a concert or going to the movies with me?"

She flashed a sexy moue. "I'd love to go out on a date with you."

Slipping into his suit jacket, Joseph reached into the breast pocket and handed Crystal his cell phone. "I'm going to need your cell number so I won't have to go through the hotel operator."

Crystal took the iPhone, programming her number. She

offered him a tentative smile, handing him back the phone. "Thank you for being a wonderful dinner guest."

Raising her hands, Joseph kissed each of her fingers. "Good night, Crystal."

Her smile widened. "Good night, Joseph."

Crystal felt his loss within seconds of his releasing her hands. Proper etiquette stipulated she walk him to the door, yet her legs refused to follow the dictates of her brain. She didn't know how long she stood there, waiting for the sound of the door opening and closing. When it didn't she followed him. He stood at the door, his hand resting on the doorknob.

"Joseph?" His name came out in a shivery whisper.

Without warning he turned and approached her, but Crystal didn't have time to catch her breath when she found herself in his arms, his mouth on hers in an explosive kiss that stole the very breath from her lungs. Her arms came up in slow motion, circling around his neck, holding him fast.

Being in Joseph's embrace, his mouth on hers, inhaling the sensually haunting scent of his body felt so good and so right. Her lips parted under his searching tongue, and she inhaled his warm, moist breath. She heard a moan and realized it had come from her. Crystal moaned again, this time in frustration. She wanted more, and the more was to sleep with him.

The kiss ended as abruptly as it had begun. Joseph released her, her arms falling away from his neck, and he retraced his steps. This time he opened and closed the door behind him without a backward glance.

It happened so quickly Crystal thought she'd imagined it, but the lingering taste of Joseph's tongue on hers, the heaviness in her breasts and the throbbing and moistness between her legs said otherwise. She knew if he hadn't ended the kiss she would've begged him to make love to her.

Walking on wobbly legs, she managed to find her way to the sofa without bumping into the coffee table, collapsing on the butter-soft leather cushion. Fists clenched, eyes closed and heart pounding a runaway rhythm, Crystal replayed the pleasure of Joseph's slow, drugging, possessive kiss in her mind over and over.

Opening her eyes, she came back to reality. The hotel owner's return to Charleston could not have come at a better time. Work was the perfect alternative to fantasizing about sleeping with a man she'd met only five days ago.

Chapter 8

Crystal found herself totally engrossed in decorating the twelve suites in the Beaumont Inn and the eight bedrooms with en suite baths in the Beaumont Bed-and-Breakfast. A hallway on the first floor permitted access between the adjacent buildings. The Charleston earthquake of 1886 that left a hundred dead and destroyed a number of buildings in the city caused little or no structural damage to the proposed inn and B and B.

She and the contractor, Roger Kincaid, were like kindred spirits because he knew exactly what she wanted whenever she explained the pieces that would go into each of the rooms. Roger and his crew had restored the interiors to their former beauty with hardwood floors, wainscoting and crown molding.

All of the fireplaces were converted from wood-burning to electric to eliminate the risk of potential fires. The upgrading of the electric and plumbing had passed inspection and all that remained was painting, hanging wallpaper, installing light fixtures and filling the rooms with furniture and accessories.

She and Roger sat at a makeshift worktable, going over paint swatches. "Miss Eaton, you'll have to let us know what colors you want in each of the rooms."

Crystal gave the contractor—a diminutive man with a ruddy complexion, shock of white unruly hair and a voice that was perfect for radio—a sidelong glance. The timbre of his voice reminded her of Joseph's—deep, velvety and beautifully modulated. Spending hours on the phone with vendors and endless trips to local antique shops had kept her so occupied she hardly gave him a passing thought until she returned to the hotel.

Once there, Crystal looked for him in the parking lot, in the lounge area off the lobby, in the elevator or on the penthouse floor whenever she left or returned. The one time she spotted him, he'd been in the lounge with several couples, and he'd acknowledged her with a nod and wave before turning his attention back to those at the table.

"That's going to be easy. I want to mix paint with wallpaper," she said, tapping a key on her laptop. A color design was displayed on the monitor. "I'm using a signature fabric with a color palette that will become the thread throughout the entire inn or B and B."

She tapped another key with splotches of paint samples with hues ranging from oyster white, French gray, pale powder blue and blue-gray cashmere. All of the rooms were numbered with a corresponding numbered color palette. Crystal suggested the owner identify each room or suite by name instead of a number. The rooms in the B and B would be named for Revolutionary War patriots and the inn for U.S. presidents. It was easier for guests to know they were staying in the Paul Revere or Thomas Paine room or George Washington or Thomas Jefferson suite than room 145 or 216.

Roger scratched his stubbly chin. "Where do you want the wallpaper other than in the bathrooms?"

"Only the inn's living room suites will be papered. Based on the architect's measurements, I've ordered enough wallpaper with some to spare. I'll stop by the shop after I leave here and let them know to deliver the rolls tomorrow at a time that's convenient for you."

The daily room rate at the inn, twice the daily rate of the B and B, included amenities of a buffet breakfast, a sit-down dinner and late-night cordials in the proposed drawing room.

Reaching into a leather portfolio, Crystal handed the contractor a loose-leaf binder with printouts of what she'd saved on her computer.

"I'm usually here at seven, so anytime after that is okay. Roger flipped through the pages, his snow-white eyebrows lifting. "You're very thorough."

She nodded, smiling. Everything she'd put in the binder was

detailed and self-explanatory. She'd labeled every wallpaper pattern, indicating in which rooms they would be hung.

"It saves a lot of time and my client's money. When do you think your crew will be able to finish painting and hanging the paper?"

Roger angled his head. "If I hire one or two more painters, I believe we can get everything done in a week. The guys who hang the paper are fast, so I know they'll finish quickly."

Tapping another key and opening the page for the calendar, Crystal typed in the date for painting and paper under the column labeled Projected Completion. Meeting the projected construction completion date meant the inn and B and B could open for business as scheduled, and more important, offset cost overruns.

"If you can achieve that, then I hope to complete decorating everything sooner than planned," she said.

"Do you have another project after this one?" Roger asked.

She nodded, smiling. "Yes, I do."

"If it is here in Charleston, then you're going to make quite a name for yourself once these hotels are up and running. Mr. Beaumont showed me the pictures of the proposed rooms, and they look like they did two hundred years ago."

"I'm just giving him what he wants," she confirmed. "The buildings are historic landmarks, which mean the interiors should embody and complement the exteriors."

Roger scratched his cheek, the raspy sound reminding Crystal of fingernails on a chalkboard. "They're going to become quite the showpiece once you decorate them."

That's what I'm hoping, Crystal mused. Decorating the inn and B and B would be her first commercial commission, and she looked forward to turning the New York City Greenwich Village town house basement into a jazz club with an excitement she found difficult to contain. It'd been four years since she was in the city that pulsed with a flutter of restless activity night or day, summer or winter.

She powered down the laptop. "Call if you need me for anything," she told Roger.

Roger stood, pulling back her chair as she rose to her feet. "No problem."

Crystal had just gotten behind the wheel of her vehicle when her cell phone rang. Reaching into her tote, she stared at the display. Tapping the talk feature, she said, "Happy New Year, Emerson." She and the highly skilled architect at Bramwell and Duncan spoke several times a year, and always exchanged birthday and Christmas cards.

"Same to you, my friend."

"Are you calling to tell me you've finally decided to strike out on your own?" Emerson Russo confided to her on more than one occasion he was seriously thinking of resigning to set up his own firm but wanted to wait until he found a competent partner.

"I wish it was about that," he said cryptically.

There was something in Emerson's voice that sent a shiver up her spine. "What's the matter?" Crystal listened, stunned, her heart pumping painfully in her chest when he revealed another woman at the firm hadn't just been harassed but sexually assaulted by the same partner who'd attempted to come on to her. "Did she report it to the police?"

"No."

"Why not?"

"Because Gillian doesn't have proof."

Unconsciously her brow furrowed. Gillian Stuart had joined the firm as an intern a month before Crystal resigned. And Emerson was talking in riddles. "You're telling me she was assaulted, yet she can't prove it? Why?"

There came a beat. "What I should've said is that she can't remember the assault because she believes she was drugged."

"Please tell me that she went to the hospital for them to test for DNA and have blood drawn and tested."

"No and no."

Crystal's heart rate kicked into a higher gear as something she didn't want to believe stabbed her brain while Emerson offered other details of the assault. "She's pregnant." The question was a statement.

"How did you know?" Emerson asked.

"Other than vaginal bruising or trauma, it's the only logical conclusion. She plans to have the baby?"

"That's what she told me. She doesn't believe in abortion. I've worked at B&D long enough to hear all types of stories about Hugh going after women, but this is a new low."

"What's Gillian going to do?"

"She plans to charge him for rape *and* sue him for paternity. I know your uncle is a judge, so hopefully because of this you'd know a lawyer who Hugh Duncan doesn't have in his pocket."

Crystal knew Emerson was right. Hugh Duncan came from an extremely wealthy and prominent political family. His father and grandfather were both U.S. representatives, and their sphere of influence was legendary throughout the state of Florida. He'd also retain a battery of attorneys to protect him personally *and* professionally.

However the Duncans weren't the only Florida family with wealth and prominence. To her knowledge the Coles might not have been as politically connected, but their name carried enough clout to make people stand up and take notice.

"Let me talk to someone, and I'll try and get back to you in a few days."

"Thanks, Crystal."

"I can't promise anything, but I'll try."

"That's all I can ask. Every time I hear about Hugh going after a woman, I relive the horror of my sister being stalked and raped."

Crystal understood Emerson's driving need to have his boss charged with rape because his younger sister took her own life the day after a jury acquitted her ex-boyfriend of unlawful kidnapping and rape because he claimed they'd had consensual sex. "Hugh has hidden behind the facade of being a family man and a pillar of the community for far too long. If Gillian can get someone to take on her case, then tell her she can count on me as a material witness."

Crystal ended the call and then sat staring through the windshield. Joseph had chided her for leaving Bramwell and Duncan rather than sue the pervert, which left him to harass other women. It was as if his words had come to fruition, because not only had he drugged a woman but he had also gotten her pregnant.

Crystal called Joseph's cell. Despite the gravity of the call, she smiled when hearing his mellifluent voice. "How are you?" she asked.

"That's what I should be asking you, neighbor. It's been a while."

"That is has. I've been busy."

"Good for you. What's up?"

Crystal sobered quickly. "Can you come to my place? I need some legal advice."

"I'll see you in about… Let's say twenty minutes."

"Thanks, Joseph." She hung up, hoping and praying he would be able to help her stop a sexual predator.

Joseph stepped into the shower stall and turned on the faucet to the programmed temperature setting. He'd spent the past hour in the hotel pool, swimming laps. Hearing Crystal's voice reminded him of how much he'd missed their easygoing camaraderie. He thought he would see her during his comings and goings, yet she'd proven elusive except for the one time he spied her walking across the lobby.

He had also been busy making frequent trips to the tea garden while also conferring with the assistant manager. An above average rainfall for the month caused drainage problems wherein an unseeded section of land flooded, but the problem was remedied by redirecting the flow of water when the man flipped a switch in the factory's engineering room.

After showering, he dressed quickly in a pair of jeans, a navy blue long-sleeved tee and running shoes, wondering why Crystal would need his legal advice when she could've called her uncle or her cousin Myles. Slipping his card key and cell phone into the back pocket of his jeans, he left the apartment.

Crystal had left her door ajar, and Joseph walked in, closing it behind him. He went completely still, staring at her descending the staircase in body-hugging black jeans and an emerald-green mock turtleneck. A smile tilted the corners of his mouth as she smiled at him.

Extending his arms, Joseph wasn't disappointed as she came into his embrace. Lowering his head, he pressed his mouth to her damp hair. She smelled delicious. Holding her reminded him of the last time he kissed her. He knew he shocked her with the impulsive action, yet he couldn't resist tasting her incredibly sexy mouth one more time. The crush of her breasts against his chest stirred the flesh between his thighs and he eased his hold on her body before she detected the growing bulge in his groin. He wondered how Crystal would react if she knew how easily she turned him on with a glance or a touch.

Reaching for her hand, he led her to the sofa, sitting and pulling her down to sit beside him. "What's the matter, sweetheart?"

Leaning against his shoulder, Crystal told Joseph what her ex-coworker had revealed to her earlier that afternoon.

Anger and rage merged, twisting his features when he clenched his teeth. "Had anyone told her about him before she agreed to let him into her home?"

Crystal shook her head. "Apparently not."

"Is she certain he drugged her?"

"She had to be, Joseph. She said Hugh called her early Black Friday to ask if she'd finished a project he needed for a Monday morning meeting. When she said no, he offered to come over and help her. Gillian told Emerson that Hugh didn't do or say anything that would make her feel uncomfortable, so she was completely relaxed when he called his favorite restaurant for dinner to be delivered to her house. Halfway through dinner she began to feel sick, believing it was something she'd eaten or drunk. Hugh told her to lie down on the sofa. Once there she must have passed out, not waking up until Saturday morning."

Back in control and shifting slightly, Joseph repositioned Crystal until she lay between his outstretched legs, his chest molded to her back. "Was there any physical evidence he'd had sex with her?"

Crystal shook her head. "No."

"What about DNA? He had to have left it on something."

"She woke up on a leather sofa, so he must have raped her there rather than in her bed, where he could've possibly left DNA. She knew he'd given her a bath because she found wet towels in the hamper. So the cretin cleaned her up and put back on the same panties in an attempt to make her believe he hadn't touched her."

"Without DNA she has no case," Joseph stated.

"Yes, she does," Crystal countered. She paused. "She's six weeks pregnant. And before you ask, no, she wasn't sleeping with another man. She broke up with her boyfriend just after Labor Day."

Joseph came out of his relaxed position as if pulled up by a taut wire. "Is she certain it isn't her boyfriend's baby?"

"Quite certain, because he always used a condom."

He quickly did the math in his head. Given eleven or twelve weeks, Gillian would've known whether she was pregnant or not. "Did she tell the bastard that she's carrying his baby?"

"Yes, and he terminated her with the excuse she was delusional, paranoid and completely burned out. However, he did give her a generous severance package, aka hush money."

"She intends to have the baby?"

Crystal nodded. "She doesn't believe in abortion," she said, repeating what Emerson told her.

Wrapping an arm around her waist, he again settled Crystal against his chest. "She's got him, sweetheart. But only after she delivers the baby can she sue for paternity. Either he'll give up his DNA if he's innocent, or he'll refuse because he knows he's the father of her child."

"If he was devious enough to drug a woman and clean up after himself, why didn't he use a condom? Didn't he think about contracting a STD?"

Joseph exhaled an audible breath. "I don't know much about sexual predators except they have little or no impulse control. Duncan probably didn't think about using protection before or during the act, but once it was over he was clearheaded enough to methodically cover up his crime. And maybe he didn't get the other women pregnant, or if he did they accepted his hush money, opting for an abortion instead of having the baby."

There came a swollen silence.

"You were right, Joseph."

"What about?"

"If I'd sued Hugh instead of resigning, Gillian wouldn't be carrying a baby as a result of rape."

Joseph kissed her hair. "It's too late to second-guess yourself. Duncan is a serial sexual predator who should spend the rest of his life in prison."

Crystal closed her eyes, wishing she had confronted Hugh rather than resign, although he would've come up with the excuse that she was either delusional or burned out like with Gillian.

For Crystal, it hadn't been what he said or did but what she perceived. On several occasions he stood too close for propriety, would deliberately cover her hand with his whenever they met to review a project and compliment her on what she was wearing. Invariably his forearm brushed her breasts when he leaned over her shoulder to place a report on her desk. It was then she noticed his erection.

Perhaps he hadn't reached the stage where he'd invite himself to her home or out to dinner, drug and rape her because she was Judge Solomon Eaton's niece. Rather than allow his continual subtle violation, she resigned.

She opened her eyes. "Who's going to put him there? No lawyer in Florida would risk going up against the Duncan family political machine."

There came another prolonged silence, and then Joseph said, "I think I know someone who would be willing to take her case." Crystal turned over, resting her chin on his breastbone. He saw a shimmer of excitement in her eyes. "I'm familiar with a lawyer specializing in sex crimes. In his former life he was a forensic psychologist, so it's the perfect marriage when it comes to defending sex crime victims."

The light in Crystal's eyes faded. "Do you think he can get her a fair trial?"

"What he'll attempt to do is *not* go to trial because Duncan's defense team will try and dissect her sex life from her first encounter to the last. And if the baby is proven to be his, they'll turn it around and say it was consensual sex, or she deliberately seduced him and got pregnant so she could sue him for paternity."

A flicker of apprehension coursed through Crystal. "Please don't tell me you're talking about a plea deal. He'll pay restitution, and then get off with a slap on the wrist so he's free to rape another woman." There was a hint of panic in her voice.

Joseph placed a hand alongside her delicate jaw. "Seth will not let him get off that easily. In order to spare Duncan's family the embarrassment of a trial, he'll suggest he plead guilty to misdemeanor rape and register as a sex offender. His offender status will depend on how many women are willing to come forward and testify to being victimized by him, and if they agree to a class-action lawsuit and win, hopefully Hugh Duncan will have a lot fewer zeroes when it comes to his net worth."

Her jaw hardened under his light touch. "This may sound vindictive, but I want him to pay for everything he's done."

Joseph's mouth replaced his hand. "He will."

"How can you be that certain?" Crystal whispered.

"I know people who can get someone to snitch on their mothers or firstborn just to save their behinds."

She froze. "What are you going to—"

"No more questions," he warned, stopping her words with a light kiss. "You asked me to help you, so please leave it at that. What I'm going to need is the phone number of your friend Emerson so I can pass it along to Seth."

Crystal nuzzled his throat, breathing a kiss there. "Thank you."

"Thank me once your predator gets what he deserves. However, I will accept a little kiss right now."

Crystal melted against his body, losing herself in the pleasurable sensations of his mouth on hers. Joseph deepened the kiss and within seconds she forgot why she'd called him. And in a moment of madness, nothing mattered except the man holding her to his heart.

She wanted him with the hunger and thirst of someone deprived of food and water. Joseph was a constant and nagging reminder of what she'd missed and had been missing for far too long. She'd been so intent on growing her interior decorating business she denied the strong passions within her.

However, if she were to become involved with Joseph, both knew it would be brief. Anything short-lived and personal fit nicely into Crystal's current lifestyle; her upcoming commission would take her away from home for prolonged periods of time and thankfully she didn't have to answer to anyone as to her whereabouts.

She'd known a few women who'd sacrificed advancing their careers because their boyfriends or husbands weren't willing to accept their need to travel for their jobs. Spending four years in a city as racially and culturally diverse as New York City and living with a man sixteen years her senior had forced Crystal to mature at a faster rate than her same-age female counterparts. There were times when she felt this gave her an advantage and other times when she found herself quite cynical about the opposite sex. And like many thirtysomething women, she looked forward to marriage and motherhood, but didn't feel an all-encompassing need to find Mr. Right before her biological clock started ticking.

A slight gasp escaped her parted lips when she felt Joseph's fingers feather under her sweater, his hands coming to rest over her breasts rising and falling heavily under the lacy fabric of her bra. "You smell and taste wonderful," he whispered, swallowing her breath as she exhaled.

Laughing softly, she began her own exploration, her hands searching under the front of his tee, encountering hard-rock muscle. "So do you," she countered in a husky whisper. Crystal bit down on her lip to keep from laughing aloud when he jerked as if burned as her thumbs grazed his nipples, the tiny buds hardening like pebbles. Within seconds, her mouth replaced her hands. She gasped again, this time when Joseph hardened quickly, the solid bulge in his groin pressing against her middle. "Jo-se-ph," she whispered, his name coming out in three syllables.

Reaching for her shoulders, Joseph managed to extricate her mouth with a minimum of effort. Lowering his head, he fastened his mouth to the side of her neck. "You see what you're doing to me, Crystal?"

She buried her face between his neck and shoulder. "What am I doing?"

"I just have to look at you or touch you and I get a hard-on."

"This isn't as one-sided as you think."

"Are you telling me you're ready to take what we have to the next level?"

Crystal gave him a long stare. "I need to know what you mean by the next level." She hadn't lied to Joseph. Her body said yes while her head still said no when it came to sharing a bed.

A smile played at the corners of his firm mouth. "I'm surprised you're asking me that. I want to make love to you, but it has to be on your terms."

Her eyes opened and Crystal couldn't stop the smile parting her lips. "Are you certain you want to hear my terms?"

Joseph eased back, his eyes searching her expression for a hint of guile, and finding none, he nodded. It was the same thing he'd said to Kiara, but with unexpected dire consequences. He knew it would be different with Crystal. She was older, more mature and secure enough to speak her mind.

"I'm very sure," he answered after a comfortable silence.

Crystal stared at the cleft in Joseph's chin, pausing as she chose her words carefully. "If we do happen to sleep together, then it would be like the Las Vegas commercial. What happens here stays here." Joseph smiled, attractive lines fanning out around his large eyes. She sobered quickly. "You wouldn't have to concern yourself about me asking you for a commitment or a declaration of marriage because I don't want or need either at this time in my life, and I'd like you to promise the same."

He knew she was referring to his disclosure to why he'd ended his relationship with Kiara. Although his life was more predictable than it had been two years ago, he still wasn't ready to marry or start a family.

"I promise."

"I'm not on birth control, so you're going to have to assume responsibility for protecting me from an unplanned pregnancy. That is, if we *do* decide to make love," she added softly.

Joseph wanted to tell Crystal the only thing better than going to bed with her would be waking up with her beside him. And it had nothing to do with sex—that was something he could get from any willing woman. Whenever they were together he experienced a level of comfortableness he hadn't thought possible.

"So I can look forward to the time when we can become friends with benefits?"

Crystal's arms went around his neck. "Yes."

"Don't worry about contraception. I'll take care of it."

Exhaling an audible breath, Crystal met his eyes. "I said all that because I need you to understand where I'm coming from."

Reaching up, he gently removed her arms. Joseph had asked Crystal what she wanted, and it was something he could very easily live with.

Joseph knew instinctively that if he'd met Crystal years ago, fallen in love with her, he would have seriously considered proposing marriage. That is, if she thought him worthy of becoming her husband.

"I understand and accept your terms. Let's go out."

Crystal sat up. "Where?"

"The Watering Hole is a local sports bar that's within walking distance from here. I want to warn you that it's a little noisy."

Rising on tiptoe, she kissed his cheek. "I don't mind noisy. I'll be right back. I have to change my shoes and get a jacket."

Cradling the back of her head, Joseph brushed a light kiss on her mouth. "I'm going to my place to get a jacket. I'll meet you at the elevator."

Chapter 9

Crystal sat next to Joseph in the booth instead of opposite him in order to hear what he was saying. When he said the Watering Hole was a little noisy she didn't know it would be from decibel-shattering music.

A dozen wall-mounted, muted televisions were tuned to various sporting events, a few displaying closed captions. Shouts of triumph and/or collective groans followed a hockey goal or basketball sailing through the net. Motown hits and '60s and '70s R&B blared from speakers as several couples seated at the bar got up to dance to Smokey Robinson and the Miracles' "Ooo Baby Baby."

Thursday night at the pub was advertised as wing night, and the rustic establishment offered more than ten different varieties of Buffalo wings, attracting hoards of college students paying a twenty-dollar flat fee each for all-you-can-eat wings with unlimited pitchers of domestic tap beer.

She and Joseph ordered fresh guacamole with grilled corn, salsa, crisp tortilla chips and virgin margaritas. They were watching the Miami Heat in a back-and-forth scoring battle with the New York Knicks.

"Yes!" Crystal said between clenched teeth while pumping her fist. The Heat's point guard had just scored his fourth three-point basket within the span of five minutes, ending and winning the game.

Joseph found it hard to conceal his own excitement. Both he and Crystal were into the basketball game, and it was the first time he saw her that relaxed. So, he thought, the prim and proper decorator did know how to let down her hair.

"That was swee-eet," Crystal crooned.

Joseph smiled. "You really like basketball."

Crystal gave him a sidelong glance. "I do. I played basketball in high school."

"Come dance with me," Joseph said close to Crystal's ear when the classic love song segued into the Temptations singing "Just My Imagination."

She didn't have time to accept or decline as Joseph grasped her hand, pulling her off the well-worn vinyl booth and leading her to the area dance floor. She had to quicken her step to keep up with him. He eased her to his chest at the same time her arms circled his slim waist inside his jacket.

Crystal rested her head on his shoulder, inhaling the lingering fragrance of his cologne that mingled with his body's natural scent. Crystal felt as if she were being pulled into a sensual vortex from which she did not want to escape.

Lowering his head, Joseph pressed his mouth to her ear. "Do you have anything planned for Friday night or Saturday?"

"What do you have in mind?" Crystal asked.

"The Heat are playing the Bobcats in Charlotte Friday night. I figure we'd drive up, stay overnight and then come back here Saturday, when we'll have dinner at the Ordinary. If you like seafood, then you'll love this place. When I make the hotel reservation I'll ask for a suite with adjoining rooms."

Crystal nuzzled his warm throat. Joseph had just gone up several approval points when he mentioned adjoining bedrooms. He hadn't assumed because they were going away together she would automatically fall into bed with him. Crystal was forced to admit to herself the more she saw Joseph the more she wanted to sleep with him. In him she found everything lacking in the men with whom she'd become involved.

Involved! She shook her head as if to banish the word. What she didn't want was to become emotionally involved with Joseph. If and when the time came that they did sleep together, she wanted it to be no more than a slackening of the sexual tension wound so tight it kept her from a restful night's sleep.

"Your offer sounds very, very tempting," she murmured.

He spun her around and around. "Tempting enough to take me up on it?"

"I think I'm going to need a little convincing."

Cradling her face in his hands, Joseph met her eyes in the semidark space. "How much convincing do you need, sweetheart?"

Crystal felt as if she and Joseph were the only two people in the crowded restaurant. Everything else ceased to exist: the music, the images flickering across the many television screens, pub regulars, college students and waitstaff. Within seconds of the question flowing from her lips, she realized it sounded like a subtle challenge for seduction. And as much as her body craved intimacy, she was ambivalent about sleeping with Joseph, wishing she was more like some women who were able to sleep with a man without becoming emotionally involved. If she and Joseph were to make love, then she had to make certain not to confuse love with lust.

"Tell me, how are you going to get tickets?"

Joseph chuckled. "I have season tickets. They were my brother's, but he gave them to me just before he left the country. Is that convincing enough?"

Pressing her forehead to his shoulder, Crystal nodded. The noise escalated when another crowd of students pushed their way into the pub, and yelling to be heard was getting annoying. "Can we please get out of here?"

Tightening his hold on her waist, Joseph led her off the dance floor and back to their booth. Signaling for the waitress, he pressed a bill into her hand.

Crystal sucked in air when they walked out of the Watering Hole. Afternoon temperatures peaking in the high '70s had dropped to mid-'60s with nightfall and the streets were filled with pedestrians taking advantage of the warm night.

Tucking her hand into the bend of his elbow, Joseph steered her out of the path of a group of rowdy teenage boys playing a game of chicken by pushing one another off the sidewalk and into the flow of traffic.

She gave him a quick glance. "How well do you know this city?"

Slowing his stride, he stared straight ahead. "Well enough to get around without getting lost." Joseph told Crystal about coming to the Holy City for the first time when he negotiated purchasing land to set up the tea garden, then again while conferring with the engineers hired to drain the swamp and surrounding land for cultivation. "Instead of commuting between here and Palm Beach, I decided to live at the Beaumont House, and whenever I have some downtime I become a tourist."

Crystal huddled closer to Joseph's side. "Would you ever consider living here permanently?"

He patted her hand. "Not really. It's not that it isn't beautiful, but I like living in Florida. How about you? Would you ever consider leaving the Sunshine State again?"

"Yes," she said truthfully, "only because I'm unencumbered."

"Unencumbered," he repeated under his breath. "I like your way of saying you're single with no children."

"It's because I have options some women my age don't have. Either they're in relationships, are married, going through a breakup or divorce or have children. All of which would make it more difficult to pick up and relocate. If I were to get my big break, the only thing I'd have to do is put my condo on the market."

They left the avenue, turning down a cobblestoned side street lined on both sides with houses with decorative wrought-iron gates and white porches. The flickering glow from streetlights reminded Crystal of Victorian-era gas lamps. "If it were raining and this street were lined with town houses, it would be the perfect setting for a Jack the Ripper–type movie," she murmured, her tone pensive.

Something within Joseph quieted; he suddenly saw what hadn't been as apparent to him as it was to Crystal. He knew that, as a decorator, she looked at everything with an artist's eye. "You're right. I think Charleston's charm is its architecture. Whenever I come here I always feel as if I've stepped back in time. It's the same when I go to Eagle Island."

"Is that where you've set up the tea garden?" Crystal asked.

"Yes. An elderly man who claims he's a direct descendant of one of the oldest black families living on the island told me about stories passed down by the griots, who talked about hundreds of large birds with wings that were wider than a man was tall that had built their nests high up in the pine and cypress trees, hence the name Eagle Island. But when the European landowners decided to build homes, they cut down many of the trees, disturbing their habitat. Later it was the pesticides that greatly reduced the numbers.

"Are there any eagles left on the island?" Crystal asked.

"I've seen a few."

"Didn't putting in the tea garden disturb their habitat?"

Joseph patted the hand tucked into the bend of his elbow. "No. That is one thing I insisted upon when the engineers dredged the land. They were not to upset the balance of nature. Although I negotiated for the sale of one hundred acres, we cleared only the land needed for planting. The rest of the garden is surrounded by water and swamp that's home to gators, water snakes, egrets and of course fish. Watching the sun rise over the swamp is an amazing experience."

"It sounds primordial," Crystal remarked reverently.

"It is," Joseph said, agreeing with her. "I did promise to take you on a tour, so anytime you're ready just let me know."

"I'm off until Tuesday, so I'm available to take the tour whenever you want to take me."

"If that's the case, then we can go either Sunday or Monday." Joseph was anxious to show Crystal the undertaking that had taken over every phase of his life for the past two years. And once the tea was harvested and processed, his focus would turn to the construction of his new home.

"How do you get to the island?" she asked.

"The way is the ferry. Unlike with Wadmalaw, there's no road connecting it to the mainland. I have to warn you that it's very rural."

"If I can play competitively on a girls' basketball team, then I'm certain I'll be able to adjust to a rustic countryside."

"Do you have another commission after this one?" he asked after a comfortable silence.

A shiver of excitement swept over Crystal. "Yes. I'm going back to New York City to decorate a jazz club. The owner inherited the town house from his grandparents, who ran a speakeasy during Prohibition in an adjoining property."

"They were never busted by the police?"

She laughed softly. "You don't get busted when you have high-ranking police officers on the take. After the repeal of Prohibition they turned it into a rooming house. Unfortunately someone smoking in bed started a fire that nearly destroyed the three-story building. Renovating it was too costly for the owners, so they boarded it up and many years later a high-profile actor bought and renovated it because he wanted homes on both coasts. By the 1980s the Lower Manhattan neighborhood was transformed into an upscale, trendy residential area.

"Last year my client decided to convert the basement into the Speak Low late-night jazz club. It's probably the only concert venue in New York City with a doorbell. Just like with a speakeasy, you'll have make reservations and be buzzed in through the front door. Then you head downstairs through a narrow, chandelier-marked hallway and into the club."

Joseph found himself intrigued with the idea of running a modern-day speakeasy.

"Have you seen it?" he asked Crystal.

She shook her head. "Not yet. However, I did see a video of the entire house and it's magnificent. It was built in 1860, a year before the start of the Civil War, but wasn't completed until 1866, because some of the men working on the house had enlisted in the Union army. I'll show it to you when we get back to the hotel. Tell me about your brother," Crystal said, deftly changing the topic of conversation. "Where is he living now?"

"Harper and two of his friends bought an uninhabited island in the Caribbean they plan to turn into a vacation retreat."

"That sounds exciting. What did he do before becoming part owner in a private island?"

Joseph waited for the light to change before he and Crystal

crossed the street leading down the block to the hotel. "He was a sports agent."

She smothered a laugh under her breath. "It looks as if your family is really into vacation resorts."

"It works for those who run them."

Crystal thought she detected a hint of wistfulness in Joseph's voice. "What about you, Joseph? What would you have done if you hadn't gone into law? Would you be managing one of the resorts?"

"No. I always knew I wanted to practice law."

"You didn't have a Plan B?" she drawled teasingly.

Dropping her hand, Joseph put his arm around Crystal's waist, pulling her closer to his side as they made their way up the path to the Beaumont House. "Not at that time. Little did I know I'd become a farmer. Now I'm going to ask you the same question. What would you have been if you hadn't become a decorator?"

"A dancer."

Joseph stopped in midstride, causing Crystal to stumble. He caught her before she lost her balance, and then stared at her as if she'd taken leave of her senses. "You're kidding."

She recovered quickly, her smile spreading to her eyes. "No! My mother decided dance lessons would make me graceful, so she signed me up for ballet and modern dance. What she didn't know was that I wanted to be an Ikette or a fly girl, and when I told her I wanted to take hip-hop classes she stopped paying for the classes. I could've gone to my father for the money, but I didn't want them arguing with each other again, so when I went to Italy and France in my junior year as an art student, I spent more time in the clubs than I did at the museums or on field trips."

"Did your parents know you were out clubbing when you should've been studying?"

"Of course not, or I would've had to beg, borrow or steal to pay for my senior year's tuition. Daddy is pretty laid-back but not so laid-back that he would approve of me clubbing when I should've been studying."

Joseph laughed loudly. "Did you pass, Miss Dancing Queen?"

"It wasn't a pass/fail course, but that's not to say I didn't keep up with my coursework."

"It's still not too late to become a rump-shaking, twerking diva," he teased.

"It is too late, Joseph. Number one, I'm too old and it's been a while since I've gone out clubbing, and I really don't need any of my clients seeing me shaking my butt like a backup dancer in a hip-hop video."

"They don't have to see you if we don't go out. Instead of hanging out at Chez Crystal, we'll go to Club José," Joseph said, grinning from ear to ear. "I'll arrange for dinner to be served in my apartment. That way we don't have to cook or clean up afterward, and then we'll dance."

Crystal's heart made a crazy flip-flop motion as she anticipated dancing again. It wasn't that she hadn't danced recently, but it was always alone.

Stopping, she turned slightly and grasped the front of Joseph's jacket. Going on tiptoe, she fastened her mouth to his, deepening the kiss before ending it. "Thank you."

Joseph's arms went around her shoulders. "You're very welcome."

He liked Crystal's spontaneity, yet what he was beginning to feel for her went beyond a mere liking. He'd asked her to establish the requisites for their relationship and she had determined the parameters as to where it would lead and end. However, the more time he spent with Crystal, the more he wanted to spend with her because it was no longer about wanting to make love to her. He wanted to do and share all of the things couples experienced when dating: weekend trips, going to the movies, dinner, dancing and eventually extended vacations.

Joseph realized his time with Crystal was limited, but he intended to take pleasure in the shared encounters she parceled out like sips of water to a man dying of thirst, while attempting to make the best of it, knowing he would be left with the memories of their time together.

"Good evening, Mr. Wilson, Miss Eaton. Beautiful night

for a walk," drawled the liveried doorman standing at the entrance to the Beaumont House. His warm greeting matched his inviting smile.

"Yes, it is," Crystal and Joseph said in unison as the man opened the door for them.

The hint of a smile tweaked a corner of her mouth. She enjoyed what little time she and Joseph were spending together. He treated her like an equal, unlike other men her age who were hell-bent on power-tripping.

Despite being born into wealth, Joseph did not flaunt it, Crystal discovered. His clothes, sans designer labels, did not come off a department rack, and other than a watch, he wore no other jewelry. There were no visible tattoos or piercings, which led her to believe he was a very conservative thirtysomething.

As they strolled hand in hand across the lobby, she experienced a measure of safeness and protection she hadn't had in a long while, and she had to admit, once again, Joseph was right when he mentioned her living with a much older man had been the result of her not growing up with her father. Crystal had thought of herself as a young sophisticate. After all, she'd grown up in Miami, spent six months in major European cities and lived in Washington, D.C., as an undergraduate student, so the decision to go to graduate school in New York City had been an easy one for her.

When she met Brian in a local coffee shop, they began an easygoing friendship that eventually led to their sleeping together—Crystal's life changed the moment he suggested she share his studio apartment. The arrangement was advantageous for both. Brian didn't have to troll clubs looking for someone with whom to sleep, and she had a live-in lover and protector. And because she wasn't his student, Brian didn't have to concern himself with reprisals from college administrators if their liaison ended badly.

Despite the differences in their ages, Crystal had a normal relationship with him. He didn't relate to her as her father and herself as his daughter. And since meeting Joseph she wondered, if they'd met years ago, how changed would she have been from the connection? At that time and even now she still felt she wasn't ready for marriage, and she didn't have to go to a psychic to know her reluctance was the result of her parents' unstable relationship with others.

She'd grown up listening to Raleigh accusing Jasmine of deliberately getting pregnant so he would marry her. What Crystal didn't understand was that if her father was so opposed to marriage, then why had he married so many times? She knew the volatile and spiteful allegations had shaped her views toward marriage, and secretly vowed she would never coerce a man into marriage because she was carrying his child.

The elevator arrived and they entered the car along with several other hotel guests. It rose quickly to the top floor. Joseph held the door as they exited. They walked abreast along the carpeted hallway. Crystal slipped the card key into the slot, waiting for the green light, and then opened the door. Kicking off her running shoes, she left them on the thick floor mat, and then hung her jacket on the coat tree by the door.

Slipping out of his jacket and dropping it on one of the chairs in the entryway, Joseph followed Crystal through the living room and into the space set up as an in-home office. He smiled when he saw her workstation. Unlike his—strewn with paper, books, newspapers and magazines—Crystal's was free of clutter.

Selena had returned the proposal he'd sent her with a number of legal queries and a cover letter from Myles Eaton. Earlier that morning he'd begun drafting a response. Crystal's neat desk, her leaving her shoes on the mat at the door and not waiting for housekeeping to come and clean up the kitchen, spoke volumes about the woman who now occupied his waking thoughts. She was a neat-freak.

Crystal pulled over another chair over to the workstation. "Come and sit down."

He stared at her enchanting profile, wondering if Crystal knew how innocently sexy she was. Joseph hadn't missed the admiring glances from men when they entered the Watering Hole. Although slender, she had curves in all the right places.

His cell phone chimed a programmed ring tone as he was sitting down. The call was from one of his frat brothers. "Excuse me, but I have to take this," he mumbled, rising slightly to take his phone out of the pocket of his jeans. "Hey, Drew. What's up?" He placed his free hand over Crystal's much smaller one while giving it a gentle squeeze.

"Frank's leaving for Denver on Tuesday, and the rest of us decided to give him a surprise send-off this weekend. We contacted his fiancée about the get-together and she's flying in Friday night. Frank still doesn't know she's coming."

Geothermal engineer Francis Lynch had accepted a position with a Denver-based energy company after his cardiologist fiancée moved from Miami to Denver. "I already have plans for this weekend." Crystal tapped Joseph's arm, garnering his attention. "Hold a minute, Drew." He placed his thumb over the mouthpiece. "What is it, baby?"

"We can take in a game some other time."

He shook his head. "No."

"Yes, we can. If you have season tickets, then we can always go to other games together," she said sotto voce.

Joseph paused, mentally weighing his options. He looked forward to spending three consecutive days with Crystal and he also wanted to see his frat brother and former college roommate once more before Frank moved across the country. Winking at her, he mouthed a thank-you. If she was talking about other games, then perhaps they would continue to see each other once they'd returned to Florida.

He removed his thumb. "I'm back, Drew. I thought Frank wasn't supposed to leave until April."

"He got the call earlier this morning that they want to bring him on board early," Drew explained.

"What are you guys planning to do?" Joseph asked, his gaze meeting and fusing with Crystal's. Light from the desk lamp cast a flattering glow over her flawless dark skin, causing him to hold his breath for several seconds. She was breathtakingly beautiful with or without makeup.

"We need you to run interference."

A slight frown appeared between Joseph's eyes as he pulled his attention back to the voice on the other end of the connection. "What do you want me to do?"

"We're going to tell Frank that everyone's coming up to Charleston Saturday night to celebrate your birthday with you."

"My birthday isn't until next weekend," Joseph reminded him.

"Next weekend is the Super Bowl and some of the brothers are flying out to the West Coast for the game. That's why we decided your birthday is the perfect excuse to hang together."

The seconds ticked off as Joseph mulled over the plan. "Okay. Count me in."

"Thank, bro. Now, I need you to give me the names of a few restaurants where we can party."

"Forget about a restaurant. If it's my birthday, we'll party here at the Beaumont House."

"Are you sure you'll have enough room? The brothers are bringing their wives and girlfriends."

Joseph smiled. "There's plenty of room. I'll arrange for the hotel to cater the party."

"Thanks, brother. We'll reimburse you later."

"Forget about it. What time should I expect you?"

"We're renting a party bus so we don't have to come in separate vehicles and—"

"And you don't have to worry about designated drivers," Joseph quipped, perceptively finishing Drew's sentence.

"Bet to that," Drew countered, laughing. "Look for us to arrive around seven."

Ending the call, Joseph placed the phone on the desk. "I'm sorry about—

"Please stop apologizing," Crystal admonished, interrupting him. "Think about the fun you'll have with your friends when they celebrate your birthday prematurely."

He draped an arm over her shoulders. "It will only be fun if you're with me."

Easing back, Crystal stared at Joseph, committing everything about his face to memory. And she knew she would only have memories once they parted. "No, Joseph. They're your friends and they'll just view me as an interloper."

Picking up his chair, Joseph moved it closer to Crystal and cradled her face between his hands. "When you asked a stranger to come with you to your cousin's house for brunch, did you think of me as an interloper?"

"No."

He smiled. "I rest my case."

Crystal affected a sexy moue, bringing his gaze to linger on her mouth. "You like saying that, don't you?"

"Only when I have to," Joseph drawled, pressing a kiss on the bridge of her nose.

"One of these days I'm going to overrule you, counselor."

Joseph's smile grew wider. "Should I be afraid?"

Crystal rubbed noses with him. "You should be very, very afraid, because you're not going to win every difference of opinion."

Curbing the urge to kiss her mouth, Joseph lowered his hands because he didn't trust himself not to take Crystal into his arms, carry her up the staircase to her bedroom, strip her naked and bury his flesh so deep inside her they'd become one in every sense of the word.

Aside from her beauty, Joseph wasn't certain what it was about Crystal that drew him to her like a moth to a flame. Perhaps it had something to do with her outspokenness. Under the veneer of poise and sophistication was a woman in complete control of her life—something he'd just come into. Joseph left the court to take on a role at ColeDiz because of family loyalty. It hadn't been easy working with Diego, whom he initially regarded as a despot. Whenever he challenged his cousin, Diego's stance softened and their working relationship had become one of mutual respect. When the CEO accused him of not being a risk taker like so many other Coles working for the family-owned company, Joseph reminded Diego his mind-set was law, not business.

He'd become a businessman who'd found himself enthralled with a businesswoman, although they were like ships passing in the night, acknowledging each other for a while before sailing on to other ports of call.

"I'm ready to see what you plan to do with the former speakeasy."

Crystal inserted the thumb drive in one of the ports on her laptop, clicking on the file for Speak Low. Joseph stared, awed by the before photos and after renderings of the basement in the Tribeca residence that had been transformed from a dark, brick-lined empty space to one with strategically placed lights between the coffered ceiling and brick walls, creating a soft, inviting atmosphere.

He shook his head in amazement. "It's stunning."

Crystal highlighted the wall with framed photographs, enlarging it. "Do you recognize these jazz greats?"

Joseph peered closer. "I know Scott Joplin, Duke Ellington, Miles Davis, John Coltrane and Charlie Parker." He paused, shaking his head. "I can't recall the others."

She pointed to the three remaining photographs. "Sidney Bechet, Fats Waller and Artie Shaw."

"How do you know so much about jazz musicians?"

"My father is a jazz enthusiast. He has a priceless collection of rare recordings of jazz greats dating back to the 1920s."

To say Joseph was in awe of Crystal's talent was putting it mildly. She was more than good at her craft. She was brilliant. "You must decorate my home once it's built, and I'm not going to take no for an answer."

Crystal closed the file, her jaw hardening as she clenched her teeth. Joseph was back to flaunting his belief in entitlement, that she couldn't or shouldn't deny him whatever he wanted. "You have no idea how long it's going to take to build your house, and I don't know where or what I'll be doing then. You have my number, so whenever you're ready, give me a call and I'll let you know if I can or can't accommodate you."

Joseph went completely still as if he'd been struck across the face. Crystal's retort was cold, waspish. "I'm sorry if you believe I'm pressuring you," he said.

A beat passed as Crystal looked at Joseph in what had become a stare-down. Twin emotions assailed her. She didn't know why he excited and exasperated her all within the same breath. "It isn't what I believe, Joseph. You were emphatic when you said you weren't going to take no for an answer."

"I shouldn't have put it that way."

Crystal tried to soften her response. "I'll let you off this time, but please don't let it happen again."

A frown marred Joseph's even features. "Damn, girl. Can't you cut me some slack? I said I was sorry."

She had no intention of relenting, not until Joseph learned that being a Cole wasn't the answer to getting everything he wanted in life. "I'll have to think about it."

It was Joseph's turn to engage in a stare-down, his large, dark eyes boring into Crystal. "Why is it I find myself completely enthralled with a woman whose beauty is comparable to the most exquisite, delicate rose? Yet when I try to touch her she's quick to remind me she has sharp thorns that draw blood. What do I have to do for you to let me in?"

"You don't have to do anything. You're already in," Crystal said in a hushed whisper. She wanted to tell Joseph that she'd allowed him to scale the wall she'd erected to keep men at a distance.

Joseph moved closer, his breath warm and moist against her cheek. "Am I really in?" he questioned. Crystal blinked, and then nodded. "Please spend the night with me." She blinked again, staring at him as if he'd spoken a language she didn't understand. "Nothing's going to happen that you don't want to happen," he continued.

Please spend the night with me. The passionately spoken query caused Crystal's breath to solidify in her throat, choking her with a raw emotion that wouldn't permit her to speak. He hadn't asked to make love to her, but just to be with him. His arrogance and entitlement aside, she knew Joseph was different, unique from the other men with whom she'd become involved. He made her more than aware of the strong passions within her, and that she'd denied her own physical needs for far too long.

He'd asked her to establish the terms of their short-lived relationship and she knew if they were going to make love, then she would have to make the first overture.

Exhaling an inaudible breath, Crystal knew she couldn't continue to ignore the truth. She wanted the man. A secret smile stole its way over her parted lips. She and Joseph had reached a point in their friendship where it had to be resolved.

"Please wait for me to pack an overnight bag."

Joseph sat stunned, unable to move, when Crystal stood and walked out of the room. She'd become an enigma, keeping him emotionally off balance. It wasn't vanity that communicated she enjoyed his company as much as he enjoyed hers; however, the hours, minutes and seconds they'd spent together hadn't totaled a full day.

He wanted more time, time in which to discover if what he felt for her was real or imaginary, only because José Ibrahim Cole-Wilson believed he was falling in love for the first time in his life.

Chapter 10

Crystal knew the moment she walked through the door to Joseph's penthouse to spend the night that she and her life would change forever. She shifted her bag from one hand to the other in an attempt to stem a sudden flash of nerves, unable to believe she was reacting like a frightened virgin about to embark on her first sexual encounter. *Pull it together, girl,* she told herself. After all, she was a thirty-year-old, sexually experienced woman who in her early twenties had lived with a man almost twice her age. Even though there hadn't been anyone since Brian, she still shouldn't be shaking like a fragile leaf in a storm.

Reaching for her bag, Joseph placed it on the floor. His eyes never left hers as he cradled her face in his hands, and she was certain he could hear and feel the runaway pumping of her heart. "If you don't want to do this, then I'll take you back to your place."

Crystal lifted her chin in a gesture he probably had no problem interpreting as defiance. "If I wasn't certain, I never would've agreed to spend the night with you."

Lowering his head and hands, taking her into an embrace, Joseph breathed a kiss under her ear. "You're certain, yet you're afraid."

"I'm not afraid," she countered.

"If you're not afraid, then why are you trembling?"

"Perhaps it comes from the anticipation of sharing your bed," she half lied.

Crystal knew Joseph had offered her the option of their sharing a bed without making love.

It was just that while her head said no, her body was screaming for a release of sexual tension and frustration building up for longer than she could remember. And she had to remind herself that both were responsible, consenting adults who were aware of where a sexual encounter would lead. There would be no declarations of love or promises of a future together. In other words, they would be friends with benefits.

"Would you feel less apprehensive if we don't make love tonight?"

Crystal tried making out his features in the muted light in the entryway. "Why are you giving me mixed messages? Didn't you say nothing's going to happen that I don't want to happen?" He nodded. "Then I say we should start with sharing the same bed." Smiling, Crystal rested a hand on his chest. "Please show me where I can shower and change."

And it wasn't for the first time Joseph felt he was falling in love with an enigma. The trembling woman in his arms was nothing like the one who'd stunned him when she broached the subject of men and women masturbating. He pressed a kiss to the soft, fragrant strands covering her head. "Come upstairs with me."

Like a trusting child, Crystal held Joseph's hand as he led her up the staircase to the second floor and into his spare bedroom. He set her bag on the padded bench at the foot of the bed, turned and walked out, closing the door behind him.

Puffing up her cheeks, she blew out a breath. She stood without moving, staring at the bag on the bench seat. Joseph had referred to her as a delicate rose with thorns, but the thorns were a necessity to keep him at a distance. And what Crystal knew as surely as she knew her own name was that she had feelings for Joseph. She could imagine herself falling in love with him. But, unlike his ex, she wouldn't try and pressure him into marrying her. However, she did think him selfish for continuing to date a woman for that long when he wasn't ready to put a ring on her finger.

Shaking her head as if coming out of a trance, Crystal opened the bag and took out her grooming supplies. Minutes later she stepped into the shower stall.

* * *

Joseph stared at his reflection in the bathroom mirror as he drew the electric shaver over his jaw and chin, knowing he'd turned the corner in his relationship with Crystal when he'd practically begged her to spend the night with him. It wasn't sex he needed from her as much as it was companionship.

He'd chided Diego time and again about being married to ColeDiz, but he'd become his cousin's clone when over the past two years he'd thought of nothing else but the overall success of the tea garden.

This time when he'd returned to Charleston, Joseph could never have predicted he would meet someone like Crystal. If he were looking for the ideal woman, then she would be it. She embodied beauty, grace, intelligence and passion. However, she'd accused him of being somewhat arrogant with an inflated sense of entitlement when in reality he wasn't either. What she thought of as arrogance was confidence to Joseph—something that had been instilled in him from childhood. His father constantly reminded him that as a Cole he was a descendent of survivors who'd endured unspeakable cruelty so that he would exist today, and at no cost should he dishonor their sacrifice.

As for entitlement, it was synonymous with his family's legacy. His great-grandfather Samuel Claridge Cole, the grandson of slaves, had established a foundation wherein his children, their children and their children's children would never have to look outside the family for financial stability.

He ran his hand over his face and throat, finding it free of stubble. Reaching for a bottle on the vanity, he uncapped it and poured a small amount into his cupped hands, then patted his cheeks, wincing against the stinging sensation. Not wanting to linger any longer, Joseph stepped into the shower stall, switched on the radio hanging from the showerhead and sang along with the latest Bruno Mars hit.

Knocking lightly on Joseph's bedroom door, Crystal entered at the same time he walked out of the bathroom in a pair of black cotton pajama pants. Her eyes widened as she stared at his smooth, broad chest. His upper body was magnificent: broad shoulders, long, ropy arms, muscled pectorals and defined abs and biceps. The drawstring waistband to his pants rode low on a pair of slim hips. She smiled. Joseph wasn't that conservative; the scales of justice were tattooed over his left breast.

"I was hoping you were decent," she said, smiling.

Joseph glanced down at his bare toes peeking out from under the hem of the pajama pants. "I usually sleep nude, but because I have company I decided it best I cover up."

She nodded. "Thank you." If she walked into the room and found him nude, Crystal wasn't certain how she would react. Seeing him in a state of half dress was enough to make her heart beat a little too quickly. When going through her lingerie drawer, she had to decide whether to wear a nightgown or pajamas, deciding on the latter at the last possible moment because she didn't want to show too much flesh. The pink-and-white cotton pants and a matching sleeveless top were definitely not risqué.

Joseph pulled back the quilt, blanket and sheet on the far side of the bed. "I like to sleep near the door. If that's okay with you," he added quickly.

"It's okay."

Crystal wasn't about to debate with Joseph which side of the bed she preferred, because even if she slept on the right side, by morning she'd find herself on the left. She strolled fluidly across the bedroom, placed her slippers next to the bedside table and got into bed. Reaching up, she turned off the lamp on her side, then settled down against the mound of pillows cradling her shoulders.

Joseph hadn't closed the wall-to-wall drapes and millions of stars winked in the clear nighttime winter sky. She went completely still when he got into bed next to her, dimming rather than turning off his bedside lamp. The warmth of his body elicited sparks of awareness that eddied throughout her.

Resting his head on a folded arm, Joseph turned on his side to face Crystal. "What's on your calendar for tomorrow?"

Shifting slightly, she stared directly at him. Light from the lamp illuminated his smooth clean-shaven jaw, while drawing her gaze to linger on his mouth. Crystal stared at Joseph through the eyes of an artist. He would've made the perfect model for drawing classes, because with his balanced features and beautifully proportioned body he was certain to have become a favorite for those drawing the male nude figure.

"I have a one o'clock appointment at a textile factory over in Goose Creek." She had to order sheets, tablecloths and towels for the inn and B and B. "What about you?"

"I'm free all day," he answered, his minty toothpaste breath sweeping over her face.

"How often do you go to the tea garden?"

"Four or five times a week, now that the project manager is in Nebraska awaiting the birth of his first child."

Her eyebrows shot up as she focused on the tattoo on his chest. "Don't you have someone else to step in for him if you're not there?"

Smiling, Joseph flashed his straight white teeth. Crystal was thinking in business mode. "There's an assistant manager who is an environmental engineer, but he's not full-time because he teaches environmental studies at the College of Charleston. I have someone who's retired and living on the island who acts as a backup and security. We've installed closed-circuit monitors in his house, and at any time of the day he's always aware of any activity at the garden."

"When do you expect to harvest your first crop?"

"Mid to late April."

Her eyes came up, meeting his. "So, you're going to hang out here until that time?"

Joseph nodded, his fingers playing in the curls touching the top of her ear. "That's the plan. I can't go back to Florida now even if I wanted to, with Shane gone. Marci's due to have her baby in another two weeks, so by the time she and baby are medically cleared to travel, they'll be back for harvesting."

Crystal couldn't believe she could feel so comfortable sharing the bed with a man of whom she'd had erotic dreams. He smelled of soap and an aftershave that matched his cologne, and she wanted to press her body to his in a silent plea for him to make love to her.

"How old will you be next weekend?" she asked after a pregnant silence.

"Thirty-one."

She smiled. "You're eight months older than me."

"When's your birthday?"

"October thirty-first."

"Damn, baby. You came out with the witches and ghouls."

"Tell me about it," she snorted delicately. "I usually celebrate it November first."

Joseph stared at her fresh-scrubbed face, wondering if Crystal knew she didn't need makeup because her complexion was flawless. "All Saints' Day was a school holiday for me growing up."

Crystal assumed Joseph would be Catholic because of his Latin ancestry. "You have Latin roots, yet your name doesn't reflect it."

"My legal name is José Ibrahim Cole-Wilson, but the only person who calls me José is my grandmother. My uncles refer to me as Joe Jr. and my sister calls me Joey."

Easing away from him and sitting up, Crystal gave him a long, penetrating stare. "I like José better than Joseph or Joe. It's softer sounding."

Pushing into a sitting position, Joseph pressed his shoulder to Crystal's. "*Abuela* would love you for saying that because she wanted all of her grandchildren to have Spanish names. My parents decided before they had their first baby that my father would name their boys and my mother their girls. My oldest brother is Anthony instead of Antonio. Then there's Harper, and the youngest is Nathan. When my mother had two boys back to back, she overruled my father because she thought they would never have a girl. So she got to name me and my sister, Bianca."

"It must have been fun growing up in a big family." There was a hint of wistfulness in Crystal's voice.

"It was chaos personified, especially when we pretended we were professional wrestlers and jumped off sofas and tables. If we didn't break lamps or some little figurine that was my mother's favorite, then it was an arm, wrist, leg or occasionally we'd dislocate a shoulder. Dad, who's an orthopedic surgeon, would put us back together and then ground us for as long it took for whatever was broken or dislocated to heal. Unfortunately for me I broke one leg and then the other in two consecutive summers, so I spent two school vacations in a cast and indoors. All of the roughhousing stopped when Marimba opened for business and Mom put us to work. I'd complain that she was breaking the law because we were too young to work, so she had us sign up for working papers and put us on the payroll."

"I suppose she rested her case," Crystal teased. Joseph cut his eyes at her, but she pretended she didn't see the threatening look. "Speaking of food, what do you plan to serve Saturday?"

His expression changed, softening. "We're going to entertain between sixteen and twenty, so it should be buffet-style." Turning over, Joseph picked up a pad and pen with the hotel's logo off his bedside table. "I like what you made when I came to your place for happy hour. Maybe we can add a few more dishes."

Crystal noted it was the second time he'd said *we.* "You can order a cheese and fruit platter. A raw bar with clams, oysters, lobster and sushi is always a big hit. I'm partial to prosciutto-wrapped asparagus and melon, prawn with various sweet and spicy dipping sauces, spinach and bacon-stuffed mushrooms and sliced tomatoes and mozzarella. That's just for the ladies."

Scribbling quickly, Joseph listed the various dishes. "What's for the guys?"

"Chicken wings, ribs and pigs in a blanket."

"What you trying to say, baby? That we're carnivores?"

Crystal folded her hands at her waist. "Who're you trying to fool? If I gave you a choice between a walnut salad in endive and a rib eye steak, you'd go for the steak."

"Man cannot live by salad alone," he quipped.

"Speaking of salads, what do you think of a Cobb salad?"

Joseph added it to the list. "Anything else you can think of?"

"Deviled eggs topped with caviar."

"Beluga, sevruga or osetra? What's the matter?" he asked when she gave him a look of astonishment.

"Beluga. I didn't think you were that familiar with different types of caviar." It was only on very special occasions and depending upon the artist that Jasmine served caviar during a showing.

"I remember my mother nearly having a meltdown when she catered a private party at the restaurant and the woman who wanted to surprise her husband insisted she wanted to serve sevruga caviar to her fancy guests. Beluga or osetra wouldn't do, because she'd heard somewhere that the golden osetra was the rarest and most mature of the osetra sturgeon. My mother contacted a gourmet shop that sold sixteen-ounce tins for twenty-five hundred dollars a pop."

Crystal did a quick calculation in her head. "That would only serve eight to sixteen, depending on the portions."

"Mom had to order enough for at least eighty. The bill alone for caviar was more than twelve thousand dollars."

Crystal shook her head in amazement. She didn't understand how some people threw away money in order to impress others. "How much was the entire bill?"

"Over a hundred grand. Mom closed the restaurant to the public, so she had to adjust the final cost. Champagne flowed like water, along with vintage wine and top-shelf liquor. There was a live band, a D.J. and rolling bars. Several couples left with someone they hadn't come to the party with, and I witnessed firsthand how drinking too much destroyed a few marriages when men and women who were married to others were seen coming out of the private party rooms adjusting their clothes."

"Damn!" she drawled, scrunching up her nose. "That is so low. The only thing worse is having sex in an airplane bathroom."

"That depends on the plane," Joseph replied, deadpan.

Crystal's jaw dropped. "You've have sex on a plane?"

Joseph did all he could not to laugh at her shocked expression. The bathroom on the Gulfstream G650 had a shower *and* enough room for a couple to make love without having to be contortionists. "No. One of these days I wouldn't mind joining the mile-high club, but only on a plane with a bathroom large enough where I don't have to straddle a toilet to get my freak on."

She scrunched up her nose again, unaware of how much Joseph had come to watch for the charming expression. It reminded him a little child smelling something malodorous.

"That's one club I don't need to join, thank you." Crystal gestured toward the phone. "I think you'd better call concierge to place your food order," she suggested.

"You're right," he agreed. Reaching for the phone, Joseph punched in the number for the concierge. He knew he wasn't giving the hotel chef a lot of time in which to prepare what he'd need for Saturday night; however, it was the Beaumont House's pledge to their penthouse guests to fulfill their requests.

"Concierge. John Porter speaking. How may I help you, Mr. Wilson?"

It took fifteen minutes for Joseph to give him the proposed menu. "I'm going to need at least two servers and one bartender. I'd really appreciate it if they can set up twenty minutes before my guests are scheduled to arrive. They're coming in together around seven, and I'd also like someone from the hotel staff to allow them access to this floor."

"That shouldn't be a problem. Is there anything else you'll need, Mr. Wilson?"

"That's all for now. Thank you so much, Mr. Porter," Joseph said, ending the call.

Turning off the lamp, he lay beside Crystal, pulling her hips against his groin, while hoping he would be able to sleep through the night without making love with her. In that instance he felt like Job, being put to the test and praying he would succeed.

He pressed a kiss to the nape of her neck. "Good night, sweetheart."

Crystal smiled in the darkened space. "Good night, darling."

It was Joseph's turn to smile. "Am I really your darling, sweetheart?"

"Tonight you are."

"What about tomorrow morning?" he asked.

"Let's take this one day at a time."

He sobered quickly. Joseph wondered if that was how their relationship would play out—one day at a time. He'd asked her to let him in and she countered saying he was in, but somehow he felt it wasn't enough. With Crystal it had to be all or nothing for him, and he wasn't prepared to accept nothing. Exhaling an inaudible sigh, Joseph closed his eyes, waiting for sleep to overtake him.

His last thought before slipping into the comforting arms of Morpheus was of his growing old with Crystal.

Ribbons of sunlight crept over the bed, caressing Crystal's cheek with warmth. She came awake with the realization she was alone. The pillow beside hers bore the imprint of Joseph's head but none of his body's heat. Moaning softly, she turned over to peer at the clock on a side table. It was minutes before eight.

Pushing into a sitting position and raising her arms above her head, she stretched like a languorous feline emerging from a long nap. Sharing a bed with Joseph certainly had its advantages. She'd slept through the night and Crystal felt more rested than she had in a while.

Her arms were still above her head when he walked into the bedroom carrying a bed tray with covered dishes from which wafted mouthwatering aromas. He'd pulled on a white tee over the pajama pants. Seeing him like that was a sight she could easily get used to.

Lowering her arms, she ran her fingers through the short strands pressed against her scalp. "Good morning."

Joseph placed the tray on the table on his side of the bed. Leaning down, he brushed a light kiss over her parted lips. "Good morning. I thought it would be fun if we'd have breakfast in bed."

Easing back, Crystal swung her legs over the side of the

mattress. "I'd like that. But I have to wash my face and brush my teeth first."

"I put your things in my bathroom," he said as she headed for the door.

Crystal stopped midstride and turned around slowly to face him. A beat passed. "Thank you."

She didn't want to read more into the action than necessary, as she turned toward the bathroom, wanting to anticipate when they would possibly share the intimacy of a bath or shower. She was realistic enough to know when they did make love it would change her. An even more terrifying realization would be falling in love with him. Shaking her head as if to banish the thought, Crystal entered the bathroom.

Crystal completed a modified ablution in record time and returned to the bedroom.

Joseph had set another tray on her side of the bed. "Come and eat before everything gets cold." Quickening her step, she practically jumped into bed, smiling as he adjusted the pillows behind her back and shoulders before settling the bamboo bed tray over her lap.

She uncovered a dish and gasped. He'd prepared a mushroom-and-spinach omelet topped with fragrant grated truffle. A smaller dish held country links and strips of crispy bacon, and another grapefruit sections.

Crystal picked up a knife and fork resting on a snowy white damask napkin, cutting into the omelet. An explosion of flavors lingered on her tongue and palate even after she'd chewed and swallowed the eggs.

"I truly can get used to eating breakfast in bed if this is what I have to look forward to," she remarked lightly.

Attractive lines appeared around Joseph's eyes when he smiled. "That can easily be arranged, sweetheart." The endearment rolled off his tongue as easily as involuntary breathing.

"Every morning I could prepare something different. It could be chicken and waffles, eggs Benedict, shrimp and grits, scones, frittatas, croissants—"

"Stop it, Joseph," she interrupted, in an attempt not to burst out laughing.

"You interrupted me before I could finish. There are also pancakes, crepes, steak and ham and eggs."

Crystal gave him a sidelong glance. "Yeah, right, and I'd end up so full that I'd never get out of bed."

"Lingering in bed can be quite pleasurable when sharing it with someone you love."

Crystal froze. The four-letter word had the same impact as a large hand going around her throat and not permitting her to swallow, breathe or even utter a sound. However, she was able to shake her head before finding her voice. "No, Joseph," she whispered. "You're not abiding by the terms."

Joseph chewed and swallowed several grapefruit sections. "What are you talking about?"

"We promised there would be no mention of love."

It was his turn to go completely still. Nothing moved. Not even his eyes. "You're wrong, because the word *love* never came up in that conversation. And what is so wrong with me saying I love being with you—in and out of bed?"

Crystal felt properly chastised. Being presumptuous, she'd misconstrued his meaning. She flashed a bright smile. "And I enjoy being with you."

Joseph touched his napkin to the corners of his mouth. "What's the matter? Does saying the word *love* bother you?"

"No. It's just that I believe it's bantered about much too freely."

"What if I tell you that I love you?"

"But you don't," she countered, and then continued eating.

A pregnant silence followed her retort until the space vibrated with tension as Joseph struggled to control his rising temper. Crystal was the most incredible *and* exasperating woman he'd ever met. "Are you a psychic, Crystal?"

She blinked. "Say what?"

"Did I stutter?"

A shiver of annoyance shimmied up her back. "No, you

didn't stutter, *Joseph*." Crystal stressed his name. "Why would you ask me that?"

"I asked because if you're able to read minds, then I applaud you. But if you can't, then don't tell me what I feel. Or is it you don't feel you're worthy to be loved?"

She snorted delicately. "Now who's being presumptuous?"

Picking up a pot of coffee, Joseph filled Crystal's cup with the steaming brew. "Will you please answer my question? Do you feel worthy of a man loving you?"

"Of course I do," she said much too quickly.

Joseph decided to press the issue. He'd found the woman in bed with him so easy to love, yet she continued to put up barriers to keep him from getting too close. "If you believe that, then why would you live with a man who didn't love you enough to marry you? And please don't tell me again that he didn't want children. I know a few married couples who've decided not to have children, but that doesn't mean they're not a family."

Biting down on her lower lip, Crystal mentally beat herself up for telling Joseph about living with Brian. Her past was her past and he had no right to pass judgment about her former lover. "Brian and I had a very satisfying relationship."

"Open your eyes, sweetheart. The man used you. Imagine his ego when as a middle-aged man he got to flaunt a beautiful young woman nearly half his age every time you were in public together. He didn't have to pay for sex because he had you." Joseph leaned closer. "I never would've treated you that shabbily."

Crystal pretended interest in adding cream to her coffee. Joseph's assessment of her relationship with Brian was similar to her parents'. "How would you have treated me?"

"If I wanted you to live with me, then I would marry you."

"Even if you weren't ready for marriage?" It was her turn to remind Joseph of why he'd ended his relationship with his longtime girlfriend.

"Maybe it wasn't so much that I wasn't ready but perhaps I'd chosen the wrong woman with which to engage in a long-term relationship."

They fell silent, concentrating on finishing breakfast. Joseph knew he'd waded out into dangerous waters bringing up the topic of marriage with Crystal. He knew her stance on the issue, but since meeting her, his had changed drastically. He wasn't the same man who'd checked into the Beaumont House in late November, and he had to thank Crystal for that.

Before meeting her, his focus had been on himself and his accomplishments. Walking into the federal courthouse alongside her uncle amid cameras and reporters on the first day of a drug kingpin's trial gave him a rush of unquestionable power. The high continued throughout the trial, ending when the jury rendered a guilty verdict.

It was ironic that his association with Solomon Eaton never crossed the line from professional to personal. It wasn't until Joseph handed in his resignation that Solomon revealed he'd received several death threats, threats targeting friends and family members. He also hadn't told Joseph that members of the U.S. Marshal Service had provided around-the-clock protection for him during the trials in which Solomon had served as a lead prosecutor for the government against high-level drug traffickers.

When he walked out of the federal courthouse and into a private office at ColeDiz International Ltd., Joseph's life took another turn he hadn't anticipated when instead of becoming immersed in corporate law he'd become a businessman and farmer.

Now his life was about to change again, and he thought of Crystal as his good-luck charm.

Everything he wanted seemed to go in his favor. Diego had found someone at ColeDiz willing to travel, leaving Joseph to concentrate on eventually taking over as CEO.

He'd revised the proposal for the jams and jellies, either deleting or updating the points set down by Myles Eaton and emailing it to him for his review. Within hours he'd received a reply. Myles had approved the proposal and final contract between ColeDiz International Resorts and Sweet Persuasions.

He hadn't lied when he told Crystal she was special, and for him she was special enough to make her a part of his life and his future.

Chapter 11

Pressing her palms together, Crystal stood next to Joseph, watching the bartender set up his bar. His arm went around her waist and she pulled her gaze away to meet his eyes. "Do you think I lit too many candles?"

"No, baby. Everything looks perfect. You're perfect." She'd placed white candles in various sizes in the fireplace and along the mantel. Watching her instruct the waitstaff where she wanted them to set up the buffet indicated this wasn't the first time she'd hosted a dinner party.

If he was pleasantly surprised as to her hosting ability, it was her appearance that rendered him mute. She'd selected a silk-lined midnight-blue cocktail dress with a slightly flaring skirt ending at her knees. Four inches of matching strappy pumps put her at the six-foot mark.

"Be careful, sweetie," she whispered, "or you're going to give me a big head."

"We'll be all right as long as I don't end up with a big head before our guests get here," he whispered in her ear.

It took a few seconds before Crystal realized what Joseph was referring to. "I don't like quickies," she whispered back.

Joseph chuckled deep in his throat. "That's something else we have in common."

Crystal nuzzled Joseph's ear with her nose. "I think your friend is going to be very surprised."

Earlier that afternoon two men from maintenance had come to set up tables near the wall-to-wall windows spanning the width of the living and dining room, leaving enough space for people to walk around.

The dining table provided seating for eight; the sofa added

three and a love seat another two, and an additional dozen padded chairs were set up around the living room to accommodate
those wishing to sit.

Joseph had turned a satellite radio to a station featuring
slow jams from the '80s and '90s, and the melodious sounds
flowed from hidden speakers installed in rooms throughout
the first floor.

The apartment phone rang, preempting Joseph's reply. He
picked up the receiver on the table in the entryway. "Our guests
are here," he announced softly.

Crystal stood beside Joseph, smiling, shaking hands and exchanging air kisses with his frat brothers when he introduced
her as his girlfriend. Like their host, all of the thirtysomething
men wore suits or blazers, tailored slacks, shirts or sweaters,
sans ties. They exchanged rough hugs with Joseph while pounding his back.

Their female companions, less effusive and very chic in tailored suits, dresses and designer shoes and matching handbags,
were dignified and gracious. All of them had left their purses
and totes on the table in the entryway.

When Joseph introduced her to Frank Lynch, his former college roommate, Crystal wondered if the tall, handsome, red-
haired, green-eyed engineer was aware the gathering was for
him and not Joseph.

Frank held her hand, dropping a kiss on her knuckles. "If I
wasn't engaged, I would seriously consider stealing you away
from Wilson."

Joseph forcibly removed Crystal's hand from his friend's,
tucking it into the fold of his elbow. "I know you're not trying
to hit on my woman," he teased with a wide grin.

Frank's fiancée, a very pretty petite woman with a light brown
complexion and a profusion of reddish brown, shoulder-length
twists, glared at him. "Francis Patrick Lynch, I hope you're not
disrespecting me and Joseph by flirting with his girlfriend!" A
chorus of guffaws followed her reprimand.

"Easy there, Brother Lynch. When your woman calls you

by your government name, then you better watch out for what comes next," mumbled Andrew "Drew" Andrews. He grew up being teased because he had the same first and last name.

"Word," drawled another of Joseph's frat brothers. "You're a better man than me, Lynch. There's no way I would upset a woman who knows how to use a scalpel, then lie down next to her and close my eyes." Francis turned a beet-red while his future wife glared at Drew.

"If you're ever in Denver and need medical assistance, don't come to my hospital, Mr. Andrews," she threatened, flashing a grin at the stocky man sporting a dark brown shaven pate and a neatly barbered goatee.

Joseph knew it was time to end the lighthearted teasing before it escalated. "Ladies and gentlemen, the bar is open. Once everyone is served we'll have a toast."

"Damn, Wilson," Drew drawled, following Joseph to where the bartender waited to take their beverage requests. "This place is outrageous. Brother, you're really living the high life."

"It'll do," Joseph said, winking at him over his shoulder.

Crystal beckoned the women closer. "Ladies, please follow me. For those who need to use the restroom, there's one just before you come to the kitchen, and there's another to the left of the staircase."

"I'm so glad Joseph came to his senses and stopped seeing that cow that used to work my last nerve," whispered Lucretia Moore, an incredibly beautiful full-figured woman with close-cropped hair bleached a becoming platinum.

Dr. Anaïs Woods nodded in agreement. "I second that, Lucie." She gave Crystal a direct stare, smiling. "You're such a welcome change from Kiara Solis, who believed her you-know-what didn't stink. We only tolerated her because she was seeing Joseph."

"How did you meet him?" asked Maria Acosta in slightly accented English.

"He used to work with my uncle." She wasn't ready to divulge that she and Joseph occupied neighboring penthouse apartments. Her answer seemed to satisfy them as they made their way toward the bar.

* * *

Glasses in hand, everyone stood in the middle of the room waiting for Joseph to make a toast. Crystal stared at the man who, despite her efforts to put up barriers to keep him at a distance, had managed to scale the hurdles to soften her heart. He'd called her a thorny rose and she had been. Now the thorns were gone and she was ready to acknowledge that she was falling inexorably in love with him.

Smiling, Joseph raised his glass of amber liquid. "First of all, I'd like to thank everyone for coming to my temporary humble abode for an evening of friendship and goodwill." This was followed by a roar of laughter. "All of you know why you're here," he continued once the laughter faded. "Except for one person. It is not to celebrate my birthday prematurely, but rather to honor a friend and brother who in another week will wake to look at the face of his beautiful future wife and the majestic Rocky Mountains." He extended his glass. "Brother Lynch, we'll miss you, man."

The shocked expression on Frank's face was priceless when his jaw dropped. "Why, you sneaky—"

"Don't blame me," Joseph said quickly, interrupting him while taking a backward step.

Drew held up a hand. "Blame me, Frank. We know how you hate goodbyes, so the brothers decided a little get-together would be the best way to show you how much we're going to miss your corny-ass jokes."

"My jokes aren't corny," Frank retorted. All of the frat brothers knew he was a frustrated standup.

"Just don't quit your day job!" someone yelled out.

Joseph laughed with the others. "Speaking of day jobs. Frank, we wish you and Anaïs all the best life has to offer."

"Frank and Anaïs!" chorused the assembly.

Frank kissed his fiancée, eliciting a round of applause. He signaled for silence. "Even though I'm here under false pretenses I still would like to thank everyone for giving me a send-off I know I'll never forget." Shifting slightly, he stared directly at Joseph. "He's probably going to try and kick my ass, but I'm going to tell it anyway." He paused. "I wouldn't be standing here if it hadn't been for Brother Wilson." Frank ignored Joseph when he shook his head.

"When I moved into my dorm room and saw Joseph Cole-Wilson standing there, my first impression was I'm going to have to compete with this pretty SOB for women because he had no idea I liked my honeys with a little color." Everyone laughed, including Joseph. "Once he found this out, he encouraged me to pledge a Black Greek Letter Organization, and that way I would become his brother in every sense of the word. We were halfway into our junior year at Cornell when I got a letter from the bursar's office saying I wouldn't be able to attend classes because my tuition payment was overdue. When I asked my father if he'd sent the check, he broke down and told me he'd lost his savings in a Ponzi scheme and that I would have to drop out. I started packing and that's when Brother Wilson told me he could get the money. I thought he was crazy, but three days later I was reinstated. At first I thought my roommate was into some funny stuff, but he finally had to admit that he asked his father to give him the money for the rest of my junior year. What I didn't know at the time was that he'd also paid for my senior year." Frank paused again as he stared down at the floor. "I owe everything I am today to Brother Wilson. Because of him I was able to graduate. Because of him I became an Alpha, which led me to meet the woman whom I love more than I ever thought possible." He extended his glass to Joseph, and then to the others in the room as tears filled his eyes. "Frat, sorors. I love you all."

There came a moment of silence. "You should be glad you're leaving, because from the look on Brother Wilson's face I know he's thinking about kicking your ass," Drew called out.

Lucretia waved her free hand. "Brother Wilson, I have a nephew who wants those new Jordans. Is it possible for you to spot him some chedda so he can style like the other kids in his class?" Her plaintive entreaty elicited another round of laughter.

Maria sucked her teeth loudly. "I'd have to be crazy to spend four hundred dollars on a pair of sneakers for my son when he'll need another pair less than six months later because he's grown out of them."

Most of the women were grumbling loudly about the cost of so-called designer sneakers, while Crystal's gaze met and fused with Joseph's as he stared at her over the rim of his glass. She'd thought him arrogant, entitled, yet in an act bordering on courage and selflessness, he'd gone to his father on behalf of his friend and roommate to ask for money.

She'd tried much too hard to tell herself that she was totally immune to him, but that was a lie. And Crystal knew she had to stop lying to herself and face reality. She wanted Joseph, all of him, for the short time they would have together.

She hadn't moved, so he wended his way through those lining up alongside the table with the food. A secret smile curved her mouth with his approach. "I like your friends," she said softly.

Lowering his head, Joseph pressed a kiss along the column of her neck. "I like them, too, but I like you a lot better. I should warn you that most of the women are also Greek, and you'll find a few AKAs among them."

Looping her arm over the sleeve of his jacket, Crystal took a sip of her wine. "Greek love," she said softly.

Joseph nodded. "Phi-Skee."

"Skee-Phi," she replied, acknowledging the bond between the Alphas and the AKAs of being the first Black Greek fraternity and sorority respectively.

It was two in the morning when she and Joseph said their goodbyes; the bartenders and waiters were clearing away all food and drink, and the maintenance staff had come to stack chairs on trolleys and reposition furniture.

Resting his hands at Crystal's waist, Joseph turned her in the direction of the staircase. "Go to bed, baby. I'll wait down here until everyone's finished."

Crystal flashed a lopsided smile. "Thank you," she slurred, leaning in and patting Joseph's chest. She knew she'd drunk too much wine when she was forced to hold on to the railing as she attempted to climb the staircase in her bare feet.

Frank's farewell celebration was nothing short of perfection. Copious amounts of food were consumed, and the bartender was kept busy filling drink requests.

Joseph changed the radio station to one featuring rap and hip-hop, Frank and Drew rolled back the rug and the living room had become a dance floor with couples dancing. As soon as the dancing began, Crystal shed her shoes and so had most of the women wearing stilettos.

Stepping off the top stair, she walked slowly along the hallway and into the master bedroom.

Folding his body down to the chair in the entryway, Joseph stretched out his legs, crossing his feet at the ankles. Given the short notice, Frank's impromptu going-away celebration was a rousing success. However, Joseph would've preferred Frank not disclose his involvement in securing the money needed for the engineering student to complete his undergraduate education at Cornell.

His thoughts shifted from Frank to Crystal when he spied the stilettos she'd taken off once the dancing had begun. He smiled. Club José had become Joe's Joint when the guys shed their jackets and the women their shoes. Joseph noticed Crystal bonding with the wives and girlfriends of his frat brothers—something Kiara had never been able to do.

He'd felt a measure of smugness when his frat brothers spoke of her beauty and graciousness. A few were bold enough to remark that Crystal was a refreshing change from his ex. Hearing their comments made him question himself as to why he'd continued to date Kiara when he knew marriage wasn't in their future. And in the end he had to admit to himself he'd been wrong to string her along, hoping he would never have to experience what he'd put Kiara through.

"Mr. Wilson, we're finished here."

Coming to his feet, Joseph nodded to the maintenance workers. They'd loaded tables and chairs on two trolleys. The bartender with his cart and the waiters were right behind them.

"Thank you, guys."

The bartender flashed a wide grin. "Awesome party." The waiters nodded in agreement.

"I agree," Joseph said without a modicum of modesty. It was one of the better get-togethers his friends had had in a while. Only the destination weddings were better. He closed the door, locking it, picked up Crystal's sexy heel, and went in and out of rooms extinguishing lights, leaving on the lamp on a side table near the staircase.

Joseph climbed the staircase, following the lingering scent of Crystal's perfume to his bedroom. Placing her shoes on the floor beside the door, he kicked off his own. She'd dimmed the lamps to the lowest setting, and there was enough light for him to see her neatly folded dress and underwear on the bench at the foot of the bed.

Undressing, he made it a concerted effort not to leave his shirt, slacks and socks scattered about the room.

Wearing only a pair of boxer briefs, he made his way to the bathroom. Crystal reclined in the Jacuzzi amid a profusion of bubbles up to her neck. She gave him a sexy, inviting smile.

"Hey, you," she said softly.

Leaning against the door frame, Joseph returned her smile. "Hey, yourself, beautiful. Would you like company?"

"I don't mind if you don't mind smelling like a girl."

Pushing away from the door, Joseph approached the tub, his thumbs anchored in the waistband of his briefs. "It will take more than smelling like a girl to make me feel less than a man," he drawled confidently.

Moisture had curled Crystal's short hair and spiked her lashes. "Bragging?" Bending slightly, he shed his underwear and stepped into the warm water. Her breathing stopped, her gaze lingering on the heavy semierect sex hanging between Joseph's muscled thighs. His genitals were an overt testimony to his masculinity.

Her gaze came up, resting on his face as he sat down opposite her in slow motion. The heat from the water spread up her chest to her face. The wine hadn't dulled her senses so much she didn't know he was giving her an up-close and personal view of his magnificent naked body. Crystal wished she could read minds, because Joseph's impassive expression gave nothing away.

"It was very noble of you to pay your roommate's tuition." She'd said the first thing that came to mind.

"That's something I really don't like to talk about."

"Why?"

Joseph closed his eyes. "I didn't do it to be noble. And I'm certain if the roles were reversed, Frank would've done the same thing for me."

"Are you certain he would've been able to come up with that much money?" she asked.

He opened his eyes. "It wasn't my money, but my father's."

"You asked your father?"

A cynical grin twisted Joseph's firm mouth. "I begged him. However, he agreed on one condition. That when I gained control of my trust I would have to pay him back plus fifty percent interest. Of course his demand was excessive, but he hadn't given me much of a choice. Two days after my twenty-fifth birthday I wrote him a check. Dad shocked me when he tore it up, saying he was proud I hadn't welched on my debt, and if he needed one friend, he'd want me to be that friend. Now, can we please drop the subject?"

Crystal now knew why Joseph was uncomfortable talking about it. He hadn't been comfortable with his father's compliment. "Yes."

She shifted slightly, the motion allowing Joseph a glimpse of a firm, rounded, water-slicked breast through fading bubbles. He hardened quickly, grateful for the remaining bubbles concealing his erection.

Crystal picked up a bath sponge and handed it to him. "Do you mind washing my back?"

Staring at her under half-lowered lids, he beckoned her. "Come down here and turn around." Joseph realized he should've refused her request when she scooted down to the opposite end, presenting him with her back. His erection brushed the small of her back, the sensation making him even harder.

He tried concentrating on drawing the sponge over her flawless dark brown skin, but his body refused to follow the dictates of his brain.

Around and around, up and down, he counted each time he touched her and after a while he lost count as the sponge moved lower down the curve of her spine to the roundness of Crystal's buttocks. Then he heard it. Her breathing had quickened. He dropped the sponge, cupping her hips, and his fingers massaged the firm flesh.

Crystal managed to escape the hold Joseph had on her bottom. Turning around, she went to her knees. Days, nights, months and years of denial surfaced, allowing her a newfound boldness when it was her turn to explore Joseph's body.

Resting her hands on either side of his face, she brushed her mouth over his in a whisper of a kiss. She tasted one corner of his mouth, then the other, knowing she was frustrating him when he brushed her hands aside and held her head captive. His explosive kiss sucked the air from her lungs, leaving her lightheaded and struggling to breathe.

Looping her arms under his shoulders, Crystal pressed her breasts to his chest in an attempt to get even closer. She was on fire, the area between her legs throbbing uncontrollably. Her hips moved sensually over his groin, silently communicating how much she needed him to assuage a rising passion threatening to incinerate her.

"Joseph." His name was a whisper.

"I feel you, baby."

Joseph released her head, pulling her to straddle his thighs before grasping his erection and slowly, methodically easing himself inside Crystal. He was met with a slight resistance, so reversing their positions and pushing his knee between her thighs, he drew back and with a strong, sure thrust of his hips buried his hardness in the hot, moist, tight flesh pulsing around his own.

The world outside ceased to exist as he lost himself in the sensual pleasure taking him to a place where he'd never been. Even when he'd fantasized about making love to Crystal, that hadn't come close to the ecstasy he now found in her arms. Fastening his mouth to the base of her throat, he pulled the tender flesh between his teeth. Then without warning he felt it. The tightening in his scrotum indicating he was going to come when he'd wanted it to last much, much longer.

"Joseph!" Crystal called his name. "Please stop!" Panic rushed through her like molten lava. She'd been so caught up in passion she'd forgotten he'd penetrated her without using protection.

Something in her voice shattered the sensual fog holding Joseph captive. He'd promised to protect her. He pulled out, every muscle in his body screaming in frustration. He held his engorged flesh tightly, struggling to stop the flow of semen straining for release. Unable to believe he'd been so irresponsible, he pressed Crystal's head to his shoulder.

"I'm sorry, baby," he apologized over and over. "Will you forgive me?"

Crystal nodded, grateful he'd stopped in time. She placed her fingers over his mouth. "Yes, I forgive you." She pressed a kiss under his ear. "Remind me not to accept an invitation to take a bath with you again."

He caught her hand and kissed each finger. "I promise it won't happen again."

"We have to be careful not to get caught up in the moment."

Joseph smiled, the gesture not meeting his eyes. Crystal didn't know his level of frustration had gone into overdrive, and he knew if they didn't get out of the Jacuzzi he would break his promise and take her again without protection.

Punching the button to turn off the Jacuzzi, he stood, bringing Crystal up with him. Stepping out of the tub, he picked her up and walked out of the bathroom. He placed her damp body on the bed, his following hers. His rapacious mouth charted a course from her mouth to the soles of her feet, seemingly wanting to taste every inch of her silky skin. And as much as he wanted to be inside her, Joseph wanted to bring her to completion.

Crystal pulled her lip between her teeth to keep from screaming. The pleasure of Joseph's tongue and teeth made her feel as if she was coming out of her skin. Closing her eyes, she arched when the heat from his mouth seared her closely trimmed mound. A scream, torn from the back of her throat, filled the bedroom as the tip of his tongue made tiny circles around her swollen clitoris.

"Please," she pleaded shamelessly, over and over, the plea becoming a litany of neediness only Joseph could assuage.

Stopping his temporary sensual assault on her body, Joseph opened the drawer to the bedside table, took out a condom and slipped it on. Spreading her legs wider with his knee, he reached for Crystal's hand and placed it on his erection; together they eased it into her vagina, both groaning in unison.

Crystal gloried in the feel of her lover's skin against hers, his touch sending tingles up and down her body, and the hardness sliding in and out of her body setting her afire. He quickened his thrusting; she followed his pace. Heat shot through her like an electric current; throwing back her head, she screamed his name, followed by long, surrendering moans of ecstasy. A peace she'd never experienced swept over her as Joseph collapsed on her body. The raspy sound of his heavy breathing reverberated in the room. After what seemed like an eternity when it was only seconds, he rolled off her and lay on his back, a muscular arm covering his face.

A secret smile curved her mouth. Her period of enforced celibacy had been more than worth it. Making love with Joseph had awakened the dormant sexuality of her body, and she looked forward to when they would make love again and again until they parted. Her smile grew wider when he reached for her hand and laced their fingers together.

"Did I hurt you?" he asked.

"No," she answered truthfully.

"You're very small."

"I'm probably tight because it's been a while since I've had sex."

Joseph didn't want to engage in a debate about how small or tight she was, but made a mental note to wait a few days before making love to her again. And he didn't want to correct her about having sex. What they'd shared went beyond sex. Letting go of her hand, he sat up and swung his legs over the side of the bed. "Don't run away," he teased softly.

"Where am I going?" she asked.

"I don't know. Maybe you're a vampire and you have to get home before the sun comes up."

Rolling over, she placed her hand over his latex-covered penis. "As long as I don't bite this, you'll be okay."

Joseph forcibly removed her hand. "We will not pretend we're vampires."

"You're the one that brought it up."

"My bad," he drawled, rising to stand.

Crystal stared at his gloriously naked body as he headed for the bathroom. She'd wanted to tell him she wasn't as small as he was large. A moan slipped past her lips when she shifted her legs. The muscles in her groin were on fire. She needed to soak in the Jacuzzi again—this time without company.

Turning over on her side and pulling the sheet up to her neck, she closed her eyes. She was drifting off to sleep when Joseph returned, molding his chest to her back. They lay together like spoons, their breathing coming in unison until they fell into a dreamless sleep.

Crystal woke at dawn to find Joseph on his back, snoring softly. She managed to slip out of bed without waking him, completing her morning ablutions in the other bathroom.

Dressed in a pair of sweats and thick cotton socks and carrying the bag containing her clothes, she went downstairs to the kitchen. She'd drunk two glasses of water while waiting for the coffeemaker to finish the brewing cycle.

"Good morning, baby."

Spinning around on the stool at the cooking island, she smiled at Joseph standing a short distance away in his bare feet and pair of jeans and long-sleeved tee. She hadn't heard him enter the kitchen. "Good morning."

He kissed her forehead. "What are you doing up so early?"

Crystal nuzzled his ear. "I had to get something to drink. My mouth is as dry as the Sahara Desert. I OD'd on cheese, caviar and sushi, which led me to drink more wine than usual."

Wrapping his arms around her waist, Joseph rested his chin on the top of her head. "How many glasses did you have?"

"I stopped counting after the second one. I suppose that's why I was slow reacting when we got caught up in the moment."

Joseph sobered suddenly. He recalled their impromptu coupling in the Jacuzzi. "I hope I pulled out in time."

Crystal said a silent prayer he had, because they'd picked the wrong time of the month to have unprotected sex. "I think I'm all right," she said with more confidence than she actually felt.

She didn't want history to repeat itself, like her parents, if she found herself carrying Joseph's baby. Jasmine had vehemently denied she'd deliberately gotten pregnant to trap Raleigh into marrying her; instead she'd accused him of getting her pregnant because he'd believed she was breaking up with him.

Despite the accusations, they married and then spent the next six or seven years blaming each other until they finally divorced. All Crystal remembered from her early childhood was the "he said, she said" rants, and it was something she vowed never to repeat with any man.

"Will you tell me if you're not all right?" Joseph asked.

"Why?"

"Because *if* you are pregnant, then we would have to get married."

Pushing against his chest, she extricated herself from his arms. "That's where you're wrong, Joseph. I doubt if I'm pregnant, or if I were to get pregnant by you, then we don't *have to do* anything except become parents to a baby girl or boy. I will not repeat with you what my parents went through. One blaming the other because my mother was pregnant with me."

Joseph froze as if he were a statue. "We are not your parents, Crystal."

Her eyes flashed fire. "I know we're not, because I'd never marry you or any other man because of a child."

Joseph refused to back down. "Don't you believe a child needs both parents?"

Crystal also refused to concede. "Not when they're at each other's throats. Every time my parents disagreed about something, they'd pull out the pregnancy card." She shook her head. "That's not going to be me. I won't be the first single mother and I definitely won't be the last one, either. And I don't know why we're arguing about marriage and babies when it isn't something we're both not ready for."

"We're not arguing," Joseph insisted. "We're having a discussion."

She rolled her eyes upward. Okay, she mused, they weren't yelling at each other, but they were having a disagreement. Unwilling to prolong the conversation, Crystal picked up the cup, filling it from the carafe with steaming black coffee. She set it down on the saucer in front of Joseph before reaching into an overhead cabinet and taking down another cup for herself.

Joseph watched Crystal intently as she spooned a teaspoon of sugar into her cup and then added a generous amount of cream. "Will you let me know? One way or the other?" he asked.

Her eyes came up, meeting his. "Yes," she answered. "I'll let you know one way or the other."

She didn't drop her gaze as she took a sip of coffee, savoring the taste and warm brew, wondering why Joseph wouldn't let it go. And for someone claiming not to be ready to embrace marriage, he'd become like a dog with a bone, insisting on it if she were actually carrying his baby.

"Thank you," he drawled.

Crystal cut her eyes at him, clenched her teeth to keep from spewing curses, all the while counting slowly to ten. She had to leave before she said something she would no doubt later regret. "As soon as I finish my coffee I'm going back to my apartment. I have quite a few things I have to take care of."

"Don't you want breakfast?"

She shook her head. "No, thank you. I'm still full from last night." Taking a sip from the cup, she met his eyes over the rim.

"I probably won't see you until tomorrow, so if you're going to the tea garden I'd like to go along with you."

"There's a prediction of rain for tonight, and if it does, then we'll have to put it off until Tuesday."

"It can't be Tuesday because I'm going up to North Carolina." She'd planned to visit many of the furniture manufacturer stores and outlets in High Point, Hickory and Jamestown for furnishings with which to decorate the inn and B and B. "I have to shop for furniture, and I probably won't be back until next weekend." Setting the cup on the countertop, Crystal rested both hands on his chest, registering the strong, steady beating of his heart under her palms. "I'll make certain to return in time for your birthday and the Super Bowl party"

Joseph covered her hands with his larger one. "I'm going to miss you."

She affected a sexy moue. "I'm going for less than a week."

His fingers tightened slightly on hers, holding her captive. "I'm still going to miss you."

Crystal knew her feelings toward Joseph were intensifying and she was becoming more confused every minute they were together. That meant their eventual separation would be even more difficult—at least for her. "And I you," she whispered.

"I'll walk you back to your place." Dipping his head, Joseph fastened his mouth to the side of her neck.

Crystal smothered a moan as she closed her eyes. What had happened to the levelheaded woman who'd come to Charleston to decorate two renovated residences for the owner of one of the city's most luxurious hotels? What she couldn't understand was why she'd permitted herself to fall under the spell of a man whose caresses, kisses and lovemaking upset her balance and rekindled a passion she'd believed impossible.

"Please, Joseph. I have to go now." He complied, picking up her bag. They walked the carpeted hallway in silence. Joseph waited until she unlocked the door, handing her the bag, then turned and retraced his steps.

Chapter 12

Crystal stared at her reflection staring back at her in the hotel's bathroom mirror. Her fervent prayer had been answered. She wasn't pregnant! Her eyes filled with tears of relief as she compressed her lips to suppress a sob.

Since coming to North Carolina, she hadn't had a restful night's sleep in four days. As long as she was busy, placing orders for only the merchandise the manufacturers had in stock, she didn't have to dwell on whether she was carrying a baby.

At night it was different when she lay in bed, trying to imagine what was going on in her womb. What she feared most was repeating her mother's life. However, the difference was that when Jasmine discovered she was carrying Raleigh Eaton's baby, they'd been seeing each other off and on for years, while with her and Joseph, it wasn't quite a month. And for her that amounted to little more than a one-night stand.

Crystal had planned to spend one more day in North Carolina before returning to Charleston. She'd ordered beds, side tables, tables and chairs, desks, chests and armoires for the inn at a company specializing in reproductions, and the furnishings for the B and B at three other furniture companies selling exclusively to wholesalers, both who had promised a two-to-three-week turnaround for delivery.

She had an appointment with several dealers selling rugs and framed prints and with another specializing in curtains and shades. Crystal had ordered floor and table lamps from local Charleston dealers, and once the items in the storage units were delivered, she would then arrange each space according to her meticulously thought out floor plans.

Her step was light, close to skipping, when she picked up her cell phone and punched in Joseph's number. She'd promised him she would let him know one way or the other as to her physical state. His phone rang four times before going to voice mail.

Crystal paused. "Joseph, this is Crystal. I'm calling to let you know I'm not…" She paused again, clearing her thoughts and mulling over how to phrase the news he would not become a father from an unplanned pregnancy. "I'm not pregnant," she finally blurted out. "I'll see you when I get back."

Joseph rolled over, loathing getting out of bed. He hadn't gotten back to the hotel until three in the morning after spending hours at the Watering Hole. He managed to get a seat at the bar and had sat there watching basketball played on the West Coast while the three glasses of beer he'd ordered sat untouched and eventually went flat. He hadn't come to drink, but for the feverish commotion that helped him forget about Crystal.

Even after some of the college students stumbled out, he continued to sit at the bar staring at the wall-mounted screen. First it was the basketball game, then an encore of a hockey game followed by continuous commentary from sports analysts and former players.

Instead of walking back to the Beaumont House, he'd hailed a taxi for the short trip. Not bothering to shower, he tossed his clothes on the floor in a heap and fell across the bed.

Reaching for his cell phone, he peered at the display. He had two missed calls. Punching in his pass code, he listened to the voice mail. Crystal's voice was flat, a monotone when she announced, "I'm not pregnant." One part of Joseph wanted her to be, because it meant they would have a lifelong connection, but Crystal was adamant about not marrying a man because she was carrying his child. And for Joseph, there was never a question of him taking care of his responsibility. He wouldn't be the first Cole male to get a woman pregnant before exchanging vows, but what he didn't want to be was a baby daddy. Even if he and Crystal didn't marry while she was pregnant, he would be more than willing to give her time to change her mind after she delivered their son or daughter. Knowing he wasn't going to be a father permitted Joseph a second chance—a chance to prove to Crystal he wanted her for herself, to show her—if she gave him a chance—how much he'd come to love her.

He listened to the second voice mail, smiling. Seth Allen had agreed to represent Gillian Stuart. He stated he was currently interviewing other women who'd worked at Bramwell and Duncan Architectural and Design who were also sexually harassed by Hugh Duncan.

Unfortunately for the perverted architect, he didn't know he was about to confront an attorney with the doggedness of a pack of wolves stalking prey.

After he tapped in Seth's number, Joseph's smile grew wider when he heard his friend's unorthodox greeting. "Talk to me."

"I got your voice mail. Thanks for taking on the case."

"What's your stake in this, Wilson?"

Joseph told him about Crystal's experience, without mentioning her name, when she worked at the architectural and design company.

"So this is personal."

"Very personal."

"What is she to you?" Seth questioned.

A beat passed. "The only thing I'm going to say is that she's very special."

Seth's whistle reverberated through the earpiece. "It sounds like you're ready to hand in your playa's card since you broke up with your ex."

Joseph wanted to tell his friend he was wrong. He'd never been a playa—hadn't even come close to ever being one. Not when he'd dated one woman exclusively for four years. "The only thing I'm going to say is I'm seriously thinking about settling down and starting a family in the very near future."

"Good for you, friend. Send me an invitation if you decide not to go the Vegas route."

"She's not the Vegas type, and I'm certain she'll want all of her family in attendance."

Joseph chatted with his friend for a few more minutes, then rang off.

It was after ten and time he got out of bed to start his day. It was Friday and Crystal had promised to return to Charleston before Sunday. Whipping back the sheet and quilt, he swung his legs over the side of the bed and made his way to the bathroom, whistling a nameless tune.

Crystal stopped at the concierge to pick up her mail before going up to the apartment. The young woman handed her a shopping bag with her name attached. Peering into the bag, she saw several magazines and the package containing the gift for Joseph's birthday.

She'd planned to leave High Point Saturday afternoon to return to Charleston, but the vendor with whom she was scheduled to meet the day before had put her in his calendar for Saturday instead of Friday.

Her decision to check out early and be on the road by sunrise on Sunday morning proved beneficial because she was able to avoid the subsequent backup on Route 17 when several vehicles collided, blocking traffic.

Pulling her wheeled suitcase, she walked into the elevator and inserted the key into the slot for the top floor. A feeling of accomplishment swept over her as the car rose quickly and silently. Crystal had managed to purchase everything she needed to complete decorating the interiors. All that remained was the delivery of the furniture and arranging them according to the approved specifications. The commission she'd estimated would take three months would be accomplished in two. Al was excited because he would be able to advertise his grand opening well in advance of the beginning of the tourist season.

The elevator doors opened at the penthouse floor, and when she exited the car Crystal took a quick glance to the right as if she expected to see Joseph. She'd sent him a text Saturday night informing him that she'd been delayed and wouldn't return until late morning.

Although Selena had insisted she not bring anything for the Super Bowl party, Crystal had decided to use some of the ingredients in the refrigerator before she had to discard them.

She planned to make an assortment of wonton dumplings filled with gingered ground pork, chicken and beef and a chili-soy dipping sauce.

Leaving her bags in the entryway, Crystal picked up the receiver to the house phone and dialed Joseph's room. He answered on the first ring, her stomach muscles tightening slightly when she heard his voice. "Honey, I'm home," she said into the mouthpiece.

"Bienvenido a casa, mi amor!"

Crystal understood *bienvenido* because of the signs in the Florida airport welcoming passengers to the various cities. And she needed no translation for *home* and *my love*. "Thank you."

"What are you up to?" he asked her.

"I have to shower before I make some appetizers for the party."

"What are you making?"

"Wonton crescents with gingered meats and a chili-soy dipping sauce."

"That sounds a lot more exciting than what I plan to make."

"What are you making?" she asked.

"Guacamole and salsa."

"I'm completely clueless when it comes to making salsa. Mine always comes out much too watery."

"Do you want me to show you how to make it?" Joseph asked.

"Yes. Why don't you come over and we'll cook together?"

He chuckled. "That sounds like a plan."

"Give me half an hour, and then come on over. I'll leave the door unlocked."

Crystal's head popped up when Joseph walked into the kitchen. He placed a wicker basket on the countertop. Seeing him again made her aware of how much she had missed him. Time away from Joseph had also forced her to acknowledge that she was falling in love with him.

If he'd thought her perfect, then she thought him spectacular—in and out of bed. She'd watched his interaction with his friends and they appeared as fond of him as he was of them. He was three *G*'s: gorgeous, generous and gracious.

Wiping her hands on a terry cloth towel, she picked up the gaily wrapped box from the shelf under the cooking island. Rounding the granite-topped island and going on tiptoe, she pressed her mouth to his ear. "Happy birthday to you," she sang softly.

Smiling, Joseph set the basket on the countertop. "You didn't have to get me anything."

"I know, but I wanted to get you a little something." Crystal held her breath as she watched Joseph unwrap the box. The expression on his face was something she should've captured with her camera phone when he gently removed the engraved monogramed Waterford crystal basketball paperweight from its packaging.

Joseph felt the solid weight of the multifaceted glass on his palm while staring at the block-lettered monogram. His gaze shifted from the paperweight to Crystal's charming expression. "You think you know me that well?" he teased.

Picking up a knife, she chopped scallions, adding them to the crushed garlic, grated ginger, soy sauce and sesame oil in a food processor. "Don't play yourself, Joseph. You know you're a basketball fanatic. I'm willing to bet that the plans for your new house will include a basketball court."

A sheepish expression crossed Joseph's features. "I'm sure it will."

"I could walk around butt-naked while a Heat game is on and you wouldn't even bat an eye."

He returned paperweight to its box, then held out his arms. "Come here, baby."

Crystal walked into his embrace, burying her face against his warm throat. She anchored her arms under his shoulders and closed her eyes. Everything about the man with whom she'd found herself captivated seeped into her. He was so indelibly imprinted on her heart and mind that she would be able to pick him out in a darkened room with hundreds of other men.

Resting his chin on her head, Joseph dropped a kiss on the

short, damp strands clinging to her scalp. His right hand moved up and down her sweatshirt-covered back as if he were comforting her. "Nothing in this world could make me ignore you with or without your clothes." He kissed her hair again. "Thank you so much for the gift. I'll treasure it forever."

Crystal wanted to tell him it wasn't easy buying a gift for a man who had everything and could buy whatever he wanted given his net worth. The wives and girlfriends of his frat brothers were forthcoming when they talked among themselves about Joseph's ex-girlfriend bragging about dating a very wealthy man. Lucretia, the most vocal in the group, admitted she had accused Kiara of being a wannabe gold digger who'd probably end up marrying a freeloader.

"You're very welcome." Crystal delighted in his strong embrace, his familiar scent, the way the contours of his body complemented her curves. She didn't want to think of the time when they would exchange goodbyes.

Pulling back slightly, Joseph angled his head, his nose nuzzling her ear, trailing kisses along her neck. She gasped softly when his teeth closed on the tender flesh as he suckled her. "Did I tell you how much I missed and love you?" he asked between clenched teeth.

Crystal closed her eyes, willing the tears pricking the backs of her lids not to fall. He loved her, while she couldn't tell him how much she'd come to love him. "You don't have to say anything. I don't know how, but there are times when I know what you're thinking."

A chuckle rumbled in Joseph's chest. "What am I thinking now?"

"Something X-rated."

He laughed again. "Wrong, sweetie. It's triple-X-rated."

"Should I be scared?"

"Not today."

Crystal opened her eyes, meeting his. "When?"

"That's up to you. You have to let me know when we can make love again."

She glanced up, mentally counting when she would be finished with her menses. "Wednesday."

Joseph counted on his fingers. "Sunday, Monday, Tuesday. I hope I can hold off—"

"Don't you dare say it," she interrupted, placing her fingers over his mouth. "If you need some release, I believe I can help you out."

"No, no and no!" he protested through her fingertips.

She dropped her arms and pushed out her lips. "Well, I did offer."

"There's no need to pout."

"I'm not pouting!"

"Yes, you are, baby."

Leaning into Joseph, Crystal ran the tip of her tongue over his lower lip, then suckled it. "To be continued."

Joseph released her. "To be continued," he repeated, as he emptied the basket with avocados, tomatoes, red and yellow onions, limes, garlic, jalapeño and cilantro.

They spent the next ninety minutes listening to the radio while preparing a concoction of spicy guacamole and salsa. Joseph assisted Crystal filling, folding and crimping wonton wrappers with pork, beef and chicken. She would wait until they got to her cousins' house to fry them in a wok.

Crystal experienced a comfortable peace while cooking alongside Joseph. Was this, she mused, how it would be if they married? That he would serve her breakfast in bed, then linger long enough to make love before they left for their respective offices?

And would they eventually have a child or maybe children raised by two loving parents? She was certain they would be gracious hosts when opening their home to friends and family.

Crystal beckoned to the man who had stolen her heart. "May I have this dance?"

Joseph took her in his arms, twirling her around and around. "So you like old-school music?"

Tilting her chin, she stared into a pair of eyes the color of rich, dark coffee. "Not really, but I like this song."

He smiled. It was Bobby Caldwell's classic blockbuster hit, "What You Won't Do for Love." Pulling her closer, Joseph pressed a kiss to her forehead.

The song ended but they continued to hold on to each other. "What do you use on your hair that makes it smell so good?" Joseph asked after a comfortable silence.

Crystal smiled against his shoulder. "Argan oil."

"I love the smell and I love you." It was the second time he'd uttered the simple declaration.

And for the second time that morning Crystal felt like crying. Falling in love should've filled her with joy, not regret, and she knew the closer the time came when she would have to leave Charleston, the more difficult it would be to keep her fragile emotions in check.

Joseph maneuvered into the driveway and around the rear to Xavier and Selena's home, parking between a minivan and a late-model SUV. Unbuckling his seat belt, he got and came around to assist Crystal. "Go on in, baby. I'll bring the food."

She grasped the handles of the tote with the ingredients she needed to cook the dumplings. "Are you sure?"

Cradling her face between his hands, he kissed her forehead. "Very sure."

Crystal climbed three steps and opened the door leading into the kitchen. Mouthwatering aromas filled the space as Xavier stood at the stove top grilling baby lamp chops.

"Hey, cuz," she called out.

"Hey, yourself. Where's your boyfriend?"

Her cousin referring to Joseph as her boyfriend didn't bother her as it did the first time they'd come to his home. "He's coming." She glanced around the gourmet kitchen. "Are we late?"

"No. Everyone got here about ten minutes ago."

"Where's Selena?"

"She's upstairs putting Lily to bed. It's a little early, but baby girl didn't take a nap this afternoon because the doorbell was constantly ringing. This year we decided to cater most of the meat dishes."

"What did you…" Her words trailed off when Joseph entered the kitchen carrying two oversize shopping bags. Moving quickly, she approached him, taking the bag with the pan of wontons. She took them out of the bag, setting them on the countertop.

Xavier lowered the flame on the grill. "Let me take that," he said to Joseph. Reaching into the bag, he removed two large glass bowls filled with guacamole and salsa. Lifting the top on the bowl with the salsa, he blew out an audible breath. "Damn! This stuff is guaranteed to singe a few eyebrows."

Joseph laughed. "Nothing a few ice-cold beers can't cure."

"No lie," Xavier drawled, grinning.

"He shouldn't have brought anything." Everyone turned to find Selena standing at the entrance to the kitchen, hands folded at her waist. She walked in and hugged and kissed Crystal. "I specifically told you not to bring anything," she said. She turned and hugged Joseph. "Thank you for coming, partner."

Joseph gave her a warm smile. "Back at you, partner."

Waving her hand at Xavier in a gesture of dismissal, Selena picked up a pair of tongs, testing the lamp chops for doneness. "Darling, I'll take over here. Why don't you and Joseph take the salsa and guacamole upstairs? Criss and I will finish up, and then we'll join you."

"Are you certain you don't need us?" Xavier asked.

Selena nodded. "*We're* very certain." Waiting until the two men were out of earshot, she turned to Crystal. "You're sleeping with him, aren't you?"

Crystal recoiled as if she'd taken a punch in the nose. However, she recovered quickly. "Why would you ask me that?"

Pulling out the collar on the man-tailored shirt, Selena traced the slight bruise on the area above Crystal's collarbone. "You have a love bite right here."

Crystal's blood warmed, her cheeks burning as she recalled Joseph biting her neck. However, she hadn't noticed the mark when getting dressed. Her hands were shaking noticeably when she fastened a button. "I guess he got a little carried away," she mumbled. Walking out of the kitchen, she washed her hands in the sink in the half bath.

"Please don't tell me you're embarrassed," Selena said when she returned.

"I'm not embarrassed that we slept together. What I don't want to do is to advertise it. Why are you looking at me like that?" she asked when the other woman shot her an incredulous look.

"What's the big secret? It's only a matter of time before your families find out you're involved with each other."

Crystal shook her head. "That's not going to happen. Whatever we have now will end once I leave Charleston." She told Selena about returning to Florida for a brief stay before traveling on to New York City and another commission. "Joseph will be here at least until late April or early May."

Selena removed the meat from the grill, placing it in a warming drawer. "So, you won't see him for a while. What's wrong with that?"

"I'm just beginning to grow my business and I can't commit to an ongoing relationship at this time."

"Is Joseph asking for a commitment?"

"No." Crystal told Selena about the terms she and Joseph agreed to with regard to their temporary liaison. "Joseph isn't ready for marriage and neither am I. We enjoy each other's company, so what happens in Charleston stays in Charleston."

"So." Selena snapped her fingers. "You're going to walk away from someone who appears so suited to you."

Opening a drawer under the countertop, Crystal took out an apron, slipping it on over her blouse and jeans. "I'm not walking away, Selena. I just can't afford to get sidetracked when it comes to my career."

"Look at me, Criss. I'm married and a mother, yet I still have a successful career."

Reaching up, Crystal took down a wok and its cover from an overhead rack. "How much do you know about my parents?"

Selena lowered her eyes. "I know your father has been married four times."

"And he's about to embark on a fifth."

"No!"

Crystal couldn't help laughing at Selena's shocked expression. "My mother and father met in college. They dated, broke up and reconciled so many times they had to have lost count. During their last separation, Daddy heard she was seeing someone in New York and he managed to woo her back. She'd stopped taking the pill, so she relied on him to protect her from an unplanned pregnancy. Within a month of earning her MFA she was scheduled to move to New York to work as an appraiser with a Manhattan auction house, but she had to decline the position once she discovered she was pregnant. She blamed Daddy for deliberately getting her pregnant to keep her from moving to New York to advance her career, while Daddy blamed her for tricking him into marriage, because he'd always said he didn't want to father a child out of wedlock."

Selena watched as Crystal poured a small amount of sunflower oil into the wok, waiting for it to heat before she placed the crescents in the hot oil. "If your father was so against marriage, then why has he married so many times?"

"I don't know. The only thing I can figure is that my father is a control freak. In other words, he wants everything to be his decision, and he believes to this day that my mother forced him into marriage. I grew up with them constantly trading insults and blame, and that's something I never want my children to experience."

Selena gave Crystal a sidelong glance. "Do you think you'll ever marry?"

"I don't know." Crystal lifted a crescent to see if the underside was crispy; she added enough water to come about halfway up the sides of each wonton and then covered the wok and waited for the water to evaporate. "Do you have a chip- and dip bowl?"

"Yes." Selena retreated to the pantry, where she stored dishes she used for entertaining. She returned to the kitchen with the large bowl. "Are you marriage-phobic?"

Selena was asking questions Crystal wasn't ready to answer, or to which she didn't have an answer. Not at that moment. She'd always believed she would eventually marry. But it wasn't something that topped her wish list. Her career had become her priority.

When she actually thought about it, Crystal realized she was more like her parents than she would openly admit. She had become a control freak like Raleigh with regard to marriage, and as fixated on interior decorating as Jasmine was with appraising, buying and selling pieces of art.

"I don't believe I am. Right now I don't feel any pressure to marry, because I'm only thirty. I know I'll probably think differently four or five years from now if I want to start a family."

Crystal raised the lid on the wok, smiling. All of the water had evaporated. Pouring the chili-soy dipping sauce into a microwave-safe bowl, she heated it. She plated the warm wontons, arranging them neatly. "I'm not going to fill the dip cup until we're upstairs."

The two women carried platters of herb-infused lamp chops and meat-infused gingered wontons with a chili-soy sauce up the staircase to the expansive theater room. Many of the invited guests had claimed leather reclining seats with cup holders, eating and drinking while watching pregame programming, while the others were serving themselves from the buffet with hot and cold dishes.

Her cousins had spared no expense when it came to renovating the space for entertaining. The contractor had installed a built-in bar with high stools, an efficiency kitchen, a bathroom, four rows of seats, with six in each row, set up theater-style, a crystal-clear mounted flat-screen taking up almost an entire wall. The opposite end of the space contained a game room with skee ball, pool and Ping-Pong tables and several vintage pinball machines. The crisp sound coming from the audio components made Crystal feel as if she were in a modern movie theater.

Crystal reacquainted herself to the guests she'd met when they attended Selena and Xavier's wedding in West Virginia. Most of the men were ex-military, some who'd attended the

Citadel with Xavier and a few who taught at the same military school where her cousin now taught military history.

Within the span of a week she'd interacted with Joseph and Xavier's friends. It was a blatant reminder of how sterile her social life had become. She still kept in touch with some of her friends in New York and the sorority sisters with whom she shared a closer bond, but it had been a while since she saw them in person. Crystal made a mental note to call her former grad school classmates to let them know she planned to spend several months in the Big Apple and looked forward to reconnecting with them.

Crystal smiled as Joseph, carrying a plate, closed the distance between them, her gaze softening when their eyes met. "I thought you could use something to eat before the game began," he said in a quiet voice.

Curbing the urge to kiss him, she lowered her eyes to the plate. "Thank you." However, she was surprised when he dipped his head and kissed her forehead.

"What do you want to drink?"

Crystal glanced up, her eyes making love to his face. "Since it's Super Sunday I'll have a beer."

Joseph lifted his eyebrows a fraction. "There're pitchers of margaritas to go along with the guacamole and salsa."

She scrunched up her nose. "I'll hit them up on my second helping."

He gave her a skeptical look. "Are you certain you're going to have room?"

Staring at her plate, Crystal measured the amount of food on her plate. "It's not that much." He'd served what she would normally eat during a cocktail hour at a wedding. It was enough to stave off hunger until the main meal.

Joseph's expression indicated doubt as he returned to the bar to get a beer for Crystal.

He asked Xavier for a beer on tap as he fixed a plate for himself. Everyone rushed to claim a seat for the coin toss, Joseph handing Crystal her glass of beer and then folding his body down next to hers. Crystal hadn't declared a favorite team because neither a Florida nor a New York team had made it to the Super Bowl, while he secretly rooted for the Atlanta Falcons.

Those having to go to work early Monday morning left after the halftime entertainment because of the three-hour time difference between the East and West Coast. Selena had filled containers with leftovers and gave each invitee a takeaway bag filled with samples of the delicious dishes.

The game resumed, going into overtime with the Falcons as Super Bowl champions, and Crystal and Joseph lingered behind to help clean up, overriding Selena's protests when they said they didn't have to get up early to go to traditional jobs.

Crystal drove Joseph's Range Rover back to the Beaumont House, parking it in his assigned space. Resting her arm over the back of his seat, she angled her head. "Your bed or mine?"

Joseph's teeth shone whitely in the diffused light coming through the windshield. "Mine."

Leaning closer, she touched her mouth to his. "Yours it is."

Chapter 13

Crystal wished she had the power to hold back time. Her heart felt like a stone in her chest when she closed her luggage. She was leaving Charleston and Joseph. Everything they shared since Super Bowl Sunday had become a permanent tattoo, imprinted in her memory for all time.

She had accompanied Joseph to Eagle Island to see the tea garden, totally awed by the ancient trees draped with Spanish moss. The earth over centuries was worn away under the hooves of horses, bare and booted feet, wagon wheels and automobile tires. Some of the houses appeared to be little more than shanties, lacking indoor plumbing, while others had been updated with a fresh coat of paint, new shutters and paved driveways.

Joseph had maneuvered slowly along the main road, waving out the driver's-side window to elderly residents sitting out on their porches.

Crystal convinced him to stop when she spied an elderly woman weaving a sweetgrass basket as her Lowcountry ancestors had done for centuries. Crystal bought a picnic basket with a cross handle, a sewing basket and an exquisite cobra basket she planned to give to her mother from the weaver's modest inventory. She knew Jasmine would exhibit the African-inspired handicrafts in the section of the gallery dedicated to African and Asian art.

If Crystal found herself awed by the untouched, primeval beauty of an island that had mostly been left to grow in wild abandonment, she experienced shock when seeing the carpet of green leaves stretching for as far as her eye could see that would eventually become a much sought after beverage drunk throughout the world.

Crystal was equally proud to give Joseph an up-close and personal view of her decorating talent when she gave him a tour of one of the completed bedrooms in the B and B. An antique reproduction of a four-poster bed with a crocheted canopy, oriental rugs, heirloom-inspired bedding, Queen Anne chairs and an ornately carved armoire with doors matching the designs on the bed's posts beckoned you to come in and stay awhile.

He'd kept his promise to take her to the Ordinary, the popular seafood hall and oyster bar located in an old Charleston bank. She'd just swallowed an oyster when she felt suddenly ill and retreated to the ladies' room. Crystal hadn't wanted to believe the oyster wasn't fresh, because she'd eaten raw oysters and clams without experiencing a reaction. She returned to their table, apologizing to Joseph, who'd ordered an assortment of cooked fish for her.

A feeling of sadness swept over her when she realized her time in Charleston was coming to an end. She'd met with Al earlier that morning for a final walk-through of what would become the Holy City's latest luxury boutique hotels. She would miss going to the hotels whenever a furniture shipment arrived and directing the deliverymen where to position each piece.

She would also miss dropping in on Selena to watch her create beautiful edible works of art and getting down on the floor to have a tea party with Lily and her dolls. Selena had kept her updated with her collaborative enterprise unwritten by ColeDiz International Ltd., which she and Joseph projected would be fully operational in another eighteen months.

Crystal refused to dwell on missing Joseph. They'd alternated sleeping in each other's apartments, making love with each other as if their very existence depended on it. Joseph hadn't mentioned he loved her again since that momentous Sunday, and for that Crystal was more than grateful. Her body spoke for her whenever she experienced unbridled ecstasy in his passionate embrace.

Three days ago when she'd mentioned her departure, she felt his immediate withdrawal. They'd continued to share a bed but did not make love. Crystal knew if they continued to have sex it would make their separating more difficult and, on her part, very emotionally tolling.

The doorbell echoed throughout the apartment, startling Crystal and shattering her musings. Leaving the bedroom, she went downstairs to answer the door. Peering through the security eye, she saw the face that would haunt her dreams for a long time.

Forcing a smile, she opened the door. "Hey," she said cheerfully. She dropped her gaze to the small shopping bag in his left hand, knowing he'd bought her a gift. They'd celebrated Valentine's Day with a promise not to exchange gifts.

Joseph stared into the face of the woman whose very presence took him to highs and, with her imminent departure, to a low he never could've imagined. His impassive expression did not change or reveal what he was feeling at that moment. "May I come in?"

Crystal opened the door wider. "Of course. Please."

He walked in, waited for Crystal to close the door and then followed her into the living room. She sat on the edge of the cushion on the love seat, while he sat inches away.

Joseph felt her tension as surely as if it were his own. He knew saying goodbye wasn't going to be easy, but he'd given himself a pep talk before coming to her apartment. Crystal had been more than forthcoming with the terms of their short-lived liaison, so he knew he should've been prepared for this day. He'd told her indirectly that he loved her, and then waited for her to acknowledge what were the three most difficult words for him to say to a woman.

He handed Crystal the bag. "I got you a little something to remember your time in the Lowcountry."

Crystal hands were trembling slightly when she reached into the bag and took out a gaily wrapped square box. Carefully she removed the shiny black-and-white-embossed paper. Biting down on her lip, she opened a black velvet box and gasped.

Joseph had given her a Cartier bracelet. The elegant eighteen-karat, oval-shaped bracelet was studded with ten round

brilliant-cut diamonds. She barely reacted to the iconic bracelet when he picked it up and snapped it around her left wrist.
Her body's heat had barely warmed the precious metal when he
picked up an ergonomic screwdriver and tightened the catch.
She looked at him as if he'd taken leave of his senses when he
put the screwdriver in the back pocket of his jeans.

Cupping the back of her head with one hand, he kissed
her hair. "I wanted to give you this for Valentine's Day, but
I changed my mind when you reminded me you didn't want
to exchange gifts. Call me whenever you want to take it off."

"I…" The protest died on Crystal's tongue as she watched
Joseph stand up and walk out of the living door, through the
door and out of her life.

She lost track of time as she stared at the love bracelet on
her wrist; the light coming in through the window shimmered
off the blue-white diamonds. Reaching into the gift bag, she
removed a small dust bag with which to store the bracelet and
an authenticity card for appraisal. What good was the dust bag
when she couldn't remove the bracelet without the screwdriver?

"Call me whenever you want to take it off." His parting
words assaulted her like invisible missiles, eliciting a foreign
emotion Crystal recognized as resentment. The arrogance Joseph had managed to repress had surfaced when he used the
little screwdriver to link them together without a promise of a
commitment, which he claimed he didn't want.

She walked into the office, picked up her cell phone and
tapped Joseph's programmed number. It rang four times before going straight to voice mail. It was obvious he'd turned off
his phone. She repeated the action, dialing his room number,
and again she heard the automated voice asking her to leave
a message.

Replacing the receiver in its cradle, she clamped her jaw
tightly. If he thought her wearing his bracelet signified they
were somehow connected, then he was wrong. The only connection was that as consenting adults, they'd had a brief sexual
encounter. Crystal knew one day if their paths were to cross

again she would not be the same person who'd come to Charleston to decorate two boutique hotels.

She picked up the phone again, asking for a bellhop to come to PH2. A quarter of an hour later, Crystal slipped behind the wheel of her SUV, turned on the engine and maneuvered out of the parking lot. The warm air coming in through the passenger-side window signaled an early spring. Tapping a button on the steering wheel, she searched the satellite radio until she found a station featuring smooth jazz.

Crystal stopped in Savannah to refuel and eat lunch and then drove nonstop to Fort Lauderdale. A smile parted her lips as she drove past the gatehouse and maneuvered down the tree-lined street leading to her town house. It felt good to be home.

A buildup of heat assailed Crystal when she walked inside. Moving quickly, she turned on the central air-conditioning to dispel the stagnant air.

Crystal mentally went through what she had to do: take a bath, check her voice mail and call and check on her mother. Hopefully Jasmine wouldn't be in drama-queen mode. Unpacking her luggage would wait for another day. She was exhausted—physically and mentally, needing at least ten hours of uninterrupted sleep.

Crystal sat in bed, her back supported by a mound of pillows. She checked her messages on her landline phone. There was a call from her father, who'd forgotten she would be in Charleston. There were a few other messages from telemarketers, and one from a sorority sister wishing her a happy New Year. She erased the messages, then dialed her mother's number.

"Hi, darling," sighed Jasmine. "I know you're back because your house number came up on the caller ID."

Crystal smiled. "I got in less than an hour ago."

"When am I going to see you?"

"It'll be either Sunday or Monday." The gallery rarely opened on those days. And besides, Crystal needed a few days to herself to adjust to being at home before taking off again. She needed time to unpack, air out the house and dust. But most of all, she wanted to spend time alone to try and sort out how she'd fallen in love with a man who made her crave him—in and out of bed.

"Please come Sunday. I have a private showing with a client on Monday."

"What time Sunday, Mother?"

"Meet me at Reynaldo's at eleven-thirty. Their brunch is exceptional."

"Don't you want me to pick you up?" Crystal asked Jasmine.

"You know I don't like riding in your car."

"Okay, Mother. I'll meet you at the restaurant."

"I have some good news to tell you."

Crystal shook her head. "You're getting married?"

"Oh, heavens no! There's no way I'm going to give up your father's alimony payments. I'll tell you about it when I see you."

She knew Jasmine wouldn't tell her no matter how much she pleaded. "Okay, Mother. I'll see you Sunday."

Adjusting the pillows under her head, Crystal reached over and turned off the lamp on the bedside table. Her mother always talked about not wanting to cut off her ex-husband's alimony payments when Crystal suspected it was the intangible connection to Raleigh that Jasmine didn't want to give up. And whenever she saw her father he would invariably ask how her mother was doing. He had to know Jasmine was doing quite well because they both lived in Miami and had on more than one occasion run into each other at social events. But because they'd come with dates they refused to acknowledge each other, and no one could be more supercilious than Jasmine Eaton.

Crystal followed the hostess to Jasmine's table, and her mother rose to greet her. She'd always thought her mother beautiful, but as Jasmine aged she'd become even more stunning. Tall and slender with stylishly coiffed prematurely gray hair, a flawless nut-brown complexion and delicate, even features caused heads to turn whenever she walked into a room. For men it was her face and body, and for women it was to see what the art dealer was wearing.

This morning Jasmine had selected a lime-green silk blouse she'd paired with a linen gabardine suit in a becoming aubergine.

"You look beautiful, Mother," Crystal admitted truthfully, pressing her cheek to Jasmine's. And she did. Her mother eschewed fillers and plastic surgery, unlike many of her fifty-something contemporaries, feared needles and going under the knife.

"So do you, darling. Please sit down."

Jasmine stared intently at Crystal. "You've put on weight. Your face is fuller."

"I got used to eating three meals a day." She loved cooking with Joseph.

Leaning back in her chair, the older woman nodded. "You look better carrying a little more weight."

Crystal stared at the uncut emerald studs in Jasmine's ears. "Not too much, otherwise we'll have to go shopping."

Jasmine raised her water goblet in a toast. "It's been a while since we've embarked on a mother–daughter shopping spree."

"It will have to wait until I get back from New York."

"When are you leaving?"

"Next week," Crystal confirmed.

A slight frown appeared between Jasmine's eyes as she sat straight. "Didn't you tell me you weren't—"

"I thought so, too," Crystal interrupted, her voice lowering and softening. "I got a call last night from my client that he'd gotten verbal approval for his liquor license, and that means the project is a definite go."

Crystal had believed she would have at least three weeks to a month before beginning her next project. She'd planned to spend a couple of weeks in Florida and another in New York reconnecting with friends before transforming the town house basement into an updated speakeasy.

"Now tell me your good news," she said, shifting the conversation away from her.

A mysterious smile played at the corners of Jasmine's mouth. "I've stopped smoking."

The three words rendered Crystal temporarily mute. "Why?"

She silently prayed her mother's decision to give up smoking wasn't health-related.

"Between smelling bad and having to bleach my teeth every six months, I decided enough is enough. But what I think really made me stop is the letter from you that was stuck under a drawer in my desk for almost twenty years. You wrote that I would never get to hold my grandbaby because I smoked."

Crystal lowered her eyes. She remembered writing the letter when she was angry with her mother for smoking in her bedroom. The stench of tobacco had lingered for days. "You're not sick, are you?"

Jasmine rested a manicured hand over her throat. "Thankfully no."

"How did you do it?"

"Hypnosis, and I'm now wearing a patch."

Crystal hated seeing her mother chain-smoking and even more inhaling the stale odor of tobacco whenever she hugged her. "Good for you." She paused. "Somehow I can't see you as a grandmother."

"Why not?" Several diners at a nearby table turned to look at Jasmine when she raised her voice. She gave them what Crystal deemed the death stare and they quickly averted their eyes. "Why wouldn't I want to become a grandmother?"

Crystal lifted her shoulders under the navy blue blazer she'd pulled on over an ice-blue silk blouse and gray slacks. When she'd selected her clothes earlier that morning, she'd made certain to wear long sleeves to conceal the bracelet circling her left wrist. The last thing she wanted was for her mother to interrogate her about it.

"It's just that I never heard you speak about wanting grandchildren."

Jasmine smiled and tiny lines fanned out around her large dark eyes. "I'm going to be fifty-four this year, and I think it's time I acknowledge that I'm not too young to be called Grandma."

"I can't imagine you allowing an infant, even if it is your grandbaby, to spit up on your clothes."

The older woman sobered. "You really don't know me, do you, Crystal? I may not have been the mother you needed when you were younger, and I'll carry that guilt to my grave. But I will never pressure you into getting married and having children just to give me a second chance to make it right with my grandbabies."

Reaching over, Crystal covered her mother's hand with her own. "None of us are born knowing how to parent, but thankfully we're given a second chance when it comes to grandbabies." She sighed. "The only thing I'm going to say is *if* or when I do make you a grandmother, you're not allowed to spoil them rotten, or they're going to have to live with you full-time."

Jasmine grinned like the Cheshire cat. "Now I know why I haven't sold the house—because there's plenty of room for them to run amok." Her four-thousand-square-foot home, set on an acre of manicured land overlooking a man-made lake, had four bedrooms and five bathrooms—more than enough room for several grandchildren to frolic in wild abandon.

"And what if they break one of your priceless artifacts?"

"It won't matter, because everything's insured."

This Jasmine Cornelia Eaton was someone Crystal truly did not know. She'd lost track of the number of times she'd begged her to stop smoking, but to no avail. And in the past she had always professed she didn't want to become a grandmother until she was at least sixty-five. What or who, Crystal mused, had been instrumental in changing her mother into someone who'd become a stranger?

"I wonder how Daddy would react to becoming a grandfather."

Jasmine rolled her eyes upward. "Maybe he'd realize he's getting much too old to continue marrying women young enough to be his daughters."

"He doesn't seem to be in a hurry to marry his latest girlfriend. Maybe he'll come to the realization that he can wine, dine and take them away on vacation without being obligated to marry them. I did call him, hoping to see him before I leave, but his assistant told me a group of homeowners and farmers in North Dakota asked to meet with him before they lease their land to oil companies for fracking and drilling."

"And knowing Raleigh, he'll look out for their interests as if they were his own."

Crystal had to agree with her mother. Raleigh Eaton had acquired a sixth sense when it came to investing and financial planning, and those who relied on his business acumen were never disappointed.

She picked up the menu, studying the selections. "What do you recommend?"

Reaching into her handbag, Jasmine took out a pair of reading glasses, perching them on the end of her nose. "The cherry-cheese blintzes are wonderful if you like something sweet, but right now I'm sort of partial to focaccia with smoked salmon and crème fraîche."

Crystal continued to scan the menu. "I think I'll start with a melon salad with a yogurt-honey dressing and a slice of mushroom quiche."

"After we order I want you to tell me about Charleston."

May first—May Day. It was a day Crystal would never forget, nor the doctor's diagnosis: *Miss Eaton, you don't have a stomach virus. We ran a few tests and you're pregnant.*

She remembered screaming without making a sound, and when she did recover her voice she couldn't stop crying. The doctor waited for her to settle down, then called in the ob-gyn to examine her.

When she revealed she hadn't missed a period, the doctor quietly explained there were women who had their period throughout their entire pregnancy, and it was only when they went into labor that it became apparent they'd been carrying a child.

A sonogram revealed she was in her second trimester and she was having a girl. How could she call Joseph and tell him she now was pregnant when they'd been apart for three months? He'd think her either crazy or a fraud—someone who wanted to trick him into marrying her. There was no way she would relive the insanity of her parents.

She instructed her father to sell her Fort Lauderdale property, then called Levi in Kentucky and asked whether she could live in his Mamaroneck, New York, condo until his return.

Initially she refused to tell her parents why she'd decided to relocate to New York, but as her condition became more apparent she set up a videoconference, informing them they were to become grandparents. What she refused to reveal was the name of her baby's father. The exception was Selena and Xavier, whom she swore to secrecy. Xavier protested, saying Joseph had a right to know he'd fathered a child until Crystal reminded him of her parents' volatile marriage.

Everything for Crystal changed when Levi fell in love with Angela Chase and accepted a position as head of pediatrics at a small hospital ten miles from Louisville. And for the second time within a decade, she would claim New York as her permanent home state.

Her pregnancy was uneventful. She delivered a healthy six-pound, two-ounce baby girl on a rainy October night. Jasmine had flown up a week before she was to give birth.

Jasmine and Raleigh alternated coming to New York to visit their granddaughter, while Crystal put her career on hold until Meredith was old enough to attend school.

She'd become her mother, but without the bitterness that had plagued Jasmine for years.

She enjoyed running while pushing her daughter along a jogging path, befriended other young mothers she met in a local park and was only reminded of the man with whom she'd fallen in love whenever someone mentioned the bracelet.

Being a new mother had its drawbacks. She'd become sleep-deprived when she had to get up every four hours to breast-feed, or when she would sleep on the floor next to the crib to feel the tiny hands or feet to check to see if Meredith's fever had spiked.

Being a new mother also had its rewards when Meredith learned to sit up, roll over, learned to say Dada, Mama, bottle, and demand more to eat when it was something she liked. The first time she stood up and took three steps before landing on her bottom Crystal cried happy tears. Her baby was now a toddler.

Crystal had just finished taking a load of wash from the dryer when her phone rang. Anchoring the wicker basket on her hip, she raced into the kitchen to answer it before it woke Meredith. "Hello."

"Is this Ms. Crystal Eaton?"

She went still. "Who's asking?"

"Are you Ms. Eaton?"

Setting down the basket, Crystal flopped down on the chair in the breakfast nook. "Yes."

"Raleigh Eaton has listed you as his emergency contact." She listened, chills washing over her body when the woman informed her that her father had come to the E.R. complaining of chest pain. An EKG indicated several blocked arteries and the attending cardiologist recommended surgery.

"Is he…?" She couldn't complete the question.

"He's stabilized, but the doctor wants to wait until you get here to explain the procedure."

"When's the surgery?"

"Tomorrow morning."

Her fear and anxiety vanished, replaced by a surge of determination. Crystal knew she had to be strong, not for herself but for her father.

Chapter 14

Sweet Silver Bells

Joseph stopped for a red light at a four-way intersection. He'd almost forgotten how heavy Miami rush-hour traffic could be. He stared into the rearview mirror unable to believe the woman who'd haunted his dreams sat a few feet behind him.

When he'd walked into the terminal and had seen Crystal, Joseph believed he'd conjured her up.

He'd been in an emotional tailspin, placing his social life on hold, while waiting for her to call him, not for him to remove the bracelet but to tell her how much he loved her and wanted to share his life with her. And Joseph had been willing to wait, wait another eighteen months or eighteen years.

If he'd changed inwardly, it had been the reverse with Crystal. Her face was fuller, her body lush, and a chin-length, layered haircut had replaced the short coif.

He had given her time, and after ColeDiz Tea's first successful harvest, Joseph checked out of the Beaumont House and found himself constantly checking his phone for her call. He'd scroll through his telephone contacts for her name, but a sense of pride—stubborn pride—wouldn't let him tap her number.

A smile tilted the corners of his mouth upward, the gesture reaching his eyes when they lingered on the angelic face of the child he and Crystal had created. Joseph quickly did the math in his head. If Merry was born in October, then he'd probably gotten Crystal pregnant the first and only time they'd had unprotected sex. His smile vanished.

Why, he thought, had she told him she wasn't pregnant when she had been?

He wanted and needed answers, answers that could wait until after her family crisis.

Crystal quickened her pace when her mother rose slowly from where she'd sat in the lobby of the small private hospital specializing in the heart. "Mama," she whispered, choking back a sob. "How is he?"

Pulling back, Jasmine cradled her face and kissed her cheek. "He's resting." She glanced over Crystal's shoulder at the tall man holding her granddaughter. "He found you."

Turning around, Crystal stared at a babbling Merry, who was pointing to the button on the collar of Joseph's shirt. "I'll explain everything to you later," she said through clenched teeth. She beckoned him closer. "Joseph, I'd like you to meet my mother."

Merry, recognizing her grandmother's familiar face, leaned over for Jasmine to take her.

"Mum, Mum," she repeated over and over. She hadn't learned to say Grandma.

Jasmine took the child from Joseph's arms. "Come here, baby girl." She gave her granddaughter a noisy kiss on the cheek. "Grandma loves you."

Joseph extended his hand to Jasmine. Now he knew where Crystal had gotten her beauty. Her mother was stunning. "I'm sorry we have to meet under these circumstances, Mrs. Eaton." He inclined his head. "I'm Joseph Cole-Wilson. Meredith's father."

Jasmine gave him a long stare. "Only someone with impaired vision would miss the resemblance, Mr. Cole-Wilson."

His mouth tightened in frustration. "Please call me Joseph, Mrs. Eaton."

There was a barely perceptible lifting of an eyebrow. It was apparent her mother wasn't going to make it easy for her granddaughter's father. When she'd finally revealed the identity of her baby's father, Jasmine feared Joseph would sue Crystal for full custody, charging her with deception.

"I haven't decided yet whether I'll allow you to call me Jasmine."

"Mother!" Crystal chastised. Her mother might have been called a lot of things, but never rude. In fact, Jasmine prided herself on having impeccable manners.

Joseph held up a hand. "It's okay, sweetie." He could've bitten off his tongue when Crystal glared at him. The endearment had slipped out unconsciously. He'd found himself in the presence of three generations of beautiful Eaton women, and two of them were giving him the stink-eye. He took a step backward. "I'll wait here, Crystal, while you go and check on your father."

Jasmine handed Crystal her visitor's badge. "He's in room 218." She held Merry at arm's length. "You need changing. And she also needs to change out of these heavy clothes." She rubbed noses with Merry. "Grandma will take you shopping and buy some pretty dresses for you."

Crystal attached the badge to the collar of her jacket. "Her diaper bag is in Joseph's car."

"I'll go and get it," he volunteered.

Waiting until Joseph walked out, Crystal shifted her attention to Jasmine. "Mama, please don't make this more complicated than it is."

"What do you intend to do, Crystal? Roll over and let him take your child?"

She shook her head. "It's not going to be like that."

"Are you sure?"

Crystal nodded. "Very sure. Joseph knows Merry and I are a package deal. He can't have one without the other."

"Have you talked about it?" Jasmine questioned.

"We don't have to talk about it," Crystal countered. *Don't you believe a child needs both parents?* She recalled Joseph's query as if he'd just spoken it. He'd grown up with both of his parents, and he wanted the same for his child or children.

The seconds ticked as Jasmine met her eyes. "Do you love him?"

She paused, wondering why her mother was bringing up something to which she knew the answer. Crystal had admitted to Jasmine that she'd fallen in love with Joseph. "Yes, Mother. I love him." She ruffled Merry's mussed curls, knowing she had to shampoo her hair, which always resulted in a test of wills. Merry didn't like water on her face. Turning on the heels of her running shoes, she headed for the elevator.

Crystal stopped in the doorway to Raleigh's private room. The handsome, elegant man who had women from eighteen to eighty flirting shamelessly to catch his attention appeared to be a shadow of his former self. The rich color in his khaki-brown complexion was missing and his wavy gray hair appeared lifeless, brittle. How, she wondered, had he aged that much since she last saw him at the Eaton family reunion the last weekend in May?

He hadn't brought his fiancée, and Crystal wondered if he'd come to his senses and decided he didn't have to have a woman in his life in order to feel complete.

She walked in, smiling when he turned to stare at her. He was hooked up to a machine monitoring his vitals. "Hi, Daddy."

Raleigh waved her closer. "Hi, baby. How did you get here so fast?"

Crystal pulled up chair next to the bed and took his hand, examining the large, slender, professionally groomed fingers. Her parents were two of a kind. Both had standing appointments for hair and nails. "I flew down, Daddy."

He smiled. "I just had the attack this morning. You managed to get a flight that fast?"

"I paid for a first-class seat."

Raleigh's smile vanished. "I'll reimburse you."

"Don't you dare talk about money when you should be thinking about getting better so you can leave this place."

"But you're not working, baby."

"Have you forgotten I have money from when you bought my condo?" Her father had purchased the condo from her, claiming he wanted to hold on to it for investment purposes.

Raleigh's eyelids fluttered. "Yeah. I forgot about that."

Crystal wondered if her father had been given something to

make him sleep. "What were you doing before you had chest pains?"

"Golfing."

She closed her eyes while shaking her head. "Daddy, you can't golf in ninety-degree weather even if it is October."

"I found that out the hard way. You know that they call a heart attack the widow maker." His eyes opened, meeting his daughter's tender gaze. "If I wasn't golfing, then I never would've known I had a couple of blocked arteries."

"That may be true," Crystal retorted, "but you're going to have to modify your diet." Even though Raleigh didn't have a problem with his weight, she knew he occasionally ate the wrong foods for a middle-aged man.

"I know. No fried, fat, or fast foods." He exhaled an audible sigh. "After surgery I'll be in ICU for a couple of days."

"You know you can't go home once you're discharged."

"Why not?"

"You need around-the-clock monitoring, Daddy. I'll have Mother set up a room for you."

"No, no and no. I'm not going to put your mother out. Besides, Tonya can take care of me."

"Who's Tonya?"

"She's my fiancée."

"The one you didn't bring to the family reunion?"

"We had words, so she decided not to come."

Crystal released his hand. "You had words? What if you have words and she walks out and you end up on the floor? You appointed me to be your medical proxy, and that means I have the final say where it concerns your health, not some stranger who'll bail on you if things aren't going her way."

"What about your mother?" Raleigh asked. "Won't she have the final say when it comes to me staying in her house?"

"I'll talk to her, Daddy." Crystal wanted to remind Raleigh that Jasmine had come to see him round the clock, and that should've been proof enough of her concern for his physical well-being.

"If she says it's okay, then I'll stay."

She noticed he was slurring his words. Rising, Crystal leaned over and kissed Raleigh's forehead. "Get some rest, Daddy. I'll come back tomorrow to see you once you're out of recovery."

Raleigh smiled. "How's my grandbaby girl?"

"All sugar and a little spice." Merry was all sweetness until it came time to wash her hair.

"That's my baby."

She kissed him again. "I love you, Daddy."

"Love you back," he slurred, his chest rising and falling in a slow, even rhythm.

She took the elevator down to the lobby, handing in the visitor's pass. Joseph sat next to Jasmine, who'd removed Merry's outer clothing, leaving her in an undershirt and a disposable diaper.

It appeared as if her mother and Joseph were engaged in a serious conversation. Crystal froze when Jasmine leaned over and pressed her mouth to Joseph's cheek at the same time his arm went around the shoulders of his daughter's grandmother. It was apparent they'd reached a compromise. Now all Crystal had to do was convince her mother to let her ex-husband recuperate under her roof.

Joseph noticed her first, coming to his feet and closing the distance between them. "How's your dad?"

Tilting her head, Crystal studied Joseph's face, trying to catch a glimpse of the man with whom she'd spent the most marvelous two months of her life. She'd gone to bed and woken up in his strong embrace. She enjoyed cooking with him, occasionally teasing him as to who could concoct the best dessert. With Joseph there were few surprises. He was even-tempered, quick to smile—attributes he'd unknowingly passed on to his daughter.

Once it was confirmed that she was carrying a girl, Crystal had come up with a number of names before settling on three. It would be Merry, Hope or Joy. But when she saw her daughter for the first time, she knew which name to choose.

Upon closer inspection, Crystal noticed the hot Florida sun had darkened Joseph's face to a deep mahogany. "He's resting.

He's scheduled for surgery tomorrow, and once he's out of re-covery he'll be in ICU for a few days."

"I told your mother that I'm going to take a couple of weeks off and hang out down here. I'll help look after Merry while you visit your father. A hospital is no place for a baby."

"Thanks for the offer, but my mother and I will take turns visiting Daddy."

"Jasmine and I have already talked about it."

Crystal's eyebrows shot up. "So now it's Jasmine instead of Mrs. Eaton?"

He smiled. "You betcha. We're now Jasmine and Joseph."

She tried not to smile but failed. "Thank you for driving us down."

Without warning, Joseph's face suddenly went grim. "I don't need your thanks, Crystal. If I'd known you had my baby, you and Merry would've come down on the company jet, because there's a Cole family mandate that has been in effect for almost fifty years that anyone with Cole blood is forbidden to fly on a commercial carrier."

Crystal suddenly felt as if she'd been threatened. "There's no way you can enforce that."

"Do you want to challenge me?"

"I thought we'd decided not to challenge or compete with each other?"

"That was then, and this is now," he countered. The lines bracketing Joseph's mouth eased. "I don't want to fight with you, Crystal. We share a child and what we want no longer matters. We have to keep in mind that anything and everything we say or do will affect our daughter. You admit to growing up with dueling parents, while if my parents argued, which I'm certain they did, they didn't do it around their children."

Crystal didn't drop her eyes. "You have to understand that I haven't had to share Merry with anyone. It's always been the two of us from the moment she was born."

Moving closer, Joseph cradled her face between his palms. "That's because you believed you didn't have a choice. That has to change, because there's no way I'm *not* going to be a part of my daughter's life."

"Do you think that's possible with you living here in Florida and me in New York?"

"Any- and everything is possible. If your father didn't have a heart attack, or if I hadn't offered to pick up a friend from the airport, who knows when we would've met again?"

Crystal placed her hands over his. "So you believed we would meet again."

Joseph nodded. "We were destined to meet again."

"You believe in destiny." Her question was a statement.

"Yes."

Crystal had no comeback. Her connection with Joseph was something she wouldn't be able to explain if her life depended upon it. When talking to Selena at the family reunion, the pastry chef had updated her as to her enterprise with ColeDiz, but not once did she divulge that Joseph had asked about her.

"I have to go. Merry needs to eat dinner and get her hair washed, and we always have a knock-down, drag-out battle royal when that occurs."

Joseph lowered his hands. "Why don't you let me wash her hair?"

"You don't know what you're in for."

He lifted his shoulders. "Well, there's only one way to find out."

They left the hospital, Crystal riding back to the house where she'd grown up with Jasmine driving, and Joseph following closely behind with Merry in her car seat.

During the ride, she scrolled through her smart phone directory, sending an email to family members about Raleigh's upcoming surgery. "I just sent every Eaton an email blast about Daddy."

Jasmine gave her a quick glance. "You know they're going to descend on Florida like college kids on spring break."

"You should be able to put up some of them. Two of your bedrooms have king-size beds and the other two queen. All of the love seats in the sitting rooms convert into beds, and so do the sofa and love seats in the living and family rooms. Those you can't accommodate can stay with Uncle Solomon and Aunt Holly."

"Why would they want to stay with me? I'm an Eaton in name only."

"Mother, stop it. You're just as much an Eaton as Selena or the others who married into the family. Even though she married Xavier, Selena thinks of herself as an Eaton because of Lily."

"Is it the same with Merry being a Cole?"

Crystal stared out the passenger-side window. Joseph had stated in no uncertain terms that Merry was a Cole, and subject to all of the edicts, mandates and decrees the name epitomized.

"Yes, Mama. The same way Merry is a Cole."

Running her hand through her hair, Jasmine pushed it off her forehead. "It used to work my last nerve when you called me Mama. But now I kind of like the sound of it."

"That's because you're a grandmama."

"I love being a grandmama."

Jasmine signaled, turning off onto a private road with a Sands Point Residents Only sign pointing the way to the gated community. She activated the eight-foot wrought-iron gate and drove through, Joseph following closely behind her late-model Jaguar sedan.

"I like Joseph," Jasmine said softly as she touched another button on the remote, the door to a two-car garage rising smoothly, quietly.

"So do I," Crystal said, as she lowered her window and waved for Joseph to pull into the garage and park beside Jasmine's car. "I told Daddy he could stay here with us once he's discharged from the hospital."

Jasmine cut off the engine. "Now you tell me."

Shifting slightly, Crystal turned to meet her mother's eyes. "Would you prefer I go to his house, Mother, where I'd run into his THOT?"

"What the heck is a THOT?"

"It's slang for ho or That Ho Over There."

It took several seconds before Jasmine caught her meaning. "No. I don't need you getting into it with your father's *lady* friend. We'll talk about this later. Let's go inside where it's cool." She pressed the back of her hand to her forehead. "I don't know why I'm so bothered by the heat."

"It's called hot flashes, Mother." Crystal gave her a saccharine smile when Jasmine rolled her eyes. "I'll be in as soon as I get my bags out of Joseph's truck."

She watched as Joseph unbuckled Merry from her car seat and gently picked her up as if she were fragile bone china. They shared a smile as Merry dropped her head to his shoulder. She knew her baby was hot and tired.

Joseph felt as if he'd entered a high-end furniture showroom with meticulously decorated spaces utilizing light, color and fabrics when walking into the living room. The result was an esthetic assault on his senses. "Who decorated the house?" he asked Crystal as held out her arms for their daughter.

Joseph's expression was similar to many who'd come to her mother's home for the first time. "Mother."

"Don't believe her," Jasmine called out as she headed for the curving staircase. "My daughter is very modest when it comes to taking credit for her incredible talent. Joseph, please come upstairs. I'll show you where you can put Crystal's luggage."

Picking up the bags off the carpeted floor, he followed Jasmine up the stark-white limestone stairs with mahogany banisters and newel posts.

"And my mother can take credit for every piece of art," Crystal said to his retreating back.

It hadn't really mattered to Joseph if the design of the interior was a singular or collaborative effort. The result was sophisticated elegance. He felt like a kid in a candy shop, not knowing where to look or what he wanted.

Craning his neck, Joseph peered in through the open doors of bedrooms on the second story. "How many bedrooms do you have?"

Jasmine smiled at him over her shoulder. "Four. Two with eastern exposure and the other two with southern to take advantage of light throughout the day. Crystal wants her father to convalesce here, which means we're going to be kept busy entertaining Eatons." She stopped at a bedroom on the east end of the hallway. "This is Crystal's room. There's a portable crib in one of the closets."

Joseph entered the bedroom suite, trying to imagine Crystal as a little girl growing up in the house with lush gardens and beautiful water views. "Do you know why she decided to live in New York?"

"That's something you'll have to ask her because I've made it a practice not to interfere when it comes to Crystal's relationships. I will tell her if she asks for my opinion, but that's where it begins and ends." Jasmine touched his arm. "I'll see you downstairs."

Begins and ends. Joseph found the two words profound. His love affair had begun when he saw her checking into her penthouse apartment, and he hadn't wanted to believe it would end when he placed the love bracelet on her wrist. He didn't know if she planned to return to New York to live once her father received medical clearance to resume his former lifestyle.

It no longer mattered if she lived in Florida or New York, because Joseph intended to be an integral part of his daughter's life with or without Crystal's consent. He hoped they would be able to resolve whatever differences they had before forcing a legal determination. Once a family court judge intervened, there would be no winners, but losers.

He set the bags at the foot of the bed before crossing the bedroom suite and opening the closet. Most of the shelves and racks were empty. Joseph found the box with the crib on a shelf with plastic storage containers filled with crib sheets and blankets wrapped in tissue paper.

Removing the crib from the box, he found the enclosed tools needed to assemble it, then slipped the fitted sheet over the mattress.

"You look as if you've done this before."

Joseph glanced to find Crystal sitting on the tapestry-covered bench at the foot of the bed. Merry sat on the carpet floor. "This is my first time putting a crib together." He stood up, watching his daughter pull herself up, using the bench for support before taking four wobbly steps. She fell on her bottom, rolled over and crawled back to the bench.

"Don't help her," Crystal said quickly when Joseph took a step. "She can do it by herself."

He stared, mesmerized by the chubby legs and feet of his daughter, who squealed in delight as she managed to take at least ten steps before collapsing on the carpet. "When did she start walking?"

Crystal saw the rapt expression on Joseph's face as he stared at Merry. "She's been walking around holding on for more than a month. It was only a couple of days ago that she decided to strike out on her own. Now that she's walking I have to child-proof the apartment."

"Your mother needs to put a gate at the top and bottom of the staircase." Going to his knees, Joseph clapped his hands. "Merry. Come to Daddy."

Merry hesitated, then let go of her grip on the bench. Arms upraised in order to maintain her balance, she walked toward Joseph laughing hysterically. She ran into his arms, squealing uncontrollably when he tossed her in the air.

Crystal pushed off the bench. "I'm going to run the water for her bath. And if you're going to wash her hair, then I recommend you take off your shirt because you're going to be drenched."

Joseph pulled Merry close to his chest, kissing her hair. "Why does her hair smell like applesauce?" he asked, walking into the bathroom.

Sitting on the edge of the garden tub, Crystal tested the temperature of the water flowing into the tub. "She's learning to feed herself and most times there's more food in her hair or on her face than what goes into her mouth."

"Is she getting enough nutrition?"

Crystal gave him a quick look and then turned off the water. "She's not underweight."

"Just checking," he said under his breath.

"After I brush her teeth, you can put her in the tub. And

please don't take your eyes off her." Crystal opened a drawer under the vanity and took out a cellophane-wrapped toothbrush. Picking up a sample tube of toothpaste, she squeezed out a minute drop and brushed the tiny white teeth, followed by holding the toothbrush under water, then running the wet bristles over Merry's teeth. She undressed her, then handed her to Joseph. "She's all yours."

Joseph knelt near the tub, his hand covering Merry's back as she splashed water; droplets of water dotted the front of his shirt. Now he knew why Crystal had warned him to take it off. She returned with a towel, face cloth and plastic bottles filled with baby wash and shampoo.

"Should I give her a bath first?"

Crystal knelt beside him. "I'll bathe her and then you can wash her hair." She took over, quickly washing the toddler, then using the retractable nozzle, rinsed the soap off the chubby body. She smiled at Joseph. "She's all yours."

Picking up the bottle of shampoo, he poured a small amount on his palm, pausing when Merry stared at him with wide, dark eyes as if she knew what was coming next.

Joseph disarmed her when he began singing a song in Spanish his grandmother had sung to him as a child. It was a nursery rhyme about the *coquí,* a tiny frog native to Puerto Rico, which spied a bug twice its size and had to figure out how to trap it for its dinner.

Merry was so engrossed in the strange words coming from him that she didn't react to his washing her hair. He repeated the ditty over and over while making the whistling sound of the *coquí,* as Merry sang along in her childish babble.

He motioned for Crystal to give him the retractable nozzle. Leaning his daughter backward, he managed to rinse the shampoo from her hair without water going onto her face and into her eyes.

Joseph lifted Merry out of the tub, handing her to her mother. "Mission accomplished."

Crystal narrowed her eyes at her daughter. "You little traitor. You give me grief every time I wash your hair."

"She wouldn't give you grief if you sing to her in Spanish and make funny sounds."

"I can make funny sounds, but I can't speak or sing in Spanish."

"Don't worry about Merry learning Spanish. My mother and grandmother will definitely teach her."

Crystal concentrated on drying Merry. How could she forget that her daughter had another set of grandparents? "When do you plan to tell them about her?"

Joseph shook his head. "I'll tell them tomorrow."

"I know it's going to be a little crazy around here after Daddy comes here to convalescence, but if they want to see Merry, then let them know they're welcome to come."

Joseph met her eyes, nodding. "I'll be certain to let them know." A beat passed. "I'd like you to answer one question for me."

Crystal blinked. "What is it?"

"Why didn't you contact me when you found out you were pregnant?"

Rocking Merry back and forth, Crystal closed her eyes. "Would you have believed I was carrying your child three months after our separation? I'm certain your first thought would've been that I'd slept with another man and was attempting to pass it off as yours." She opened her eyes, seeing an expression of indecision flit over Joseph's features. "I got my period every month for the first six months, so I'd assumed I *wasn't* pregnant. I'd gained a few pounds, but it wasn't enough to make me believe I was carrying a child.

"I knew something wasn't quite right when certain foods I used to eat gave me heartburn, so I stopped eating spicy dishes. Then I knew something was wrong when I started throwing up. A doctor's visit confirmed I didn't have a stomach virus but that I was pregnant. The doctor didn't know how far along I was until a sonogram indicated I was in my second trimester and I was having a girl. It took a while even before I told my parents and even longer to tell them who the baby's father was."

"So you decided to have the baby and raise it by yourself."

"What other option did I have, Joseph?"

Rubbing his thumb over her cheekbone, Joseph leaned in closer and kissed her. "You could've called me even if you were carrying another man's baby. I would've claimed it as my own because I love you. I love you and anything that is a part of you."

A single tear found its way down Crystal's cheek as she cried without making a sound. What had she done? She'd cheated Joseph out of the first year of his daughter's life and Merry did not have her father in her life.

"What are we going to do, Joseph?"

He caught the tear on his tongue, tasting the saltiness. "We're not going to do anything until your father is better. I don't want to put any pressure on you about what I want for us and our daughter's future."

Crystal looped her free arm around Joseph's neck. She pressed her forehead to his. "Thank you." She wanted to tell him that she loved him, had always loved him, yet the words were lodged in her throat. "I think it's time we put *our* daughter to bed."

Joseph stared at Merry, blissfully asleep in her mother's arms. "Do you give her a bottle before she goes to sleep?"

"No, because I don't want food on her teeth overnight. She's learned to drink from a sippy cup and I only use a bottle when traveling. I told *your* daughter the next time she bites the top off the nipple it will be her last bottle."

"So, she's *my* daughter when she does something naughty, and I assume she's *your* daughter when she's a good girl."

A warm smile spread across Crystal's face like the rising sun. "You learn fast, don't you?"

Joseph stood, cupping a hand under Crystal's elbow to assist her in standing. "I need to learn one more thing."

"What's that?"

"How to put on a diaper."

Crystal blew him a kiss. "Let's go, Daddy. Class is in session."

Chapter 15

"Is this some kind of sick joke?"

Joseph knew he'd shocked his mother when she stared at him as if he'd lost his mind. He slowly shook his head. "No, Mom, it's not a joke. I just found out today that I have a daughter."

Raquel Cole-Wilson buried her face in her hands, her shoulders shaking as she tried not to break down. "Why? How?"

Moving closer to his mother on the love seat in the family room, Joseph draped an arm around her shoulders. He told her what Crystal had revealed about her atypical pregnancy. "If I hadn't walked into that terminal, I would've spent the rest of my life not knowing that I had a daughter."

Sniffling, Raquel pressed her fingertips to her eyes. "Thank goodness you did. Now, when are we going to meet your little Merry?"

"Who are we going to meet?"

Joseph stood up when his father walked into the room, giving him a rough embrace. "My daughter."

"Your what!"

Whenever he looked at his father, Joseph knew what he would look like in another thirty years. Those who saw them together claimed he was Joseph Sr.'s younger clone.

Raquel patted the cushion beside her. "Sit down, Joseph," she said in Spanish, "and let our son explain to you what he discovered earlier today."

Joseph watched his father's expression change from shock to amusement. "I know you guys have been bitchin' about wanting grandchildren, so you've got your wish. It didn't happen the way any of us would've liked or wanted, but what's important is that she's here."

Joseph Sr. grunted. "I can't believe you got involved with Judge Eaton's niece. When are you getting married?"

"Please, Dad. Don't get ahead of yourself."

"You're not going to marry her?"

"Don't put words in my mouth, Dad!"

Raquel placed a hand on her husband's fisted one. "*M'ijo,* please. You have to let your children handle their own affairs."

"And don't forget, *m'ija,* that we didn't raise our sons to be baby daddies."

Joseph pushed to his feet. "Crystal and I have yet to discuss our future, but in the meantime if you want to meet your granddaughter, then please let me know."

Raquel stood. "What about tomorrow?" She looked at her husband, then her son. "I'll get Eduardo to cover for me," she said quickly.

An inner voice told Joseph his mother would not wait until Monday. It was the only day in the week when Marimba closed for business. "I'll call Crystal to let her know you're coming. What about you, Dad?"

"I'm coming, too."

"Good. I'll let you know what time I'll pick you up." He kissed his mother and then rested a hand on his father's head. *"Buenas noches."*

He left the house through a side door and to his truck parked in the circular driveway. As soon as he stared the engine, Joseph activated the Bluetooth feature, tapping the screen for Diego's cell. "Yo, *primo.* I'm calling to tell you that I'm taking the next two weeks off."

"What's wrong?"

Joseph smiled. "Nothing's wrong. In fact, everything is wonderful."

"Is this about a woman?"

His smile faded. "How did you know?"

"Come on, José. You've been moping around, working twice as hard and putting longer hours than necessary for more than a year. At first I thought it was because you wanted to take over as CEO now rather than later, but when I asked you about it you said you were in no hurry to run ColeDiz. That's when I figured it had to be a woman. Am I right or am I wrong?"

His smile was back. "You're right." Joseph had no intention of telling Diego about Crystal, because once his parents met her, the entire Cole grapevine would explode.

Diego's laugh filled the truck. "Take all the time you need, *primo*."

"How about six weeks?" Joseph's query was followed by a swollen silence. "Diego?"

"I don't have a problem with six weeks. Six weeks brings us to the end of the year. Are you trying to say we should plan on a New Year's Eve wedding celebration?"

"No, I'm not." Joseph wanted nothing more than to exchange vows with Crystal with friends and family members in attendance, yet even if he proposed, he wasn't certain she would accept. The only thing that was a certainty was his love for her.

Joseph stared through the windshield, driving along streets he navigated without concentrating. He decelerated and then maneuvered onto the road where his new home was nearing completion.

Construction had been delayed several times when either the materials the contractor ordered from Europe were unavailable or the inventory wasn't enough to complete a floor or the tiles for the swimming pool. Joseph hadn't put his condo on the market, wanting to do so just before he was scheduled to move into the house to list it with a Realtor.

He stopped and stared at the house's subtle Mediterranean-styled architecture with ocean views. His landscape architect cousin, Regina Spencer, and her daughter, Eden, had drawn up the plans to design the grounds with tropical landscaping and formal hedges. The roof, made up of French clay tiles with a foam setting, made it more resistant to hurricane-force wind.

Putting the truck in gear, Joseph drove the short distance to the apartment in a high-rise he'd called home for the past decade. He wasn't superstitious by nature, yet he could dismiss the fact that the completion of his home coincided with his reuniting with Crystal. Call it coincidence, serendipity, chance, providence or good karma. It was all good.

Crystal exchanged a smile with Joseph when Raquel sat Merry on her knee and sang the "Itsy-Bitsy Spider," while at the same simulating a spider crawling up her arm. It had taken the toddler a while to warm up to her paternal grandmother until Raquel launched into the *coquí* song Joseph had distracted her with the night before.

Dr. Joseph Cole-Wilson appeared visibly stunned by the existence of the little girl, and had spent the past half hour staring at her.

Rising to her feet, Crystal nodded to Joseph. "Joseph, will you please help in the kitchen?"

She now felt comfortable enough to leave Merry alone to bond with her grandparents. She'd felt apprehensive meeting Joseph's parents for the first time, while at the same time she welcomed their presence because it helped her not dwell on her father's surgical procedure.

The hospital had promised to call her once he was transferred to ICU. She wanted to see him even if sedated to reassure herself he had survived hours of surgery.

Joseph took her hand, pulling her into the kitchen, and covered her mouth with his in a passionate kiss that stole her breath. "You don't know how long I've wanted to do that," he explained, staring deeply into her startled gaze.

Crystal's curved her arms under his shoulders, holding on to him like a drowning swimmer. "It's my fault for not trusting—"

"Don't you dare apologize," he warned, cutting her off and kissing the end of her nose. "You did what you believed you had to do, so the issue is moot. Your only concern should be making certain your father regains his health."

She rose on tiptoe, burying her face against his warm throat. "I spent the night tossing and turning because I couldn't stop thinking about Daddy. I…" Her words trailed off when the phone rang. Pulling out of Joseph's embrace, she picked up the receiver on the wall phone. Crystal went completely still when she listened to the woman asking that she come to the hospital to straighten out a familial conflict. Her father's fiancée was making a scene because it was against hospital policy to give someone other than family the status on a patient. "I'll be there as soon as possible." She hung up and shook her head.

"What's the matter?" Joseph asked, seeing the distress on her face.

"I have to go to the hospital. My father's fiancée is acting up because they won't give her any information on him. I need to use your truck. Wait. Who's going to look after Merry?" Jasmine had gone into the gallery to meet with a client.

"Calm down, sweetie. I'll drive you to the hospital while my parents take care of Merry."

She shook her head. "I can't dump her on them."

"It has nothing to do with dumping. They're her grandparents, Crystal."

Pressing her fingertips to her temples, Crystal attempted to massage away the tension tightening around her forehead. She'd found herself between a rock and a hard place. She had enough to worry about without having to deal with a woman who thought nothing of going off on strangers.

"Okay. Please let's go so I can get this over with."

Crystal didn't know what to expect from her father's fiancée, but it wasn't the tiny woman wearing body-hugging designer jeans while teetering in five-inch, seven-hundred-dollar pumps. A thick fringe of fake lashes obscured her vision so much she had to tilt her chin to see. The size of the diamond solitaire on her left hand screamed *six figures*.

However, Crystal could see why Raleigh had been attracted to her. Her smooth tawny brown complexion, doll-like features and short, coiffed black hair made her a standout.

"Ms. Davis, only Raleigh's immediate family members are allowed to see him while he's in ICU. Once he's out you'll be able to see him."

Tonya gave Crystal a once-over look and then wrinkled her

nose as if smelling something malodorous. "I am family. Leigh and I are going to be married on Christmas Eve."

"It's not Christmas Eve and you're not his wife."

"Look, bitch!" Tonya screamed, garnering the attention of those sitting at the visitors' desk. "No one in this hospital is going to stop me from seeing my fiancé. Leigh told me all about you. How you were always jealous of his wives, and that you wouldn't have anything to do with them. Well, let me school you about Tonya Davis. I always get my way, so I want you to put my name on the damn list before I sue you and this hospital."

Crystal struggled to control her temper. "If you don't get out of my face, this bitch will forget her home training and make you regret waking up this morning."

Tonya fluttered her lashes. "Don't you dare threaten me."

"And don't you dare try to intimidate me," Crystal countered. "Now please leave this hospital before I have security escort you out."

"Hey, baby. Are you all right?"

Crystal turned around to find Joseph standing a few feet away. She didn't know how much he'd overheard. "My father's fiancée was just leaving. She was under the impression that she's immediate family, but I think we've cleared up her misunderstanding. Right, Ms. Davis?"

"Wrong, bitch!" Tonya pointed an air-brushed nail at Joseph. "And who the hell are you?"

Joseph gave her a feral grin. "You don't want to know. Now, if you continue to insult my client I'll be forced to sue you for defamation of character."

Tonya pushed out her lips. "You don't scare me, slick."

Joseph signaled to a security guard who'd come to check out the commotion. "My client's father is currently undergoing heart surgery, and this woman isn't on the list of authorized visitors. Could you please escort her off the premises?"

The guard crooked a finger at Tonya. "Let's go, miss." Tonya wasn't given a choice when she strutted across the lobby and through the sliding doors.

Curving an arm around Crystal's waist, Joseph led her out

of the hospital to the nearby parking lot. "I can't believe your father left your mother for *that*."

Crystal grunted under her breath. "She looks good compared to some of the others. However, what she has is less class than his other wives, excluding my mother, of course. I talked Mother into agreeing to let Daddy convalesce at her house, but there's no way she's going to let Tonya Davis cross her threshold."

"The fact that your mother lives in a private, gated community will definitely keep her at a distance."

Crystal wanted to agree with Joseph, yet she knew Tonya wasn't going to sit around and wait for Raleigh Eaton to come back to her. "I have to rent a car because I don't want to rely on you and Mother to chauffer me around."

"I can arrange for you use one of ColeDiz's company cars."

"I don't work for ColeDiz."

Opening the passenger-side door, Joseph waited for Crystal to sit before rounding the vehicle to sit beside her. "I'll drive the company car and you can use this tank."

She gave him a smile. "That sounds like a plan."

Crystal pressed her nose to the oval window of the sleek corporate jet, watching the snowy New York State landscape come closer with the aircraft's descent. She was returning to New York after five weeks, not as a resident but a vacationer.

The days and nights had passed so quickly Crystal had to check the calendar to verify the date. Her father appeared quite content living and recuperating under the roof of his first wife. He cooperated with his therapist and dietitian and slowly resumed many of the activities he'd enjoyed before the heart attack. Raleigh enjoyed reading to his granddaughter, swimming in the in-ground pool, while keeping in contact with his many clients via the internet.

After several volatile telephone conversations with Tonya, he called off their engagement and Crystal celebrated in private because the toxic relationship had begun to adversely affect his convalescence.

Every weekend, she and Jasmine entertained Eatons, whether

from New Jersey, Pennsylvania, West Virginia, Washington, D.C., Kentucky, South Carolina or Texas, who'd come to visit with Raleigh.

And as promised Joseph took a leave of absence from ColeDiz, spending every spare moment with Merry, who reveled in her new mode of independent locomotion. Crystal noticed she was getting taller and slimmer and adding words to her ever-increasing vocabulary. She followed Joseph around as if he were the Pied Piper, and a few times Crystal felt as if she were losing her baby to a man she'd come to love beyond description.

Joseph had surprised her one day when he suggested going for an afternoon drive. She knew when he maneuvered up an unpaved path to a newly constructed house that he wanted her to see the inside of his home. He hadn't asked her to decorate the mansion again, yet she knew it was what he wanted. Their relationship had changed from former lovers to friends and parents of a little girl.

Crystal didn't know what she would've done if Joseph hadn't been there to see to Merry's needs, because there were times when she'd experienced emotional overload. The home health aide saw to Raleigh's basic physical demands until he was able to shower and dress himself. A cleaning service came in twice a week to do housework, leaving Crysal the jobs of making beds, putting up loads of laundry and cooking. Even with Jasmine taking time off and occasionally closing the gallery when her assistant wasn't available, Crystal had assumed the full responsibility of running a household.

In the past it had only been herself, and then as a stay-at-home mother with Merry. Her days were very structured because she was able to accomplish many of her tasks around her daughter's nap time, but all that had changed since returning to Florida.

Two nights ago, Joseph had come into her bedroom and announced he was taking her away for a week. He'd made arrangements with Jasmine and hired a housekeeper to take care of everything during their absence.

When asked about Merry, he said Raquel would share in babysitting their granddaughter. Both grandmothers soothed her fear of leaving her child for the first time, and Crystal reluctantly agreed to get away and relax.

Now her ears popped from the loss of cabin pressure as the pilot brought the jet down smoothly on a private runway, taxiing until it came to a complete stop.

When she'd boarded the jet, a flight attendant informed her an onboard chef would offer breakfast as soon as they were airborne. Crystal got to see firsthand the exquisite service afforded anyone flying in the ColeDiz Gulfstream G650 business jet.

Joseph unbuckled his seat belt, stood up and extended his hand. "Let's go, sweetie."

Crystal slipped her arms into her ski jacket.

"Where are we going?" It seemed like the umpteenth time she'd asked Joseph that question, and his answer was always the same: *You'll see.*

"We're going to a cabin in the woods."

She stared at his broad shoulders under a heavy fisherman's knit sweater. "I'm not an outdoorsy girl, Joseph. I've never been one to rough it in the wilderness."

"You won't have to rough it. You'll have all of the conveniences of home."

Joseph shook the hand of the pilot. The flight attendant lowered the steps as the copilot gathered their luggage.

He descended the stairs, holding tightly on to Crystal as snowflakes swirled around them. The meteorologists had predicted snow, and thankfully they'd landed as it had begun.

Joseph had just thanked the remaining members of the flight crew when the door and trunk to a car parked on the tarmac opened. The driver opened the rear door and in under a minute Joseph and Crystal were seated in the rear of the heated sedan and their bags stored in the trunk.

She stared out the side window. The snow was coming down faster. "How far is the cabin in the woods?"

"Not too far."

Crystal watched the passing landscape through a curtain

of falling snow as the driver maneuvered up a winding road, coming to a stop in front of a cabin surrounded by towering pine trees.

Joseph helped her out and they sprinted to the front door, leaving the driver to follow with their bags. He unlocked the door, and a blast of warmth forced Crystal to take a backward step. "Nice!" The single word slipped out unbidden.

She flipped a wall switch, and light from table lamps illuminated the space with a wood-burning stove, a leather sofa group, a love seat and club chairs with footstools. Rugs made of animal skin and fur covered the rustic wooden floor. She untied her snow boots, leaving them on the mat inside the door, then took off her jacket and hung it on a wall hook.

Crystal took a quick tour of the cabin. She found a kitchen with a fully stocked refrigerator/freezer. It was rustic with the modern convenience of indoor plumbing. A king-size bed took up most of the space in the small bedroom. It'd been a long time since she'd shared a bed with Joseph, and she looked forward to falling asleep and waking up in his embrace. She'd been too overwhelmed caring for her father and her daughter to think about making love.

Most nights when she went to bed she fell asleep within minutes of her head touching the pillow. Whenever Joseph's body would innocently brush against hers, the urges she'd repressed surfaced. And once he told her he was taking her away, Crystal wasn't certain whether he wanted to use the occasion for them to sleep together again, but this time she was prepared. She'd purchased a supply of condoms.

Opening another door, she discovered a miniscule bathroom with a shower stall, vanity and commode.

The last door at the rear of the cabin doubled as a wood-shed, mudroom and laundry room. Heat, running water and electricity.

Crystal had returned to the living/dining area when Joseph shouldered the door closed and set the bags down. He met her eyes. "Is it too primitive for you?"

"It's perfect. How did you find this place?"

"It belongs to my parents." Joseph didn't see her jaw drop with his disclosure. "Dad pays someone to look after it when he's not here. That's why the fridge is full. My dad went to college and medical school in New England, where he'd learned to ski. One winter he came up here to ski and discovered he couldn't get lodging because everything was booked up. So the next spring he bought this place. My mother doesn't like cold-weather sports, so she hangs out here in the cabin while Dad's on the slopes."

Crystal sat on a club chair, resting her sock-covered feet on the footstool. "Do you ski?"

"No. And I have no interest in learning. What about you?"

Crystal shook her head. "I don't like being cold."

Sitting opposite her, Joseph gave Crystal a long, penetrating stare. "I don't want you to think I brought you here because I want to seduce you."

"What should I think, Joseph?"

"That I love you and I care what happens to you. I saw you wearing yourself down taking care of your father and our daughter. Maybe I'm selfish, but I need you and Merry needs you."

She lowered her eyes, staring at her clasped fingers. "What do you want, Joseph?"

Joseph's gaze lingered on the hair framing her lovely face. "I want you to learn to trust me. I'm no longer a stranger to you, so you should know that I'll never deliberately break your heart."

"I've always trusted you."

"Did you really, Crystal? You were the one who said I wouldn't believe that you were carrying my baby because we'd been separated for months."

"I suppose I underestimated you."

"Yes, you did."

She glared at him. "You don't have to sound so smug."

"Smug or arrogant?" he teased.

"Both," she said, smiling. "But I wouldn't have you any other way." Crystal paused, knowing what she was going to tell Joseph would change her forever. "I love you, José Ibrahim Cole-Wilson. I love your subtle arrogance, your insufferable sense of entitlement, your generosity, your patience and the way you make me feel whenever we make love."

"I have a laundry list of why I love you, Crystal Riesa Eaton."

"How do you know my middle name?" She rarely used her middle name or even initial except on official documents.

Joseph's smile was as intimate as a kiss. "Your uncle told me."

"Which one?"

"Solomon." He had reunited with his mentor when Solomon came to visit his brother. Joseph and the jurist spent hours together discussing law. Solomon admitted he knew who'd fathered Merry the instant he saw her, but he respected his niece's decision not to identify her daughter's father.

"Why would Uncle Solomon tell you my middle name?"

"He alluded to our names on a marriage license, and when we do decide to marry, he wants the honor of officiating. He's aware of the Cole family tradition of marrying on New Year's Eve."

Crystal slumped back in the chair. "You want to marry?"

Joseph shook his head. "No, Crystal. I don't want to marry. I want to marry *you*."

Her eyelids fluttered. "You're ready for marriage?"

His whole face spread into a smile. "I was ready the first night you came to Club José for dinner." He sobered. "I don't know what there was about you that tied me up in knots, and I regretted ever giving you a choice as to where our relationship would lead. And I knew that what happens in Charleston stays in Charleston was nothing more than a boatload of BS, yet I went along with it because I didn't want to do to you what my ex had done to me, and that is pressure you into doing something you didn't or couldn't do."

Crystal knew it was time to stop fooling herself into believing she didn't want Joseph as a part of her life and future. She gave the man sitting across from her with his hands sandwiched between his denim-covered knees a direct stare. "Ask me, Joseph."

He blinked once. "Ask you what?"

"Ask me to marry you."

His hands moved to his knees. "Don't play with my head."

"I'm not playing. If you don't ask me now, then the topic is moot, counselor."

Coming off the chair, Joseph went to his knees in front of Crystal. His eyes came up to meet hers. He held her hands in a gentle grip. "Crystal Riesa Eaton, will you do me the honor of becoming my wife?"

Crystal smiled tentatively, knowing her response would change both of them forever. "Yes, José Ibrahim Cole-Wilson. I will marry you."

She didn't have time to react when she found herself in Joseph's arms, his mouth covering hers in an explosive kiss.

They would marry New Year's Eve in West Palm Beach like Coles in the past. However, this wedding was certain to attract a lot of attention because it would join two of Florida's most prominent families—the Eatons and the Coles.

Epilogue

Crystal, staring at her reflection in the full-length mirror on the closet door, didn't believe she was about to become Mrs. Joseph Cole-Wilson. When she and Joseph informed their families they would marry on New Year's Eve at the Cole family compound, Jasmine called a preeminent Miami wedding planner to coordinate what was to become the wedding of the season.

Invitations were mailed to every Cole and Eaton, and as the acceptances were received, the quandary as where to house their out-of-town guests became an exercise in logistics.

All of the Coles had arrived on Christmas Eve in time for their annual weeklong family reunion, while the Eatons who'd reserved blocks of rooms in various West Palm Beach hotels arrived throughout the holiday week. They joined the many Coles the night before for a rehearsal dinner in the mansion's grand ballroom.

Two other images appeared in the mirror, and Crystal turned to find her mother and father dressed in their wedding finery as father and mother of the bride. Jasmine was stunning in a black-and-white-striped satin gown with long sleeves and a squared neckline. Raleigh looked very handsome in a black tuxedo, a white dress shirt and a black-and-white-striped silk tie.

Crystal held her arms out at her sides. "How do I look?" She'd selected a platinum A-line Melissa Sweet silk duchesse satin gown with a sweep train and cap sleeves. Five-inch Christian Louboutin white satin pumps and a tulle cathedral-length veil secured in the chignon on the nape of her neck completed her wedding dress.

Jasmine crossed her hands over her chest as she blinked back tears before they fell and ruined her makeup. She exhaled a soft gasp. "You look like an angel. Doesn't she, Raleigh?"

Raleigh crossed the room and took his daughter's hands, bringing them to his mouth and kissing her fingers. "Yes, she does." He checked his watch. "It's time we head downstairs because we don't want everyone to think you're going to be a runaway bride."

Crystal smiled up at her father. He'd regained the healthy color in his face and his once dull hair was lustrously silver. A network of fine lines around his shiny dark eyes added rather than detracted from his middle-aged attractiveness. She'd thought herself blessed to have two parents that complemented each other in so many ways they'd sought to deny or ignore.

She pressed her cheek to Raleigh's clean-shaven one. "The only place I'm running tonight is into the arms of my husband."

Smiling, Raleigh winked at his daughter. "It's hard to put into words, but I…I'm so proud of you, Crystal. I'm sure you learned from your parents how not to make the same mistakes we did. You and Joseph are marrying because you love each other, but it's taken more than thirty years for your mother and me to face the truth that we belong together."

Crystal's jaw dropped as she tried processing what she'd just heard. "You and Mother?"

Jasmine crossed the room, her arms going around the waist of her daughter and ex-husband. "Your father says he likes living with me and we've decided to give it a trial run for a little while. And if we find out we like the arrangement, then maybe we'll think about making it permanent."

Crystal's hands and knees were shaking so much she feared she would collapse where she stood. If someone had told her having Raleigh convalescence at his ex-wife's house would lead to reconciliation, she would've said they were liars.

"This is the best wedding gift anyone could ever give me," she said tearfully.

"Come, darling," Jasmine crooned. "I heard someone say Joseph has been pacing nonstop, wearing a hole in one of the rugs."

Looping her arms over her mother's and father's, Crystal walked out of the bedroom and down a hallway in the twenty-four-room mansion Samuel Claridge Cole had built for his Cuban-born wife and their children in 1928.

Crystal walked into the sitting room amid the excited chatter of her bridesmaids. And in keeping with the holiday-themed colors of black and silver, six of the Eaton women wore black gowns in styles that flattered their bodies. The exception was Selena. As matron of honor her gown was shimmering silver. All wore feathered headpieces, which made them look like graceful black-and-gray swans. Their groomsmen counterparts were huddled together taking bets as to which college football teams would win the various bowl games taking place on New Year's Day.

Initially she only wanted one bridal attendant, but when Joseph revealed he'd chosen his former college roommate as his best man and also his brothers and three male cousins as groomsmen, Crystal knew she had to step up her game and solicit the participation of every thirtysomething Eaton woman, of whom two had married into the family. Angela Chase, of the Louisville, Kentucky, Chases, had become the latest Eaton woman when she married Dr. Levi Eaton in June.

Raleigh cleared his throat, garnering everyone's attention. There was a chorus of gasps and murmurs of approval from the assembly. "I told you she'd look like a model," Selena crowed proudly. As the matron of honor, she'd assumed the responsibility of helping Crystal into her wedding attire.

Raleigh stood straight. "It's time we move into position. I want my daughter married before midnight. That way her husband can claim her as a dependent on this year's tax return." Those familiar with Raleigh Eaton's gift for investing in profitable companies, which paid off handsomely for himself and his clients, laughed.

Jasmine shook her head. "Spoken like a true financial planner."

The bridal party lined up as couples to process out of the house and through a door leading to the Japanese garden. Crystal was given the choice of exchanging vows in the Coles' Japanese or English garden, and she'd chosen the former. And as promised, her uncle Solomon would do the officiating.

From where she stood with her father, Crystal could hear the music of a string quartet coming through the many speakers set up around the twelve-acre property surrounded by tropical foliage, exotic gardens and the reflection of light sparkling off lake waters.

Her knees began to shake and it must have been noticeable because Raleigh tightened his hold around her waist. "It's all right, baby girl. It will be over before you know it."

Closing her eyes, Crystal relaxed as the music changed, segueing into the familiar strains of the "Wedding March."

Raleigh kissed his daughter's hair. "That's our cue."

Crystal felt as if she were a spectator instead of the center attraction when she proceeded over the stone path to where Joseph stood with Frank Lynch.

Joseph, like all of the Cole men, had continued another tradition: they all sported white neckpieces. She smiled at Merry, who'd fallen asleep in Raquel's arms. It was well past her bedtime and only the children over the age of sixteen were permitted to stay up beyond the mandated one o'clock curfew. Joseph had explained that the in-ground pool was covered because the younger children had a habit of jumping into the pool—fully clothed.

The weather was perfect for an outdoor nighttime gathering. Daytime temperatures, topping out close to ninety, had dropped to a balmy seventy-eight with a light breeze coming off the water. A full moon and a clear sky littered with millions of stars silvered the landscape with light.

Joseph stared numbly at the woman moving closer and closer like a vision in a dream. He'd felt himself in suspended animation from the time he slipped the engagement ring on Crystal's finger once they'd returned from New York until less than an hour ago when he began dressing for his wedding. Whenever he woke to find her beside him, he realized the woman in his bed was one he'd willingly give up his life to protect.

"Who gives this woman in marriage?" asked Solomon, his sonorous voice carrying easily in the still of the night.

Raleigh smiled at his brother. "I do." He placed Crystal's hand in Joseph's and then stepped back to sit beside Jasmine.

Judge Solomon Eaton nodded to his former clerk. "Do you, José, take Crystal to be your wife, to love, honor and cherish from this day forth?"

Joseph stared into Crystal's eyes. "I do."

Solomon turned to his niece. "Do you, Crystal, take José, to be your husband, to love, honor and cherish from this day forth?"

She smiled. "I do."

Solomon placed his hands over their clasped hands after they'd exchanged rings. "As you've pledged yourselves each to the other, I do now, by the virtue of the authority vested in me by the state of Florida, pronounce your husband and wife for as long as you both shall live. José, you may kiss your bride."

Joseph dipped Crystal low, kissing her passionately to thunderous applause and wolf whistles. "That's how we Coles do it, baby," he whispered against her lips, easing her upright.

A warming heat filled her chest and face. "You'll pay for that, *mi amor,*" she teased with a wide grin. Seconds later fireworks lit up the sky in brilliant color, signaling the beginning of a new year.

Amid a shower of rice, birdseed and flower petals, Joseph and his wife traversed the stone path to a footbridge, where they posed with attendants and family members for wedding pictures and then stood in a receiving line greeting everyone who'd come to celebrate their new life together.

It seemed like an eternity before Crystal was seated at the bridal table with the rest of the wedding party. Guests who were served hors d'oeuvres during the cocktail hour took their seats for the champagne toast offered by Frank Lynch. Raleigh and Selena also offered passionate toasts.

The live Latin band alternated with the DJ for nonstop music throughout the night. Joseph and Crystal shared their first dance as husband and wife, dancing to the Flamingos doo-wop classic "I Only Have Eyes for You."

Crystal danced with her father while Joseph spun Raquel over the dance floor in a spirited salsa. The pulsing Latin rhythms set the stage for a night of unrestrained merriment. Members of the waitstaff and a dozen bartenders circulated efficiently, serving and mixing drinks for nearly three hundred guests. Those of questionable age requesting alcoholic beverages were carded to ascertain whether they were of legal age to drink.

At exactly one o'clock, all those under sixteen were ushered into the house, but not without them protesting loudly.

It was close to four in the morning when Joseph's teenage female cousins crowded around the DJ. The year before, their male cousins had put on an impromptu show during Jason and Greer Cole's reception, stripping down to their boxer-briefs and gyrating à la Channing Tatum's *Magic Mike* to Rihanna's "We Found Love."

Joseph pressed his shoulder to Crystal's. "Watch this, sweetie." He quickly explained what the eight young women had planned to do. "Last year it was the boys, and this year it's their turn."

Crystal laughed until her sides hurt when the young women in matching costumes revealing a prudent amount of skin twerked to Beyoncé's "Crazy In Love." Everyone laughed, gyrated and sang along while their mothers shook their heads in exasperation. The DJ segued into hits made popular by Florida-based artists Flo Rida, Pitbull and Jason Derulo.

Shedding her veil and stilettos, Crystal danced continuously until it came time for her to cut the cake. Instead of tossing her bouquet, she handed it to landscape architect Eden Spencer. "You're next," she whispered, pressing her cheek to the tall, pretty woman with the dimpled smile.

Joseph tapped her arm to get her attention. "It's time we go in and change. We have to board the jet in an hour." They'd planned to honeymoon at one of the family's vacation resorts in the Caribbean. It would be the second time in two months

Crystal would leave her daughter with her overly indulgent grandparents.

The past year had become one she would remember forever. She'd reunited with the love of her life, her parents had reconciled, Merry had met her paternal grandparents and she and Joseph had shared a momentous Christmas and New Year's with their extended family and friends. And she looked forward to the coming months during which she would be kept busy decorating her new home.

Crystal never could've imagined, when checking into the Beaumont House, that the man occupying the neighboring penthouse suite would make her his wife and the mother of his child, but not necessarily in that order.

Reaching for her husband's hand and standing on tiptoe in her bare feet, she touched her lips to his. *"Te amo,"* she whispered in Spanish. Joseph had begun teaching her Spanish, beginning with words of love.

Joseph made love to his wife with his eyes. *"Y yo a ti, mi amor y mi corazón."*

They managed to slip into the house through a side door undetected, to change, and when they reemerged they were ready to begin the year anew as husband, wife, father and mother.

* * * * *

REQUEST YOUR FREE BOOKS!

2 FREE NOVELS PLUS 2 FREE GIFTS!

KIMANI™ ROMANCE

Love's ultimate destination!

KROM13R